NOTES FROM UNDERGROUND

NOTES FROM UNDERGROUND

ROGER SCRUTON

BEAUFORT
BOOKS

Library of Congress Cataloging-in-Publication Data
Scruton, Roger.
  Underground notes / by Roger Scruton. — First Edition.
     pages cm
  Includes bibliographical references and index.
  ISBN 978-0-8253-0728-7 (hardcover : alk. paper)
  1. Underground movements—Prague (Czech Republic)—20th century—Fiction. 2. Communism—Prague (Czech Republic)—20th century—Fiction. 3. Prague (Czech Republic)—20th century—History—Fiction. I. Title.
  PR6069.C78U53 2014
  823'.914—dc23
                           2013036890

For inquiries about volume orders, please contact:

Beaufort Books
27 West 20th Street, Suite 1102
New York, NY 10011
sales@beaufortbooks.com

Published in the United States by Beaufort Books
www.beaufortbooks.com

Distributed by Midpoint Trade Books
www.midpointtrade.com

Printed in the United States of America

Interior design by Neuwirth & Associates, Inc.
Cover Design by Michael Short

10 9 8 7 6 5 4 3 1

CONTENTS

AUTHOR'S NOTE

This is a story about truth, but it is not a true story, and, with a few obvious exceptions, the characters involved in it are fictions. I have tried to evoke the atmosphere of Prague around 1985; in doing so, I have taken some topographical liberties, though incidental references to political and cultural realities are largely accurate. In reading Czech words you need only know that ě is pronounced "ye"; that č, ř, š, ť and ž are softened forms of those consonants; that accents lengthen the vowels over which they stand; that ch is a hard form of h, as in loch, while c is a soft "ts"; and that the stress falls almost always on the first syllable in any word. People are addressed in the vocative case, so Betka becomes Betko, *miláček* (darling) becomes *miláčku*, etc. The initials StB were used to refer to the *Státní bezpečnost*, state security apparatus, or secret police.

The poem on p. 108 is my translation from Ivan Martin Jirous: *Magorovy labutí písně* (The Swan-Songs of Magor), Prague, Torst, 2006, and I thank the publishers for their kind permission to make use of the original. I wish also to thank Barbara Day for constant information, insight and encouragement.

ROGER SCRUTON
Malmesbury, 2012

NOTES FROM UNDERGROUND

CHAPTER 1

THE POLICE MUST have been in our apartment for at least an hour when I arrived. Mother was standing in the kitchen, a large policeman blocking her passage to the room where we lived. Everything was in disarray: the drawers open, the beds unmade and pulled away from the wall, our few possessions piled on the table or pushed in little heaps into the corners. Two more policemen filled the living space. One was thumbing through our samizdat library with slow, patulous fingers. His face was sharp and white, with wisps of soft beard on his chin. The other, who was taking notes in an official-looking notebook with a black plastic cover, looked up as I entered, and I recognized the smooth-shaven officer who had taken my identity card on the bus. He took the card from his pocket, and handed it to me with a sarcastic curl of the lip.

"We don't need this now," he said.

I looked at him in silence, and then at my mother.

"I told them the truth," she said, and fastened her eyes on mine. Mother's eyes were dark, with a ring of shadow, and were the most striking feature in her slender face.

"About what?"

"About the typewriter, the paper, the covers—that I took them without permission."

Mother was a meek woman, who never raised her voice and did not easily meet another's gaze. But her reckless, almost joyful tone said more to me than all the quiet complaints against misfortune that she had uttered down the years. The chance had been offered to sacrifice herself. And in seizing it she was paying her moral debt to Dad. But her words and looks went through me like a knife. It was not she but I who had prepared this sacrifice: prepared it in those long months underground, when I had lived with purely imaginary companions, and forgotten the only real one. She turned to the smooth-faced officer and nodded, as though to indicate that, whatever had been done to disturb the moral order, she alone was to blame. The patched clothes of yellowish wool and cotton clung to her slim form like the fur of some dingy animal: they were part of her, the outgrowth over years of unceasing poverty. His clean grey-green uniform, with four brass buttons above a brown leather belt, wrapped his body like a banner. The smart green shirt and tie, the laced leather boots and brass-buttoned pockets, were the marks of a power that had no need to take note of this frail woman dressed in re-stitched rags and hand-me-downs. The sight filled me with anger and with fear.

"And who," said the policeman, picking a volume from the table, "is this Comrade Underground, that Mr. Reichl was reading on the bus?"

"How should I know?" Mother answered quickly. "They come with their manuscripts, and I make them into books. They don't leave their names."

"And of course they pay you, Soudružko Reichlová. Stealing property in socialist ownership, operating an unlicensed business, and possibly Article 98, subversion of the Republic in collusion with foreign powers. It doesn't look good."

Mother stiffened, affecting what dignity she could.

"Nobody pays me; I do it for love," she replied.

"For love!" the policeman repeated with a laugh.

He nodded to his large colleague who, taking the handcuffs from his belt, locked them quickly onto Mother's wrists. She blanched and stared before her, avoiding their eyes.

"We're taking her for interrogation," the smooth-faced policeman said, addressing me. "At Bartolomějská. We will probably need you tomorrow."

They gathered up our library in a plastic sack, and took the books, the typewriter, and Mother too, to the car that was waiting outside. I stared at our desecrated room, and a kind of blankness came over me, as though the self, the I, the being identical with me, had been suddenly blown away and only scattered thoughts drifted here and there in my head like bits of paper in a windswept lot. And one little regret kept returning, which was that the last volume of *Rumors* had been lost—the volume in which here and there I had pencilled, though so lightly that only I could read them, my thoughts for some future, official, fully-public edition.

CHAPTER 2

AS THE AUTHOR of *Rumors*, I was Soudruh Androš, Comrade Underground, and it was how I thought of myself, almost forgetting at times that I was also Jan Reichl. The samizdat writers, the long-haired dissidents, the unofficial rock bands, the clandestine priests—all belonged beneath the city, in a place where a forbidden life went on. We described that place with an English word, for English was a symbol of freedom. It was the "underground" haunted by the "underers," the *androši*.

I was young then, the age when I should have been getting a university education, except that Dad had sacrificed my right to it. Not that he had done anything heroic, so far as we know. It was in the early 1970s, the time of "normalization" following the Soviet invasion of our country, and people were looking around for some quiet and unobtrusive way to understand what we had lost. Dad organized a reading group in our village, where he was headmaster of the school, and a few retired people would assemble each week to discuss the banished prophets—Dostoevsky, Kafka, Camus—whose words they would ponder in search of an exit from the maze. I was thirteen when my father was arrested. It was the last time I saw him, and he remains in my feelings as he was for me then—not Father, but *Tati*, Dad.

There were loud noises in the middle of the night: Mother weeping, boots stamping on the stairway of the block where we lived. My sister, Ivana, and I slept in the sitting room, on a bed that was rolled up each morning to make room for the work table. We could see through the glass door into the tiny lobby, where Dad stood in his pajamas, his handcuffed wrists in front of him, his face white and frozen. He was found guilty of subversion in collaboration with a foreign power. We never knew which foreign power they had in mind. The power of literature, maybe. Or perhaps his reading parties were the cover for something more serious that they chose not to reveal. Anyway, he got five years hard labor. Three years on, we were told that a mine had collapsed, burying a dozen enemies of the people. Dad was one of them.

By that time we had moved to Prague. They had discovered a seam of coal under our village. They sold the village to a Hollywood movie company, to provide footage for B movies about the Second World War. Just two years ago, in a cinema in Washington, I saw one of them: *The Love Song of Captain Mendel*—about a Jewish captain in the American army, on a private mission to rescue a family of Jews from the last train to Auschwitz. In the concluding battle you see the onion-dome of our church sway above the rooftops, bits of molding falling away, the Virgin in her niche suddenly breaking free and flying as though to save the child in her arms, and then the whole thing sliding down in a cloud of debris. In the background, the baroque palace that was my father's school springs apart like a firework, sending out shoots of stucco on long arms of dust. I went back to the cinema three times to watch it. On the third visit I took some of the students from my class on "Everyday life in Communist Europe." I had intended to draw their attention to the battle scene, to say, "Do you recall the church, the statue of the Virgin, the whole thing blown to smithereens? Well, that was my village." But Jake said how cheesy the movie was; Meg wondered what the story had to with their course on International Relations; Alice dismissed Captain Mendel as a drip. I bought them pizza and, as they bandied about their cheerful opinions, recalled in silence those times of fear.

The destruction of our village was not reported in the press. All we were told was that we had been relocated "for economic reasons." As the family of a criminal we were entitled only to an undivided space with a kitchen and toilet, in a block made of cast concrete panels near the Gottwaldova Metro station, named, then, after the thug who led the Communist Party to power in 1948. Mother was given a job as cleaner in a paper factory down in the valley: they paid her next to nothing, but since the factory was producing next to nothing, there were no grounds for complaint. That, we were made to understand, is what socialism means. My sister and I were put in the local school, where we learned some math and science. But our teachers were informed of our criminal connections, and took care to avoid us. We were shunned, too, by our classmates, and when Ivana finished high school and left to work in a shoe factory near Brandýs nad Orlicí, in the Pardubice region, I began a life of isolation.

Mother had made friends with an under-manager at the paper factory, and had been promoted to senior caretaker. She often spent her evenings with her protector, which I didn't begrudge her, for she did not deserve the joyless life to which events had condemned her. Despite the under-manager, mother remained faithful in her feelings to Dad, mourning him quietly, and treating his few possessions with a special reverence. Among these possessions was a collection of long-playing records, including the operas of Janáček in Supraphon versions from the 1960s, and some gloomy abstract pictures that Dad had painted as a student after the war. There was also a trunk of books—not large by bibliophile standards, but occupying the central space in our narrow room, and used in the evenings to support the plank from which we ate. They had taken Dad's manuscripts, and a packet of letters; but they had left the books, maybe in the hope that a fresh batch of criminals would spring from them, and a fresh series of arrests.

In the trunk, I found the Czech classics—Mácha, Neruda, Vrchlický, Němcová, Hašek—and beneath them the guilty texts that had destroyed my father. I read them avidly, and was especially thankful that Dad had taught us to read in English and German, devoting an hour before supper each day to the task. There was Kafka's *Trial* and *Castle*, the first in an old German edition with a foreword by Max Brod; there was *The Radetzky March* by Joseph Roth and Zweig's *Die Welt von Gestern—The World of Yesterday*—describing what we had lost when President Wilson decided to dismember the Austro-Hungarian Empire, and to liberate the Czechs and Slovaks from their alleged oppressors.

Zweig evoked an enchanted world, ordered towards comfort and high culture. He told me that I lived in a place where everything reliable and good had been twice destroyed, like pieces in a peaceful game of chess swept to the floor by the hand of some passing sadist. And he wrote of a spiritual force that had rotted things from within: the religion of Progress, which forbade humanity to stand still, not even for a moment, making it a sin to enjoy the luminous present and all the depths that shine in it, as they shone for me in those two Mahler symphonies—5 and 6—that had acquired a special place in Dad's collection of records. But it occurred to me that Dad, too, had subscribed to this religion, believing, after the Nazi defeat, in a new order of things, in which electricity and abstract painting, surrealist poetry and cooperative farms, education and reinforced concrete, were all mixed together as on a celebratory stamp, to stick to our country and post it into the future. And it was because he had dreamed of this future, in which all conflicts would be resolved and every human being would have a share, that Dad had become a teacher, only to watch in good-natured dismay as the hand of the sadist once again swept all the pieces from the table.

The trunk also contained a complete set of Dostoevsky in Czech, from which one title stood out as though addressed to me directly: *Notes from Underground*. This was the book that I would carry with me after school, when I took the steps down from the Metro station into the valley, along a narrow path to the railway crossing, and then over the polluted stream called Botič, to the chapel of the Holy Family below the Nusle steps.

The chapel—a tiny box with a pepperpot cap—was boarded up, with barbed wire wrapped around the windows. It was a piece of flotsam in the ocean of unowned spaces that the Communists had created. Some maples were growing above it, hemmed in by the steps and the torn fence of wire above the railway, on which trains plunged into a tunnel a few yards below. This place was my destination, because nobody else would visit it save a few squirrels, a starling or two, and God. Here I would sit in all weathers on the damp earth under the trees, studying the text that promised an explanation not only of Dad's momentous crime but also of me.

I spent many hours thus, rehearsing my longed-for identity as the underground man. But I could never remember anything of the book apart from the title and its strange cantankerous tone of voice. Each day I would carry back with me to our cramped little room— where Mother slept on one side of the trunk and I on the other—a summary of the last ten pages. And each day the memory of them would seep away, as though I were trying to fill an uphill pool from a leaking bucket. Of course, the atmosphere remained, and with it the knowledge that there is another life, a life belowground where Dad lay buried and where the rules of daylight don't apply. I felt some of the extremism of Dostoevsky's prose—the rage that condemns each feeling as a fake. But what was the alternative? I was a lonely adolescent, in a lonely country, where the rules were made for the sake of people who did not pay the cost of them. Our daylight world was one of slogans in which no one believed, of vague prohibitions and joyless celebrations of our benign enslavement. It was a world without friendship, in which every gathering was an object of suspicion, and in which people spoke in whispers for fear that even the most innocent remark could accuse the speaker of a crime.

I left high school and, although not allowed to graduate, I was required by law to take a job. I applied for a position as sweeper with the City Council, and was assigned a length of street in Smíchov: two hundred meters of broken pavement behind the Husovy sady, the orchard of Jan Hus, from which I had to gather the rubbish into an adjacent bin on wheels, and which I was to keep clear of snow in the winter. It was not a demanding job, and no one bothered me as I leaned against my bin and imagined the world away. But it was at this time that I began those travels underground that led at last to Mother's arrest.

CHAPTER 3

THE PRAGUE METRO was of recent construction and the Communists were proud of it. It was a symbol of progress in a city whose beauty and antiquity were a standing offense to the proletarian future. Moreover, its rolling stock was made in the Soviet Union and had the same machine-age look as the dams, chimneys, and pylons on the hundred crown note, four of which I received each fortnight in a rough brown envelope that had been initialed and rubber-stamped by Mr. Krutský, the district superintendent. I traveled to work on the Metro and then, because my work finished at midday, I would go back and forth on a single ticket, changing trains and sometimes staying underground for two hours at a time before taking the Red Line out towards Gottwaldova.

The silence of our world was more intense underground. Even at rush hour, when the cars were full and people stood holding the handrails and staring past each other's ears, there was no noise apart from the roar of the train and the automated voice that told us that the doors were closing. Nobody exchanged greetings or apologies; no face smiled or departed in the slightest particular from the mask that everyone adopted, as the instinctive sign of a blameless inner emptiness, from which no forbidden thought could ever emerge.

Some passengers would be reading. A few read the sports and TV pages of *Rudé právo* or *Mladá fronta*; one or two read the official weeklies. Some read the permitted novels that would appear each Thursday in nicely printed hardcover editions. Once or twice I would catch sight of a foreign text, concealed in a paper wrapper and hastily put away when strange eyes fell upon it. And a few old people would occupy themselves with shabby editions of the classics, Němcová's *Babička* or Jan Neruda's stories of Malá Strana, the Little Side, describing the life that once flowed in those ancient streets around the Castle.

It took me a couple of years to get through Dad's library. After a while, I started to take notes. I would write down phrases, sometimes single words, that seemed to sound in that underground silence with a special force. There was a phrase from Kafka's diaries that particularly struck me: *the true path*, it said, *is a tight rope, stretched just above the ground.* I sat pondering that phrase for an hour, wondering what it was telling me. My own path was also a tight rope; but it was stretched belowground, and the interludes of daylight bore no relation to the steps that I took. And another phrase: *the wish for an unthinking, reckless solitude.* The solitude that I saw around me was conscious, premeditated, and full of timidity. The idea of a reckless solitude filled me with warmth, as though I were not alone in my loneliness, but embraced by it. And because I had discovered this phrase in a book, a book that might have been published in the wake of that Writers' Union Congress in 1967, when the all-too-obvious things about Kafka's country were being all-too-obviously said, but which was not published then and was soon unpublishable in any case, it had a special authority for me. Such phrases were the proof of my inner reality, and they could never be taken away.

Life underground is ordered in its own way. There are two voices: the inner voice of thought, which constantly changes in response to the page in front of you, and the public voice, to which no personality attaches, but which announces the opening and the closing of the doors. A toneless female voice governed the Green Line, a toneless male voice the Red.

"*Ukončete výstup a nástup, dveře se zavírají.*"

"Stop getting on and off, the doors are closing." Later, after the changes, when the blank mask of subservience had been replaced by the blank smile of commerce, the word "please," found its way into the message: "*Ukončete prosím výstup a nástup, dveře se zavírají.*"

I am struck by this because, in that little word, "please," is summarized all that separates the days that I am describing from the days in which I write.

My underground journeys, in those times of hiding, were ordered by short sharp barks of command. They were the voice of daylight, dividing and fragmenting our spells in the tomb. My thoughts took on a new urgency whenever they sounded: they reminded me that I did not belong to the world above, that I had cast off its rules and its goals, and that my life was here inside me, protected by my own personal strategies from whatever the rules required. In some way, I was mortifying that voice by my refusal to credit its authority. The whole bleak system of commands that spoke through it, and which reached to the perimeter of my being, was brought to nothing by the countervailing force of my thinking.

But what was I thinking? For a year or more I knew only that I was thinking, and thinking hard, and that my thoughts isolated and protected me. My life was one of neat, closed beginnings, like a book of preludes. I was living in the catacombs, worshipping strange gods, the close companion of martyrs and outcasts. Distant murmurs in the darkness suggested the presence of others like me, people who were breathing the same exhausted air, and whose thoughts were drifting along the same forbidden tracks. Of course, I had a view of my situation. When I thought of Dad, a kind of gasping disgust besieged me. My throat became dry as though I had swallowed some of the dust that had choked him to death, and a lump formed in my stomach, so that sometimes I bent over and fought back the desire to vomit. What I felt was beyond anger, beyond resentment. It was an existential feeling, like the nausea that Sartre describes in the novel that I had found in the trunk, in an English translation heavily marked by Dad's pencil. And over the months, my thoughts began to crystallize.

I came to the conclusion that the daylight world was not a world of outward oppression, that the stuff we heard on Radio Free Europe about our condition was really the most superficial propaganda and that the "evil empire" in whose grip we were held was an empire of our own devising. Two years after I discovered Dostoevsky's book, I began to understand its purport. The real slavery, he was telling us, is a disease of the will, a kind of self-entrapment, whereby we build up for ourselves expectations that we know will be defeated. For instance, there was Dad's hope that, by establishing a group in our little town to read those not-quite-forbidden classics, he would find a way out of the maze—a hope that he knew to be nonsense, and which therefore held him in a vise-like grip of self-contradiction, all the time that he waited for that fatal knock at the door. For instance, there was the habit I had acquired of writing letters to the Minister of Justice, demanding my constitutional right to a higher education—letters to which I received, and expected, no reply, and yet which served to perpetuate an irrational belief in miracles. For instance, there was Mother's absurd belief that she could, with the under-manager's support, get permission to travel to Yugoslavia, on one of those holidays from which people regularly escaped to the West—a belief that caused her to look always with despair on the few scant savings she had made, and which would sometimes cause her to weep bitter tears of frustration, as though it were only the lack of money that prevented us from traveling.

The illusions and deceptions that haunted the daylight world were stopped at the threshold of the underground as though by a spell, to stay wailing and whimpering as I sank out of view. No sooner had the doors of the train closed behind me than I would begin my study of the other passengers. In those days, when silence meant safety, and contact meant danger, each person seemed to be surrounded by a bottle of glass. Eyes would stare from their bottles as though sight had long ago expired in them, and the features even of the youngest bore the shadows that come from suspicion and fear. I was surrounded by faces that did not so much avoid the eyes of others as strive with all their might to deny that others were real, to live inside their bottles as though transported through a dream, unconnected to the things that vaguely moved in the space beyond. Because of this, I could study without embarrassment the types of my countrymen and women.

In those days, clothes, posture, body rhythm, and character all showed the marks of central distribution. Ours was a collectivized way of life, and to stand out was a mistake. All around me I saw the same mustard-colored jerkins of nylon and cord; the same plastic shoes, with ribbed soles, looking as though glued together without stitching and all dust-covered and unpolished. I saw the same oilskin and mock-leather shopping bags with ruined zips and frayed handles. Men had navy blue pants shiny at the knees and large rough hands that rested in their laps, dry-skinned and motionless like old potatoes.

Of course, there were people, women especially, who attempted a measure of gaiety. But the result had a random and absurd appearance, adding to the general impression of drabness precisely through its futile attempt to escape from it: the woman with ham-shaped thighs in bright blue trousers and a pullover of mauve and orange stripes, who looked as though she had taken her clothes from a dressing-up box; the one with paste jewelry hanging in large dollops from her neck and ears like rotting fruit, wobbling precariously on high heels that might at any moment snap under her weight. All such attempts at difference had the opposite effect to the one intended. For they emphasized that, in the midst of this randomness, you saw only the one identical expression: eyes staring into the distance, and lips held firmly shut as though against some pervasive infection. Our people had collectively solved their shared problem, which was how to keep the mask in place, while showing that it is only a mask. People collaborated in the great deception, so as not to be deceived.

On the other hand—and this was the intriguing part—each person exhibited some revealing detail, betraying the accidents that no central authority had yet been able to banish. Hence I could sort them into categories, endow each with a private life, sometimes a family circle, and maybe a record of deals and betrayals whereby they had found their passage through. The woman with the worn green jacket, for instance, whose greying hairs fussed around her ears and whose blue eyes, set wide apart, stared sightlessly at the carriage door. Her thin lips had been open once or twice in anger and in passion, though they were closed now on her secrets and her grief. Her husband, the Professor, had left her for a younger woman, a Party member like himself, whom he had helped in her university career. She had tried her luck with other men, and then settled down to a life on the edge of things, teaching Russian in the local gymnasium, going alone to the theater and cinema, and sometimes lingering afterwards over a beer in the Lucerna Music Bar. There she would read the books of free verse that were written for would-be intellectuals, and which were even published, with kitsch illustrations of doe-eyed lovers, in the official press: verse going everywhere, carried about the page on a breeze of white paper, always fresh, naïve, and purposeless, like spring blossom blown from a tree. And in this verse, she caught glimpses of her stolen soul. "I am what the poet writes," she thinks. "I am the inflammation made by words, when they rub against the world."

Or the young man in the leather jacket sitting across from me, whose nervous hands were shuffling papers in his lap, and whose flaccid mouth seemed to be chewing some unpleasant substance that had lodged between his teeth. He had wanted to study for a doctorate, had been called for an interview, to be told that he must report on the neighbors who shared a staircase with his family. He had discussed the matter in whispers with his timid sister, but when they told him that his family would be moved out of town, to one of the estates of paneled towers beyond Žižkov, if he did not do as they required, he gave in. He told himself that it was for his sister's sake, since she must not leave her school in Nové Město, which was the best in Prague. But he needed that doctorate if he was to travel, and was it such a price to pay, to submit each week an account of the visitors who stood for a moment at the door beneath his own? And had he not acquired his own distinctive underground view of them, imagining a life for each, and wondering how they would fare when the fatal visit came? For a while he deceived himself thus. And then came the stale sense of alienation which, like some cheap restaurant gravy, made every experience taste the same.

Gradually, the underground people responded to my unobserved observing, like seeds sprouting under a laboratory sunlamp. I entered the Metro at the end of my shift around midday to take up a seat beside the doors, where I would read one of Dad's books, overscoring his pencil marks with marks of my own. Between midday and two o'clock, the trains were comparatively empty, and I had my best chance to warm those silent faces into life. With some of them I became intimate, listening to their imagined confessions and adding confessions and plans of my own. With others I kept my distance, inventing lives armor-plated against sympathy, which repelled my unmeant offers of assistance. Of course, the faces changed continually, and sometimes I had no more than a minute or two to attach a life to them. But there were regulars, too: people who would get on at a certain time and a certain stop, and travel to a fixed destination. With several of these, I would renew the conversation each day, and especially with those who were in some way marked out from the crowd—say, by a Bible hidden in paper wrappings, which only I had noticed, or by a pair of hand-knitted gloves, in which I could discern the record of a very private affection.

Relationships sprang up all around me, and I was a part of them, as I was part of the intrigues and angers that had closed these faces against the world. And among those guarded faces I looked everywhere for the one who might have been Dad, had his life been permitted. The one in the greasy yellow Mackintosh, who holds a crumpled trilby on his knees and looks fixedly ahead as though for an official photograph: is that he? Or the one in the corduroy trousers with a stick, who staggers slightly because he carries a large packet wrapped in brown paper under his spare arm, and who wears on his round sallow face an expression of innocent bewilderment reminiscent of a Čapek drawing: could that be what Dad has come to?

I watch this man for a while, noting that no one surrenders a seat to him and all stare past him as though embarrassed by his presence. The parcel constantly slips from his armpit and must be hoisted up, sometimes by the hand that grips the stick, so rendering the whole body unstable. At one point he falls backwards against the knees of a girl in an expensive-looking woolen dress, who brushes him away disgustedly. Inside the parcel I imagine precious texts—Chekhov's stories, Nezval's poems, and yes, Dostoevsky's *Notes from Underground*—which he had lent to some other member of his reading circle and is now returning to the trunk back home. But Dad would not have faced the world with so defeated a look, would not have accepted, as this poor creature accepts, being kicked about like a helpless animal. And, thinking of this, I am once again overcome by that choking feeling, which causes me to withdraw from all thinking and stare at the carriage floor.

In the underground there was sadness and longing; there was self-interest and suspicion. There was also sex: sex that drove on fiercely to its imagined goal. Don't get me wrong. I am not the kind of pervert who works himself into a lather over a girl who has no idea that he is watching her, and whom he treats merely as a prop in his own games of fantasy. I had hung out with girls after school, snatched kisses and sometimes more. But those whispered encounters on the edge of things were furtive and uncertain, as though at any moment a door would open and we would be hauled away in chains. Desire was something else, something that grows in solitude. I wanted my women to live in the same solitude that I did. And I wanted to invite them to beat against the wall of that solitude, breaking at last into a place that was fully imagined, and recklessly shared.

For instance, there was a fresh-faced girl who got on at Holešovice each day just after two, and who traveled the Red Line to Muzeum; she wore a loose corduroy jacket that concealed the contours of her body and created a kind of softness around her. Her hands were smooth, tanned, with long fingers that held open the pages of a book—usually a novel; and her clear grey eyes would sometimes look up from the page and address the world, as though in search of the person who would answer to the words that she read. And this was the important point: it was only those eyes that still sought for contact, eyes which had not been sprayed with the official lacquer of sightlessness, that could arouse true desire.

After a while I managed to catch her glance. She looked at me curiously for several seconds before returning to her book. When she glanced up again it was in my direction, and her gaze rested for a moment on the book that I held before me, as though wishing me to know that this, at least, we had in common, that both of us lived in books, and sought in books for the things that had been erased from the daylight world. At Muzeum, she got up quickly and went out, vanishing into the crowd. But the next day she was back in the same seat, and when her eyes met mine they made a slight flutter of recognition before turning to her book. And then, at Hlavní nádraží, just one stop before her usual destination, she suddenly twisted in her seat, so that the corduroy jacket fell open, revealing the smooth line of her breasts, and a long, taut body on whose contours I allowed my eyes to dwell. She got up without a glance in my direction and left; the automated voice announced the closing doors, and the doors opened wide within me.

This game continued, with variations, to the point where we knew to the minute which train we should catch and which carriage we should sit in, contriving to arrive unnoticed in the foreseen place. It dawned on us simultaneously that the moment of consummation could no longer be postponed. We had positioned ourselves opposite each other, our books open in trembling hands. Her jacket was loose, and the top two buttons of her blouse were undone. I could see the rhythmic breathing of her breast, and feel the hot light of her eyes that watched me when I looked away, and looked away when I watched. We remained like this, gripped by the invisible vise that united us, until we reached her usual stop at Muzeum. To my surprise, she did not get out, but stayed sitting in the same pose, avoiding eyes only to provoke them, until my own stop of Gottwaldova. It was there that she acknowledged the imagined space in which we stood together, naked and aroused. For a long moment we stared deep into that strange metaphysical emptiness which is the source and the target of desire. Those grey eyes were translucent, and through their hazy screen I glimpsed the prowling animal as it fastened its will to mine. Her lips were parted in a kiss, and our two bodies trembled in unison; in a single moment our books slipped from our laps to the floor of the carriage and the voice told us that the doors were closing.

She reached down quickly, seized the book, and was instantly out of the carriage. A second later the train was moving. The next day I took the red line to Holešovice, and crossed the platform at the usual time, onto the train back into town. I did not expect her to appear, nor did she. The affair was over, and I never saw her again.

CHAPTER 4

IT WAS ABOUT the time of that episode that life at home began to change. Through the under-manager, Mother had obtained a typewriter, together with a supply of thin blue paper and carbon sheets that enabled her to make copies, nine at a time. Each evening after supper she would clear the table and begin to type, usually from hand-written manuscripts that appeared while I was journeying underground. The little room that we shared became a samizdat publishing house, for which Mother chose the name Edice Bez moci—The Powerless Press, after an essay by Václav Havel, "The Power of the Powerless," which everyone was reading in editions smuggled in from the West. She could type a short book of a hundred A4 pages in a week, and when she had finished, she would staple the pages into an elegant *papier mâché* binding, the boards of which were another gift from the under-manager. Mother met her authors at the back door of the paper factory and she described them to me: long-haired young men with Habsburg beards, often flamboyantly but shabbily dressed in the dissident manner, with loose kerchiefs and long coats of navy or bottle-green velvet, retrieved from the wardrobes of the dead. Often they would be carrying letters of recommendation from political convicts, or from students and colleagues of Professor Patočka, first spokesman of Charter 77, whom I was told the police had murdered eight years before.

Mother told me about this in a quiet whisper, knowing that it was never safe to speak too loudly in a place where criminals were housed. Why this little circle of dissident authors had picked on Mother she did not explain. They were simply a part of the unassuming life—the life in defeat—that she had made her own. But she spoke with pride of her new contacts, and of the work that she performed on their behalf. She had discovered her own subterranean path to the really real. Her authors would collect the finished product from the back door of the paper factory; but if she liked what she had typed she would keep a copy for herself, so that within a year we had a 30-volume library of samizdat beneath her bed: works of philosophy, translations of Western authors and Russian dissidents, and even a volume or two of fiction.

Dad had never permitted television, describing it as a *kreténská bedna*, a box for morons. On moving to Prague, however, and coming face to face with our isolation, we had succumbed. Like everyone, we had followed the Sunday sitcom, *Hospital at the City's End*, by Jaroslav Dietl, which showed ordinary people doing ordinary things, just as though the world of Karel Čapek were with us still, and those chess pieces had not been swept from the table. One of the first acts of Mother's new occupation was to push the TV into a corner of the room, beneath a pile of wafer-thin A4 paper on which a stapling machine—another gift from the factory—stood like a crown. The TV had been telling us to renounce our futile resistance and to join the normal world. And in turning its face to the wall and our backs to temptation, we knew that we were doing this for Dad.

Mother had by now abandoned her hopes of becoming a respectable citizen with a proper home and a right to travel. She became active in ways that she had never been when Dad was alive—allowing people even to come to our door in order to borrow one of the volumes from our not-so-secret library. It was thus that I met Betka—but I will come to that. Like Mother, I brought the underground each evening to our little room. While she was typing, I would sit across from her at our improvised table and write out the stories that I had divined in those sightless eyes. And I left the stories for my mother to read. One day I discovered that she had typed them and bound them: I was the owner of nine copies of *Pověsti—Rumors*—by Soudruh Androš, the name I had written on the title page. And I asked her to show them to her friends.

This was a mistake. I should have kept those stories to myself, refused the feeble chance of fame that my mother held out to me. I should have stayed belowground, and not allowed my dreams to escape so easily into the daylight, to become those "fried wings, cut from Mercury's ankles," of which Vladimír Holan wrote. And there was another mistake, too, though one whose significance I would understand only very much later. The quantities of samizdat were growing; almost everyone who fancied himself as an author could issue his definitive indictment of the system in the nine permitted copies. And his sales would equal those of Havel, Kundera, Patočka. He stood among those famous non-persons like an intruder poking his head into an official photograph. The world of samizdat was an equal world, in which no distinction was made on grounds of talent. No editorial committee, no marketing department, no team of publicity experts interfered in the process whereby two hundred handwritten pages became a hundred pages of type, so that—in the future world of free markets and open competition—we criminals were often looked down upon, as people who had claimed the title of author without establishing a right to it. Even those dearest to us would then sniff the smell of failure, and serve us the meager remainders of literary glory with sidelong pitying glances.

But again I am anticipating. At the time it seemed that my mother had finally compensated me for the loss of an education, and redeemed the four years that had begun when I huddled over Dostoevsky's novel by the chapel of the Holy Family, in the little copse of maples between the railway and the Nusle steps. I had graduated to a higher form of underground, where small candles of admiration lit the coffered catacombs, and where forbidden authors paraded in the shadows before their secretive fans. I was on the way to being noticed, maybe on the way to being loved. For the news of Soudruh Androš was already spreading across the city. Mother made a point of lending the precious copies of *Rumors* to her authors, indicating that she knew the identity of Comrade Underground, but preferred to keep the knowledge to herself. It was because of *Rumors* that I gained a life, and because of *Rumors* that she lost one.

It began on the Green Line between Můstek and Leninova. It was four o'clock on a winter afternoon and the train was crowded, so that at first I did not notice the girl in a white coat of felt, who stood against the partition, half-hidden by the large man in a boiler suit, whose criminal biography I was at the time composing. At Malá Strana, the man got off, to reveal her profile, the delicate face framed by brown hair pulled back in a chignon, the long white neck rising swan-like from the soft white collar of her coat, the flesh like translucent petals around her silver eyes.

Love at first sight sometimes occurs in the world of normal people; in the underground love exists in no other form. Of course, a small process of checking occurs after that initial *coup-de-foudre*: does she read books, for instance, is she artistic, how tactfully does she dress, and with what awareness that the dreariness is inescapable? But all such questions were answered at once when the girl in the white coat sat down opposite me, and took from her bag a volume of poetry and a notebook, her white unvarnished fingers moving student-like across the pages—the page in which she read, and the page in which she wrote, holding an old ink fountain-pen with navy-blue marbling, of the kind that had long since disappeared from our sparsely provisioned stationers. The girl never raised her eyes, and when she got out at Leninova, which was the end of the line, I did what I had never done with any of my characters before: I followed her into the street.

It was dark in the world above, and a faulty streetlamp flickered above the silent crowd at the bus stop. The white coat signaled her presence like a halo and I joined the queue. The gritty aroma of coal smoke, more a taste than a smell, spotted the winter evening. The pavement was islanded by waterlogged potholes, and to avoid them, the queue at the bus stop made elaborate zigzags and circles. There was no sound apart from the clanking and grinding of the trams around October Revolution Square, and the occasional sputter of a Trabant taking the corner in a cloud of oil-smoke. Two police cars stood in the pool of darkness by the Metro, their occupants motionless and scarcely visible. Despite the cold, I was sweating, and when the bus approached a wave of heat seemed to sweep before it, so that I swayed back on the pavement and splashed in a puddle. The crowd pushed into the bus, and I had to fight my way in behind them as the doors closed on my back. She was by the driver, holding the strap above her head so that the white coat slid back along her arm. All I could see was the slender wrist and the white fingers that gripped the strap. She wore a silver bangle, but no ring. There were lights in the bus; but to me it was as if the whole length of it lay in darkness, apart from that wrist and those fingers, shining above the silent heads like a lamp of alabaster. I was reminded of an old book of Rodin's sculptures that Mother kept beside her bed, in which were photographs of sculpted hands—hands full of prayer and tenderness, of a kind that had long since gone from the world.

The hand dropped from the strap like a bird shot from its perch. I saw then that the people in the bus were more than normally rigid, their faces frozen in expressions of fabricated innocence. Security checks were frequent, and it did not surprise me that the two policemen were interested in the girl in the white coat. They were men like me, after all, anxious to show off their power to an attractive female. But compared with them I could offer no protection, and when I caught sight of her pale face, nodding quiescently as they thumbed the pages of her notebook, I felt a stab of futility and helplessness.

The bus was approaching Divoká Šárka, the cluster of housing blocks on the edge of Prague where the bus line terminated, when the policemen reached me. By then, there was only a handful of passengers. I was sitting in the rear. The girl in white was also seated, at the front of the bus. Her hands were folded in her lap, her eyes fixed on the darkness beyond the window. I tried not to look at her. I tried to think of nothing, hoping that the policemen would ignore me. Then one of them turned in my direction, and the words *"občanský průkaz"*—identity card—sounded in that peculiar contemptuous tone that spelled out the impassable distance between the citizen and those who controlled him. At first I pretended that the command was addressed to someone else. But the policeman was standing in front of me, his hand outstretched, his clean-shaven face wrinkled into a scowl. His mud-colored eyes lay flat, glistening and expressionless on the surface of his face, as though they had been painted there. I took the red booklet from my pocket and handed it to him, my attention fixed on the girl who was getting up to leave. As the bus slowed down, the policeman turned to his companion, to check my details against a list that the other was carrying.

In a moment the bus had stopped, the girl had gotten out, and I too was on the pavement. From the corner of my eye I glimpsed the policemen watching me with quiet interest. But the bus was moving now towards the terminus, and I was walking rapidly down a small street opposite the bus stop, between expensive-looking villas. I

[ROGER SCRUTON]

crossed what seemed to be a railway line, whose rails were half-covered by grass, and then turned a corner into a street of broken concrete paving, to either side of which rose blocks of cheap housing. The buildings had a raw and unfinished appearance, like a stage set on which I was practicing my lines. I found myself by an old-fashioned gate of wooden palings, which opened onto a straggling orchard between two apartment houses where a few dim lights were shining. A street lamp cast a yellow glow across the orchard, faintly illuminating a little farmhouse that stood at its end. She was walking between the trees towards the door of the house. Her steps were light but sure, and she swung her bag beside her in the relaxed way of a person coming home.

Tall trashcans stood beside one of the blocks, and I hid among them to watch her. I tried to imagine the home that she had made in that old house—maybe her grandparents had run the little farm before it had been confiscated and the land turned over to housing. Maybe her mother had been allowed to stay here after the grandparents died, and maybe the girl had spent all her years in this place perched above the gorge of Wild Šárka. I imagined her in the role of Šárka, the legendary princess who had led an army of women in the futile attempt to liberate her homeland. I heard in my mind some snatches of Fibich's opera: there was an old performance from Brno that had been one of Dad's favorite records. I remembered him singing along with it—the aria in which Prince Ctirad communes with himself as he wanders through enchanted woods, soon to come across the lovely form of Šárka bound to a tree. In legends, we Czechs are capable of heroic deeds: and behind these great myths we hide our little lies. Why did Dad come striding then into my consciousness? Why had I metamorphosed into Prince Ctirad, as he would do on those Sunday afternoons before the catastrophe, when the plug was pulled on our illusions and all the lights went out? Why had the pent-up longing of my underground life suddenly spilled out in this act of madness, so that—having left my real self, the self reduced to a number on an identity card, in the hands of a policeman—I was pretending to conquer a fair princess who, according to the stupid fairy tale, must also conquer me?

She had taken the key from her pocket and was turning it in the lock when I cried out. It was not only the card that I had left behind: my canvas workbag, too, the bag containing my own copy of *Rumors*, and along with it the book of essays that Mother had just produced—essays by foreign writers, on the state of our desecrated country. I ran towards the wooden gate and into the road, not daring to show my face to the girl whose peace I had disturbed. I reached the terminus to discover that the bus had turned back to the city; I could see only the red and orange glow of its lights as it sped down the hill. I ran beyond the little pool of light surrounding the buildings, down the dark road towards the place where the bus routes unite. When I plunged underground at last at the Leninova Metro, I felt the wailing monsters of that upper world burst through the barrier to sit around me in the train.

CHAPTER 5

WHEN THEY HAD pushed her into the stairwell and slammed the door, I sat on Mother's unmade bed and stared at the faded patch on the wall where a photograph of Dad had hung. They had thrown the photograph into a corner with the other pictures, including a couple of the grey-green abstracts that Dad had painted in his youth. I must have sat there for several hours, observing the scraps of thought that rustled on the edges of my mind. I was awoken the next day by the sound of rain in the courtyard below and on the kitchen window. I noticed the book about Rodin's sculptures, which had been knocked from the bedside table onto the floor. It was open to a pair of hands entitled *La Cathédrale*. I saw the hands of the girl in white as they grasped the key to the farmhouse door. Who was waiting beyond that door? Did she raise those hands to another's face, and were they now at rest on some other person? I felt cold and hollow inside.

I got up from the bed and went into the kitchen. Our apartment was on the sixth floor, two floors below the roof, and water from a blocked gutter poured across the window. Through the stream I could see the street below, a narrow lane between faceless blocks. A parked police car wriggled in the lens of flowing water as though dancing on a grave. I knew that I should go down to Gottwaldova to ring my sister from the public telephone. But the thought of that car trailing slowly behind me as I walked through the rain gave me a feeling almost of shame. In this new world, I was a naked victim, my defenses confiscated. For a moment I almost resented Mother, who had freed the door behind which they were always waiting. And then I went back and sat on her bed.

Of course, it was I who had freed that door, not Mother. During the days that followed, I viewed her with a kind of numbness. "Mom died today. Or yesterday maybe. I don't know." Such were the chilling words that open the English translation of Camus's *L'Étranger*, which I had found in Dad's trunk. And they express my state of mind during the days that followed, as I crawled with my burden of guilt, unable to examine it, and unable to put it down.

I ate the scraps in the kitchen as a mouse would, without reference to time. Eventually, in the grey light of a December morning, I awoke to the ringing of the doorbell. I was lying on Mother's bed. Images of hands were rummaging in my half-awoken mind: her hands in hand-cuffs, Rodin's hands, the hands that held the plastic strap on the bus to Divoká Šárka, Dad's hands, also in handcuffs, held before him like buffers as he was roughly pushed through the door. I looked at the alarm clock, which lay on its back in the middle of the room. It was 8:30, an hour and a half after the time I should report for work. Probably I had already missed a day. I went into the kitchen and looked down at the street: the rain had stopped now and the police car had gone. For a second, I believed that this was not happening to me; that the thing called "I" was elsewhere, and that the whole episode was a fiction in the mind of Comrade Underground.

The doorbell rang again. Whoever it was had come for Mother and Mother was a non-person, whom it was a mistake to know.

Better, therefore, to remain hidden. I went back to her bed and sat down as quietly as I could. Footsteps shuffled outside the door for a moment and then retreated to the stairs. But there they ceased; and in a moment they had changed direction, were approaching our door, and had stopped outside. The doorbell did not ring, but I felt the visitor standing there, breathing softly. I tiptoed across to the spyglass, in whose distorting eye I perceived the face of a young woman with brown hair and a long white neck bound in a rose-pink kerchief.

I opened the door, and there she was, the girl from Divoká Šárka, looking at me from candid silver eyes, her wide pale forehead glinting in the light that entered the stairwell from our living room. Her lower lids were like mother-of-pearl, as though the eyes shone through them. Her cheeks were flushed and glowing with the December cold, so that the lips between them seemed unusually pale and soft. Her face had a childlike seriousness, and she wore no makeup, the brown hair shining like a crown above her brow. Her gloved hands clutched a canvas bag, and she was wearing a loose denim jacket and trousers, the unofficial uniform of the student class. She stood on straight legs, looking at me with a steady page-like poise, as though expecting a command.

"I have something for Paní Reichlová," she said. "My name is…"

I stopped her short and pointed to the ceiling. She gave me a look, pinching in her nose so that tiny wrinkles lay like folds of white silk along its edges. She was so beautiful that I was afraid to speak. This was not a fiction; it was happening to *me*—and because I had lost myself to her I had also gained myself. For the first time in my life, I knew who I was: not Soudruh Androš, not even Jan Reichl, but the man facing *her*.

"One moment," I said, and indicating that she stay on the threshold, I took a sheet of paper from the table by Mother's bed. On it I wrote: "Meet you at the Chapel of the Holy Family, below the Nusle Steps, in fifteen minutes. Not safe to talk."

She took the paper and stared at it. Then she looked up, held my eyes for a moment, nodded and handed the paper back to me. In a moment she had vanished and I was left standing in the doorway, my legs trembling. This was the real thing, and for sure I would make one mistake after another. But mistakes were a proof of reality, and nothing less than reality would now content me. Shamefully, I had put aside the thought of Mother, forgotten the need to let Ivana know what had happened, forgotten my work and my routine. Mother had retreated to the horizon of my world. As I took my steps down the hill, across the railway to the swollen Botič, I thought only of the girl, and of all the things that I would say to her.

She was standing among the maples, staring across the torn barbed-wire fence towards the railway. I was going recklessly forward, as oblivious of her safety as I had been of Mother's. Still, a small voice of common sense told me to walk on past the chapel and to climb the steps before descending again to meet the girl. There was no one behind me, no one in view at all, save an old woman in a torn shawl, who carried a dog under one arm while pulling herself up the steps with the other. Her face had that stony grey color that was routine among old people then, and I felt a spasm of pity, wondering how she lived and whether the dog were her only companion. Next to the steps, standing among leafless trees, was an old log house, of the kind that the wealthier sort would build in the years of the National Revival, and I stood for a moment and stared at it. The windows were shuttered, the garden overgrown with weeds, and shingles were missing from the roof. But the idea entered my head to live in such a place, to build there a home for myself and the girl from Divoká Šárka, where we would spend our young days in studious isolation, laughing behind closed shutters at the world to which we did not belong. I was so lost in this thought that I did not notice that someone was standing beside me.

"I don't think you were followed," she said in a voice that was soft and clear like a child's. "I assume you are Paní Reichlová's son."

"Jan Reichl," I said. It felt like a pseudonym. "And you?"

"Alžběta," she replied. "Alžběta Palková. But they call me Betka. Not Bětka, but Betka. Someone passed one of your mother's books to me, and I said I would return it."

She nodded as she spoke, as though seeking agreement. There was something eager in her manner that overcame my reticence. It did not occur to me to ask how she knew our address, or why she had come to our apartment at a time when neither I nor my mother should have been home. I wanted to share my trouble, and her steady eyes and unaffected gestures were like a door opened onto a sunlit garden. As I told her about Mother, she continued to nod, looking into my eyes as though the story were written there. I did not mention my part in Mother's downfall, only the fact that the police had raided us and discovered her crime. And then Betka touched my arm and pointed to the chapel, indicating that we should stand behind it, where we would not be seen.

She took a volume of samizdat from her bag. It was *Rumors* by Soudruh Androš. I stared at it in silence.

"The person who borrowed this was particularly insistent that I return it straightaway. To tell you the truth, I want to keep it. It is so close to my way of seeing things."

"Your way of seeing things?"

"Well…" She stopped suddenly and looked at me. "What are we going to do about your mother?"

I had been alone with my thoughts for so long that I could hardly grasp the meaning of her "we." Was she including me in her life, or asking me to include her in mine? Only the candid look reminded me that it was not I but Mother who concerned her.

"What do you suggest? A lawyer perhaps?"

"Are you crazy? The last time this happened to a friend of mine they jailed the lawyer too. It is a crime to defend people who have committed no crime."

I looked at her in astonishment.

"Does this happen often to friends of yours?"

"Not often, no. You are pretty safe with me. Unless…"

"Unless what?"

She was standing a pace away from me, her back to the chapel, her eyes fixed on the Nusle steps.

"Do you see that old woman?" she asked.

I turned my eyes in the direction of hers. The woman with the dog was coming down now, handing her body from step to step, gripping the rail and muttering.

"Like the poodle in *Faust*," she went on, "he comes in many forms."

"Who?"

"Mephistopheles. The spirit who always denies."

The old woman had reached the bottom of the steps and was passing out of view. In the Prague of those days, there was a peculiar emptiness that supervened, in the wake of people who were too much looked at. The specter of the city followed them into the void, and in its wake you saw a pillaged graveyard—dilapidated buildings, cracked pavements, crumbling façades with the air of tombs, and the sad un-cared-for trees that the dead had planted. This emptiness haunted me whenever I came up from underground. But never before had I seen it as I saw it then, standing beside a woman who put on display not only her beauty and energy, but her education, too, and who stood above the emptiness as a mother stands above the troubles of her child. I was seized by the conviction that this woman whom I had loved from the moment I saw her had also been sent to rescue me.

She took the glove from her right hand and warmed her fingers in her mouth. I wanted to take the hand in mine and warm it properly. I thrust my hands deeper into the pockets of my coat.

"So what should we do?" I asked.

"The only thing that works is a campaign," she said. "In the Western press."

"And who can organize that?"

"Not someone who lives underground."

"So where do *you* live, Betka?"

Betka looked at me, and I was out of my depth. How could I find words for this girl who did not whisper, did not hide as others hid from the hidden witness? I thought of Mother. That innocent woman, who had deserved only the very best of life and received only the worst, was now being broken on the wheel of their questions. The spasm of guilt that I felt was like smoke from the turbine of my excitement, which curled away above the chapel and was lost in the void. Words at home had never been direct. The world lay beyond our walls like a threat; we occasionally alluded to it, but never described it as it was. Our conversations were a kind of embroidered silence, each of us buried in the fiction of another life, a life of reckless solitude. All my dealings aboveground had been shaped by the same imperative—to conceal, to retreat, to make my pain so small that I could pack it into a hollow tooth and bite on it.

"I want to say that I live in the real world," she said. "But they abolished it long ago."

I muttered something, but she continued to look at me as though waiting for a confession. Still the words would not come.

"I think I know who wrote these stories," she went on. "It was you, wasn't it?"

"Could be."

"I understand you," she went on, "because I dreamed you up. And this book lies on the edge of my dream."

She had taken the volume of *Rumors* from her bag and held it out to me.

"Keep it. It is safer with you."

She replaced it with a smile.

"So there you are," she said, "back in my dream."

"I like it inside your dream. I like it very much."

"Only miracles happen in dreams. And you can't rely on miracles. We should go, by the way."

She nodded in the direction of the steps, which the old woman was once again ascending, the limp dog pressed to her side. She walked away.

"Follow me," she said, "and I won't look back."

I followed at a distance, my eyes fixed on her slender figure, which seemed to melt the space in which it moved. She went up the steps two at a time, and walked quickly through the streets of Vinohrady towards the center of town. The traffic was sparse and slow, as though it had lost direction. The shop windows displayed goods that were no longer obtainable but immortalized in contrived pyramids of boxes and tins. Noises were abrupt: the squeal of tram wheels against the rails, the patter of falling stucco from the facades, the occasional siren of a police car. People moved silently, their shoulders shrinking as they passed each other, their eyes fixed on the ground. The buildings stood behind wooden scaffolds like decrepit old people propped on Zimmer frames. Betka was a living woman in the land of the dead, and a glow surrounded her as she moved.

She stopped in the Charles Square, by the New Town Hall, from the windows of which, in 1419, the Hussite leader Jan Želivský had thrown thirteen town councillors to their deaths. Defenestration is a Czech tradition, the only one that the Communists had retained. The monument to Želivský stands in the square, reminding us of our national virtues. No monument commemorates those thirteen councillors. I caught up with Betka, where she stood beneath the effigy of the hero, and she walked on at my side.

"Here is the plan," she said. "You live as normal. You ask to visit your mother. You give nothing away. And you make yourself known."

"Known to whom?"

"Look, Jan..."

"Honza," I corrected.

"Look, Honza, there is only one path to safety, and that lies to the West of us. There is no safety underground. There is no safety for the ordinary person. You have to be known to the Western embassies. You have to be mentioned on the BBC and Radio Free Europe. You have to be a movement, like Charter 77. And then you raise the cost of destroying you, to the point where they might not attempt it."

"Is that how you live?"

She did not answer me, but walked on with quick, determined steps. We were descending towards the Vltava, on the far bank of which was the street where I would lean each morning against my bin and imagine the lives of passers-by. A mist hung above the river, shifting from side to side like the blanket on a troubled sleeper. A cold white sun peered through the clouds, shedding its light on the walls of the castle, above which the dark form of the cathedral lay like some huge animal that had died there, its frozen limbs locked into the sky. For a long time we did not speak. I followed beside her as though obeying orders, confident that I had acquired a destination and that she was leading me there.

She stopped outside a shop where plain bold letters spelled *Antikvariát* above a large window encrusted with dirt. She took my arm and guided me through the door. A worn-looking man with spectacles and a Habsburg beard looked up from behind the counter, where he was unpacking musical scores from a brown paper parcel. "*Dobrý den,*" she said in sing-song tones, and, "ahoj, Betko," he replied, hardly turning from his work.

"My favorite place," she said, leading me deep into the shop. The wooden shelves were packed with scores, many of them bound in leather. Betka's eyes brightened as she ran her finger along the spines, and the flesh around her eyes again had that mother-of-pearl translucency, as though a light had been switched on behind.

"You see what we were," she said, "when our country began. Music in every household, and look how beautifully engraved."

She had taken down a volume of Janáček's piano music—*On an Overgrown Path*. How strong and definite the notes looked on the page, as though nothing could sweep them away. And yet, Betka said, all this was a memory: few played the piano, fewer lived in a home that contained one. And the latest editions of this masterpiece contain all the printing errors of the original, since no one in the official publishing house has the competence or the authority to correct them. She asked me if I could read music.

"No. But we listened to it at home. That was one of Dad's favorites."

"Oh?" She looked up at me. "You speak in the past tense."

"Yes. He died."

I wanted to tell her the story. And in that moment it struck me vividly that I had told no one, shared this death with no one apart from Mother and Ivana, both of whom had been as reluctant to speak of it as I was. Slowly, she replaced the score and said, "I used to play this, back home. On my grandfather's piano."

"Where was home?"

"A little place near Brno. I came here to study."

"So you're a student?"

"No, that finished two years ago."

"So what do you do, Betka?"

She peered at a grey cloth spine on which the gold leaf had faded. "Oh, things. And what do you do?"

She took down another score and buried her head in it: songs by Schubert, with the Czech text hand-written above the German in old-fashioned characters. I briefly described my job; she smiled to herself, and changed the subject. She spoke for some time enthusiastically about the old culture of music-making, how people would gather to sing and play in every home, and how sad it made her to think that this rarely happened. She herself had learned to play the lute, so as to join a baroque ensemble that performed from time to time in the houses of friends. She was proud of this part of her life. Between people touched by that ancient music, she said, whoever they were and however tainted by the system, there were, for the moment, no secrets. While speaking she went through the shelves with firm methodical hands, putting aside the volumes that pleased her, and eventually carrying a little pile across to the counter. I was amazed by this, since secondhand books were coveted possessions, and far too expensive for people like me.

"Can you really afford all that, Betka?" I asked.

"Of course not. I have a friend who is building a library. He collects what I recommend. Here, Petr," she said, handing the books across the counter. "I will tell Vilém you are keeping them for him."

"He must have everything by now," the man said.

"He's getting there." Turning to me, she added, "We can go now. First me, then you. I will see you in ten minutes on the Střelecký Island. I'll be sitting there."

She didn't wait for a reply but vanished through the door of the shop. When I found her she was sitting calmly on a wooden bench, staring out across the river, her face to the sun. I tried hard to understand how someone could be so conscious of being followed, yet entirely and naturally calm. It was as though Betka created around herself a space of her own, a space where the rules did not apply. I sat next to that space, on the cold bench that sent a shock through my body. And her face in the sunlight shone back at the sun.

"You don't mind if I speak frankly, Honza?"

"How could I mind?"

"Oh, people do. They prefer whispered suspicions. But I hate that. I want to live. Do you want to live?"

"Now, yes."

She looked at me directly. It was a look that I was to know well in time: a curious, disarming look from wide, still eyes, which caused me to surrender completely to whatever she proposed. I had the chance then to look into those eyes that had so enchanted me on the Metro to Leninova. From an angle they did indeed have a silver sheen, peering through her lashes like the moon through trees. But this sheen was only the rough summary of their magic. The pupils were greenish-grey with a rim of royal blue, and in the center was a little apricot button, holding the whole tissue tight. Around that small sun revolved a tranquil solar system of glances, drawing the tide of my desire.

"So, Honza. Here is what we shall do. You must report to work as normal. You must go to the police station at Bartolomějská, and be scrupulously correct when they question you. Then I shall introduce you to the people you need to know. I shall fight for you, in my own way, but first I must teach you to live aboveground."

"But why should you do this?" I asked.

"For you."

"You don't know me."

She smiled, and took the copy of *Rumors* from her bag.

"I have this window where you stand."

We walked for a while on the Střelecký Island. And when, from time to time, I took her hand, she did not look at me, but smiled to herself and returned the slight pressure of my fingers. I told her about Dad, about Ivana, about my underground journeys, and she listened attentively. But about herself she was reticent, admitting only that she was living an independent life the details of which were of no interest to me. She took a notebook from her pocket and tore a sheet of paper from the center. On it she wrote the address of someone called Rudolf Gotthart, telling me that she would introduce me on Friday to his weekly seminar, and that I was to be there at 6 o'clock, before the seminar began. She wrote with a ballpoint, and I fought back the desire to ask why she did not use her fountain pen. She was never to know that it was I who had followed her to Divoká Šárka and whose cry had sounded from the trashcans by her door.

Then I noticed another thing. She was not wearing the bangle that I had seen then on her wrist. A curious thought entered my mind: that she had two quite separate lives. The thought no sooner occurred than it became a knife of jealousy. The girl who cultivated dissidents, who was exploring the world of samizdat, who was in some strange way excited by the opportunity to recreate me as a hero and a martyr, was the holiday version of another being entirely. I imagined her as mistress to some slick Party member with the right to foreign travel, who provided a nice old farmhouse on the edge of Prague, and the spare cash to kit herself in bourgeois style. So sharp was this thought that I groaned aloud.

"Are you OK?" she asked.

"You haven't told me about yourself, Betka."

"You'll learn."

"But when this kind of thing happens…"

"What kind of thing?"

"Well, you could call it love."

She screwed up her face like a child.

"Let's not start on that. I take risks, but not that one."

"But why do you take the others?"

"Because I want to live. Like I said."

"But why do this for me?"

She looked at me and laughed. Her laughter was close-knit and undulating, like a sloping lawn in the sun.

"I was crawling underground and look what I found! Why shouldn't I bring it up into the daylight and watch it blink?"

"Not very flattering to me."

"Very flattering, actually, if you knew."

Quite without warning, she kissed me on the cheek and strode away to the stone staircase that led to the bridge across the river. She paused on the turn of the steps and looked back in my direction.

"Meet me tomorrow, in the Café Slavia at three. If I am with someone, ignore me. If I am on my own, greet me as a friend."

And with that, she walked briskly onto the bridge and into town. I hesitated for a moment, wishing to follow her. Then I went in the opposite direction.

CHAPTER 6

I CALLED IN at the workshop in one of the little alleys where Smíchov meets the shore road and where each morning I collected my broom, dustpan, and orange street-sweeper's jacket from Mr. Krutský. He raised his dumpling-colored face and laid big hands on the desk, vainly trying to focus his watery grey eyes. Never in all my dealings with him had Mr. Krutský fixed his look on me. Always, his eyes seemed to stray from side to side, as though he feared a door would open somewhere and a hand reach out for his throat.

"The StB were here yesterday," he said, "asking for you. That means trouble."

"My trouble, not yours. And anyway, you can't fire me. I am at the bottom of the ladder. There's nowhere down from here."

"But where were you when they came?"

"I had a headache. I'm sorry. I will work late."

"And now I have to report on you," said Mr. Krutský, with a weary sigh.

"Is that what they told you?"

"Once a week, to be collected."

I shrugged.

"Shouldn't be too difficult. I'll write it for you."

Taking my broom and dustpan from the rack, and my bright orange jacket from the peg, I left for the Husovy sady. I spent the rest of that morning in a state of euphoria. It hurts to confess this. It hurts to confess that I was glad of Mother's arrest, glad of the misfortune that had befallen us, glad that I was officially a non-person. I had come up from underground. I was breathing real air, the air that Betka breathed, and I was going to live in another way, in a space that we shared. Side by side with Betka I would live in truth. What a cliché! And what a lie! But I am coming to that.

I telephoned Ivana from the public phone at Můstek. She lived with a woman whose old townhouse in Brandýs had been taken by the Party in exchange for a couple of rooms in a new block of apartments. The old woman was worn down enough to be indifferent to her lodger's history. But when I told my sister of Mother's arrest, she said "hush" as though refusing to be implicated in a crime. By speaking in whispers I reshaped the story as a legend. Ivana was tense, scant, and embarrassed, reluctant to be dragged beyond the confines of her world. She had opted for a clean life within the system, and wanted nothing more to do with crime. I was not surprised when she hung up on me.

I went that afternoon to the central police station, which occupies one side of Bartolomějská street: a warren of offices and cells behind old facades, punctured at one point by a window of small square panes, stretching over five floors. I entered by the old headquarters building from the First Republic, which looks as though sculpted from a single piece of coarse red sandstone. Formalized bas-reliefs of workers, miners, and peasants remind the passer-by of what is needed in the life-long business of avoiding arrest. I waited in a dirty room with a window in one wall, behind which an official face appeared, seldom the same face and always staring blankly at my request for news of Mrs. Reichlová. Uniformed figures moved purposefully in and out of the room, ignoring me. A woman entered with a shopping bag of groceries, crowned by a bunch of flowers. She went through a door to the other side of the window, nodding as she passed.

I began to notice a strange humming in the room, as though an insect were trapped somewhere and uselessly beating its wings. After a while it seemed as though the humming were coming from inside me. I felt an overwhelming urge to sit down, but there were no chairs, only a kind of ledge around the wall on which you could briefly lodge your thighs.

I propped myself up as best I could. Faces floated past, melting and then hardening as they drifted away. Perhaps an hour passed before one of them fixed itself in front of me, and the humming crystallized as words. The officer's thin grey face seemed to have been sharpened to an edge, as though to cut through whatever pretenses stood in front of it. He spoke in curt, simplified phrases, as though controlled by a machine that allowed only limited options.

"Mrs. Reichlová has been transferred to Ruzyně."

"I am her son, and have a right to visit her."

The words sounded in the room as though spoken by someone else. Everything that concerned Mother had been removed behind a screen, and I saw only shadows outlined against it.

"The Criminal Code forbids visits during interrogation."

He looked at me intently for a moment, and then added, "We need to speak to you, too."

"Is she not entitled to a lawyer?"

"We have appointed a lawyer who will present the case for the defense."

Without waiting for a reply he turned on his heels and marched to the door. Reaching it, he turned slowly around.

"Stay there," he said.

I did as he told me. It was not I who waited, but another who had usurped my body. I was far away, rejoicing still in Betka, and hardly thinking of Mother. When the officer returned it was to beckon me to the door in which he stood. I found myself squeezed against him in a lift, surrounded by his sweaty smell and unable to avoid his intensely staring green eyes between which a knife-blade of nose made short sharp cuts in my direction. He did not push me or guide me but somehow distilled me into a large room, where I sat in a chair against the wall as he took up position behind a desk in front of me. Another officer, who I understood to be the principal interrogator, was standing in the center of the room, and began pacing up and down. He was a soft-featured man of about forty, and addressed me with a schoolmasterly concern for my future. Of course I asked to be a witness at her trial, and the sharp-faced policeman, who was now taking notes, smiled at my request without recording it. I answered their questions with shrugs and evasions, hardly caring what I said. But when they asked me why I was on the bus to Divoká Šárka and whom exactly I was visiting there, I felt a burst of alarm. I told them that I had never intended to get on that bus, that I was distracted by the presence of police, and that I had got off at the last stop without thinking, in a state of somnambulism. The sharp-faced officer again smiled. This time he wrote down my words.

"Of course," he said, looking up, "we will learn in due course whom you were visiting."

He closed his notebook and lit a cigarette. A third man in plain clothes entered from an adjoining room and began to discuss repairs to a Mercedes, and how to obtain parts for it. As the three talked I began to take note of my surroundings. We were in a room with high windows. I looked out onto a semi-circular opening in the wall of St. Bartholomew's Church, which peered at me like the half-open eye of a man who has been beaten. On the wall facing me was a poster showing the hatchet face of Felix Dzerzhinsky, Lenin's chief of secret police, above his famous slogan: "Clean hands, cool head, warm heart." I recalled another saying of Dzerzhinsky's, from a book that Mother had produced about the Russian Revolution: "We represent in ourselves organized terror—this must be said very clearly." But it wasn't said clearly around here. The only hint of it was another poster announcing things that were forbidden: smoking, talking when not addressed by an officer, putting your hands in your pockets, consulting papers, taking notes.

I was seated in a simple chair in a row of four. The officers were standing around the desk, which looked as though it had been there since the days of the First Republic. At one point, the sharp-faced one left with his notebook and began talking loudly in the adjoining room. I stared for a while, then drifted away. Nothing of what was happening seemed to concern me. I thought of Betka's words to me. What had she meant about bringing me up into the daylight so as to watch me blink? What was she planning—for that she was planning something I did not doubt. They were still talking among themselves when, without deciding to do any such thing, I got up and went towards the door.

"What are you doing?" the interrogator cried.

"I assumed you didn't want me anymore."

"Just wait there."

The interrogator left for the adjoining room, and returned after a while with two sheets of paper, on which questions and answers had been typed.

"Read it," he said. "And when you have read it, sign."

The rough grey paper rubbed against my fingers like a file. Some of the words had been typed over with x's; others were fragments of communist jargon that I could not possibly have used. I had apparently denied all knowledge of my mother's reactionary beliefs and counter-revolutionary actions, and the words—*zpátečnický* and *kontrarevoluční*—were like pieces of an old jigsaw forced into the unfilled places of a puzzle to which they did not belong.

"What if I don't agree?"

"Sign it, I said."

I must have signed; I don't remember. Afterwards I went back to Gottwaldova. I did not return to my life underground. I had emerged from the catacombs into a wholly new kind of loneliness, an assuageable loneliness that came from wanting what was real. When I left work the next day I wandered along the banks of the river for an hour. It was a raw December day, and a thin sunlight placed golden crowns on all the houses. I remember one of them, a plain white house which still retained its stucco, with an attic story where stone nymphs punctuated a balustrade. I remember it because of an unusual feature, which was the figure of a woman leaning from the attic window and looking down on the Smetana embankment. People didn't lean much out of windows in those days, and certainly not in places where they could be so easily seen. She was young, dark, with strangely lopsided features, as though one side of her face had been assembled without reference to the other. She seemed to be watching me, and I did something unpremeditated and foolhardy: I waved at her. She looked back at me with a puzzled expression, and then promptly closed the window. Recalled now, the experience has the character of a premonition. The world was full of warnings, and I rejoiced in ignoring them.

Betka was sitting in a window of the Slavia, at one of the marble tables that have since been modernized away. I should have been intimidated by this place frequented by intellectuals and spies. I had heard that a circle of dissidents, who had gathered around the poet Jiří Kolář before his emigration in 1980, still met from time to time at his favorite table. And surely the man filling in the *Mladá fronta* crossword, whose table commanded a view of the whole interior, was the resident corner-cop. It surprised me that Betka was sitting there, calmly immersed in a book, one finger in the handle of a cup that she had just put down.

The Slavia had maintained some memory of its past, as the place where the cheerful believers in our nation had drunk together while the band played dumkas and polkas from the dais. The few tired waiters wore the shreds of old uniforms, with white collars and black bow ties; the tables and chairs were unchanged from the Jugendstil pattern acquired in the last days of Austro-Hungary, and against the wall of the dais, next to an upright piano, a double bass leaned as though exhausted from its labors. A few tidily-dressed men sat at one table, staring silently into glasses of wine. Two women whispered in a corner, one of them toying with a necklace of imitation pearls, as though debating whether the time had come to strangle herself. The place was another warning, and Betka was inviting me to ignore it.

She had tied up her hair in a chignon, and the sight of her pale neck aroused in me a love quite unlike any that had haunted my travels underground. I wanted to make her my own. I sat down, and she looked up with a smile. She put a scrap of paper in her book, closed it, and pushed it into the center of the table. It was the *Heretical Essays* by Jan Patočka, published in Canada by an exile press. I asked her how she had acquired this work by a famous non-person, first spokesman of Charter 77, who had been interrogated to death, so I had been told, by the StB, and whose dense, laden prose had been one of the weights under Mother's bed.

"No need to know," she answered. "But it's pretty unreadable stuff."

"He wrote that way because he was wrestling with darkness," I protested.

"His own darkness."

It had not occurred to me that a famous dissident might be frankly criticized. It was part of our impotence, that the few touchstones could not be shifted. Betka moved in an illuminated space of her own, in which nothing was protected, and all was provisional.

I found myself talking to her as though coming home from a long adventure, and it dawned on me that my conversations with Betka were the first real conversations in my life. I was speaking to her of my failed education and my journeys underground. I talked about Dostoevsky and Kafka, and she nodded her encouragement, saying hardly a word. How ordinary my confidences sounded, but how special was the glance with which she greeted them. There was a kind of ingenuous amazement in her features, as though I had fallen into her world in just the way she had fallen into mine. And when I had finished, she held my hand gently for a moment and said "Jan," as though baptizing me.

I asked her about her parents.

"They are irrelevant," she answered. "Not the kind of people you would want to know."

"But what do they do?"

She looked down at her hands, which lay as though discarded on the table.

"They are divorced. Dad manages an export business, but I never see him."

A Party member, then. It could hardly have been otherwise, since she was so rich and so free.

"And you?" I asked. "Do you live with one of them?"

She looked at me for some moments with an ambiguous stare.

"Not really," she said. "At least not with Dad."

She was silent for a while and I placed my hand on hers.

"That was your mother's mistake," she said suddenly, "not to be known. There she was, an ordinary person, deviating from the official routines like Winston Smith in *Nineteen Eight-Four*, and she hadn't told anyone about it. Anyone who matters, that is. Public criminals have an electric halo and cannot be touched. Private criminals are defenseless."

I thought ruefully of Dad and nodded my agreement.

"But how did they discover her?"

Her question was like a mirror, in which I saw my own frightened face.

"I guess they came across one of her books. It wouldn't be difficult to discover where the paper came from."

She looked at me curiously, as though knowing there was more that I could tell. Slowly she withdrew her hand from under mine.

"They could arrest you, too, of course," she said. "But what would they gain by it? Think of it this way, Honza. You have been given an opportunity. You can step into the light. And there is nothing more that they can take from you."

"If they don't take you."

"Oh, they can't take *me*."

Without warning she got up and beckoned to the waiter. Before I could detain her, she had paid for our coffees and was walking to the door. I caught up with her outside, but she turned away from me. "You go that way," she said, "and I go this way. I'll see you at Rudolf's on Friday. Meet you in the street outside at a quarter to six. I want to introduce you to him first, before the seminar starts. OK?"

In time I got used to his habit of hers, of bringing things abruptly to a close as though terminating an interview. I came to think of it as proof of her superior reality, that she appeared and disappeared through doors whose existence I had not guessed at and which opened without warning when my mind was elsewhere.

CHAPTER 7

THE NEXT TWO days were the strangest I had known. I was alone in our cupboard at Gottwaldova, and yet for the first time not alone. I ate scraps of food from the corner shop—black bread and dusty sausage—and drank beer that I brought up in a jug from the *hostinec* at the end of our street. And my little meals were celebrations, which I shared in my imagination with the girl who had disinterred me. I hardly thought of Mother: she was like a numb spot in my consciousness from which my thoughts rebounded to another place, the place where Betka stood. And that was why Betka so astonished me. Here was a girl who did not whisper, as Mother did; who did not look at me askance who did not seem shifty, uncertain, and as though haunted by some unconfessed failing as she tried out her repertoire of permitted words. Here was a girl with the frank manner, the ironical glances, and the occasional bursts of laughter that I remembered from a week of Westerns inexplicably shown at the cinema next to Dad's school. This manner has become so familiar to me now, after fourteen years in an American university, that I no longer take note of it. But then it could only amaze me. Her unfathomable self-assurance: how and from whom had she acquired it? Her easy smile and untroubled sympathy: what sun of love had warmed these seeds in her?

Her image filled my thoughts as I swept my little patch of street, and as I walked on the Petřín hill after work. It was snowing now, and my worn-out shoes gave little protection against the cold. But I did not mind: my frozen toes reminded me that I was walking above-ground, that I had emerged into a colder and clearer world. I saw before me her eyes set wide apart, her high Slavic cheeks with their faint sheen where the bone showed, her pale lips that lay sleepily against each other beneath her opal nose, her brown hair tied in a bun. Always she appeared to me as I had first encountered her, the delicate neck in a barely visible foulard of pink cotton, and a coat of white felt from the sleeves of which pale hands emerged, busying themselves with a notebook in which her inner life was written down. And when, from time to time, I put her image back in the box from which I had lifted it, it was into the little farmhouse trapped between housing blocks in Divoká Šárka.

Rudolf's apartment was situated in a street of nineteenth-century houses on the hill of Letná. Wooden scaffold had been fixed to the façade to protect against falling stucco, and Betka was waiting for me, leaning against one of the posts, and wrapped like a child against the cold. She smiled softly at my approach but turned away from my attempted kiss and led me quickly into the cold grey foyer of the house. By the bank of letter boxes, she turned to me.

"They can know that I know you," she said. "But nothing more."

And she walked quickly towards the stone stairs.

Always they were present, watching her. And always she shrugged them off, reminding me, as though from a sense of duty, of the unseen eyes that followed us. She pressed a bell on the second floor and the door opened at once with a whispered greeting from an unseen face. We left our shoes in the hallway and were bundled silently into a large room lined with bookshelves that climbed the walls right up to the high rococo cornices.

Rudolf was thin, bald, wiry, with a firm, square jaw set in his face like a piece of steel machinery. His cheeks seemed clamped against his nose like metal plates, and his grey eyes stared intently from beneath eyebrows that resembled thick wire brushes. His movements were jerky, almost robotic, and he had about him an air of defiance, as though fighting in a corner from his last reserve of strength. Betka introduced me as Paní Reichlová's son, and it was apparent that already Mother's case was well known in Rudolf's circle. He wanted to hear exactly what had happened, how the StB had discovered her work, and what books she had been working on. I answered as best I could. But Rudolf did not listen as one person listens to another. Rather, he gathered up my words and weighed them, as though assessing their worth. And all the while those eyes were watching, not blinking, not moving, but unnaturally alert as though instructed by some homunculus deep in Rudolf's skull.

Among the few people I had met, Rudolf was without exception the most disconcerting, and standing in his gaze I felt like an impostor, as though I were making unjustified and presumptuous use of Mother's affliction in order to claim a parity of heroism that I in no way deserved. Everything I said to him, about Mother, about my reading, even about Dad, seemed somehow false and inauthentic. And he listened as though it seemed that way also to him, as though he had heard it all before and as though I were cribbing from a standard text that all his young visitors would parrot. Looking around at his book-lined room, I felt a despair at my lack of education, even a certain bitterness, thinking that it would have been worthwhile losing whatever Rudolf had lost in order to have gained the knowledge for which they had punished him.

He told me that I could join his seminar, and that they were reading the *Two Studies of Masaryk* by Patočka. It was one of the books that Mother had worked on, and which had been taken away from beneath her bed. I asked him how I could obtain a copy. He said it wasn't necessary, that the relevant pages would be read aloud. And he added that there would be special seminars from time to time, with visitors from the West, who would inform us of the latest scholarship, and help us to remember.

"To remember what?" I asked.

He looked at me long and hard.

"To remember what we are."

He said it like a slogan, something to be repeated in moments of doubt, when his little band of followers might be tempted to give up on him. I glanced around at Betka, but she was lost in the shelves of books. Rudolf and she ignored each other, and she was clearly a familiar presence in his life. I noticed that she had taken off the thick brown jacket and woolen scarf that had wrapped her and thrown them on one of Rudolf's leather-covered armchairs, as though they belonged there. I was troubled by the thought, which somehow suggested that the life I was building had no certain foundations. Yet I must build it: there was no other way.

Rudolf was lecturing me now, telling me that in 1848, when the Austrian authorities had cracked down on the national revival, only two professors were dismissed from the university, and even then it had caused a major scandal, whereas now… I was made to understand that anybody who was anybody in the life of the mind had been driven from the system, and that the "parallel polis" to which Rudolf belonged was the true place of refuge, the temple where ancestral gods kept vigil over our collective soul. Moreover, he implied, just by being washed up in this way on the shore of dissidence, deprived of all weapons and without the instruments of worldly success, you showed your superior title to the life of the mind. He swept the air as he spoke, including books, furniture, a few gloomy pictures, and the enigmatic Betka in his gesture, and emphasizing the impassable gap between the hope contained in this cluttered interior and the unending nothingness outside.

Beyond the window it was snowing hard, and flakes clung to the window, glowing gold and silver from the streetlight below. I saw that the path to which Rudolf pointed was obligatory, and it was a path of no return. He advised me always to carry the equipment, such as soap and toothbrush, that I would need in jail.

"They can keep us for forty-eight hours," he said, "and from time to time it strikes them as the right thing to do."

I turned to Betka, who was sitting now in one of the armchairs.

"Has it happened to you?" I asked, and she shook her head as though ridding herself of the question.

"Alžběta is our guardian angel," said Rudolf. "We are safe when she is here."

After a while, the visitors—*moji žáci*, my pupils, as Rudolf described them—began to arrive. Someone had left the door ajar, so they entered quietly, discarding their shoes, leaving their coats in a pile by the door, and whispering their greetings as though assembling for some dangerous adventure. A few were young, the boys with long hair and shabby clothes like Western pop stars, the girls neatly dressed, one or two wearing a cross on a gold or silver chain. Some were middle-aged—scholarly men with waistcoats and beards, matronly women in long woolen skirts, an elderly couple who entered hand in hand, stumbling slightly, and a few ill-dressed men who seemed to have been brought in off the street, with shifty gestures and blank faces suggesting they had been recruited against their will. A tall man of a certain age, with finely chiseled features and a shock of white hair, bent beneath the lintel as he entered the room, looking deferentially from side to side like a once-proud nobleman who had lost everything, and was now the debtor of those who used to serve him. I learned that he was the poet Z. D., famous in his day but long since deprived of the right to publish. Other faces, too, were familiar, though I could not put a name to them. One in particular stood out: a man of about thirty-five in a greasy mechanic's outfit, who wore a wooden cross on a leather thong around his neck and whose pale face and slow-moving brown eyes were suffused with a strange softness. He sat down on the floor next to Betka and smiled at her; returning his smile, she leaned forward to stroke his arm.

This was my first experience of a social gathering, and I was overwhelmed by it. I had known imaginary friendships and invented love affairs; but real love and friendship are learned by example, and—except for Dad who betrayed me and Mother whom I betrayed—the examples had never come my way. Of course there was Ivana; but observing this room of drop-outs and criminals, I imagined the shudder of disdain with which she would instinctively shield herself from entering it. Here, littered across the carpet like the aftermath of battle, were the remains of our true society: people who had declared their solidarity, and whose need for each other was revealed in the tenderness with which they wove their whispered greetings from filaments of air. I was seized with a burning desire to be part of what I saw, and I took my place on the floor beside Betka, my heart pounding with excitement. And yet she seemed so cool, so calm, as though this gathering were one form of life among many, and nothing special for her. She looked on the people who greeted her as though from a place of safety, a guardian angel, just as Rudolf said.

Rudolf took up position behind his desk, on which stood a large lamp of frosted glass, borne aloft by a naked nymph in bronze. He stood, slightly leaning on the desk, and began to talk, his white hands circling in the air, his lips moving from side to side as though printing the words, the words themselves dark and serious, since all smiles had been sucked from them. I saw that Rudolf's standing in his world was as high as any to be achieved in the official life outside. Here was authority, visible, tangible, the power of the powerless in a wiry torso. Whatever privations he had suffered, they were the price of a far greater freedom, which was the freedom to command the thoughts and feelings of an audience, and to come before them as a guide.

I looked around at the books shelved side by side from floor to ceiling, some leather-bound in glazed cases, others with the neat cloth covers of the First Republic, their spines embossed with streamlined lettering, their irregular sizes and experimental colors the outward signs of the same freedom that spoke through Rudolf—a freedom that lived in words, and which was exhaled like a breeze when you opened the covers of a book. Rudolf was reading from the book on his desk, the *Two Studies of Masaryk*, some copies of which Mother had managed to distribute, but which Rudolf seemed to possess in a neat edition from an exile press. The passage spoke of the twentieth-century wars, of the reckless night in which the price of everyday senselessness is paid.

Patočka's drastic words, mixing philosophical technicalities and frightening invocations of an all-encompassing destruction, were like spells, summoning the ghosts of our ruined country into the room. And around me I sensed the held breath, the intent stares into nothing that bound us together in a conspiracy of apartness. In the new kind of night, Rudolf read, into which the soldier goes without purpose, lies the reality of sacrifice, and in sacrifice an awareness of freedom. My own reality as a soul, whose nature is to care, is brought home to me; in the moment of sacrifice comes an intimation of the meaning that daylight had bleached away. In that moment I break out of the prison of the everyday, and there, in life at the apex, I experience the only form of *polis* which we may now attain, the "solidarity of the shattered."

I write these words now in suburban Washington, looking down on a quiet street where mothers pass with prams and wheelchairs, and a few old people walk their dogs. And the words are like dream

[ROGER SCRUTON]

debris, washed up in the weary light of dawn. It is only with a certain effort that I recall their sound in Czech. But when Rudolf pronounced them on that evening twenty years ago, a shudder passed through the room. This *solidarita otřesených* was a presence among us and I felt it on my arm like the grip of a neighbor in a shared moment of fear. No tragedy, no ritual performance, no encounter of warriors on the eve of battle, could have been more charged with feeling than the room in which we sat. We were assembled on that floor in a state of total togetherness. We were side by side, sharing life, hope, and danger in our own threatened space. The faces all around were focusing on Nothing with intense and seeking stares. I had the impression that it wanted only the fatal knock on the door for a great smile of acceptance to sweep across our faces like a burst of sunlight. Betka, however, seemed to withhold herself, and I let my eyes dwell on that calm, collected face, astonished by its beauty.

When Rudolf had finished reading, he looked round in a kind of triumph, emphasizing with his fierce eyes and rigid posture that we had been led into another realm, where truth alone was the goal. He alluded to writers whom I had never encountered, to books that I could never have read, to a world of reasoning and feeling that stood before me like a pool into which I wanted to jump and be cleansed of my isolation. And he illustrated everything with thoughts of his own, connecting the most abstruse arguments to our daily routines of selfishness.

"All the things that are required of us," he said, "like queuing for essentials, pulling strings, reporting on our friends and colleagues, marching on May Day, are so much easier to do for selfish than for noble motives. Who could queue for two hours simply in order that a child in Africa should be saved from starving? Who could betray his colleagues in order to prepare his own martyrdom as their leader? But to do these things for a loaf of bread—nothing is easier."

He went on to compare us to those people in the ancient world whose city has been destroyed and who have been led away into slavery. No motive remains that will keep us to the path of honor and justice. We steal from each other, even what we love. We become scavengers. And when one of us shows that it need not be so, that he, for one, is prepared to make a sacrifice, there is suddenly joy and light and for a brief moment we remember what we were. And then we go back to captivity, for we have nothing else.

They were simple thoughts. But Rudolf linked them to such a wealth of philosophy and culture that I found myself shaking with desire for the path of truth and sacrifice that he described. He held my attention as the hand of eternity holds the apple of time, and I watched as the thin dust of humanity was blown across that apple and then polished away. My underground life, I saw, had been another form of selfishness and fragmentation. I had been avoiding even the fear that I should have been feeling, the fear that I saw all around me and which, had I opened my heart to it, would have saved my mother from her fate. This fear was real; I heard it in Ivana's voice on the telephone, as she shut the door on the life that we had shared. I saw it in Mother's face as she was led away. It was the all-pervading substance from which *Rumors* had crystallized, the stuff from which my underground friends and lovers had been composed. And yet I had avoided it until this moment, had allowed myself to fall in love with the girl beside me precisely because she showed no sign of it. The new life required me to acknowledge fear and to open my heart to it. And by fighting this fear in myself, I would be fighting it in the world around me.

Rudolf stopped speaking and discussion began. I looked on eagerly, astonished to find myself in a gathering where questions were posed as though they were common property and where knowledge was assumed, not displayed. At a certain point, Rudolf's wife, Helena, entered, carrying a tray of *chlebíčky*: she was a small woman, with a soft wrinkled face like a dried apricot. She smiled timidly at the guests as they helped themselves to the little circles of bread, on each of which a piece of cheese and a slice of gherkin had been balanced like a hat.

Never since Dad's death had there been guests in our apartment. I associated hospitality with the gatherings of apparatchiks, with their expensive leather coats and plump mistresses wrapped in fur. Hospitality belonged to the unapproachable world of *them*, where it signified not kindness or compassion but the insolence of privilege. Yet, here before me was the vivid disproof of that: powerless people offering and receiving gifts. A new dimension of being was outlined before me in a dramatic tableau that invited me to change my life. Someone was talking next to me of a poem that ended with just those words—*musíš změnit svůj život*, you must change your life. The poem was by Rilke, whose *Duino Elegies* had found their way into Dad's trunk, and the discussion of it spread like laughter through the gathering. I smiled at Rudolf, and then at Betka. I did not mind that the bread was stale or the cheese hard and acrid, with the texture of a toenail. That was the way we lived. I was standing in a sunbeam, and had lost all consciousness of the surrounding storm.

I find it hard to recapture the experience now, for that dreamscape has been swept away. Here in America's capital, where the ripe fruit of abundance hangs from every tree, where days end in parties, where friends come and go with easy hilarity and where fear is a specialist product, to be bought and sold in videos or downloaded from the Internet, how can I conjure a world where words were kept close like secrets, and friendship had the furtiveness of sin? All I can say is that I left the seminar as though walking on air. As we descended the stairs, Betka told me to meet her the next day on the Střelecký Island. Her light touch in the street, as she looked in my eyes and said "You go that way," and then promptly turned in the opposite direction, was a promise, an assurance that life had already changed for us, and that we had no need to make a display. I walked down to the river, imagining her on the bus to Divoká Šárka, neatly bundled against the window, showing tissue-paper eyelids as she looked down on her book. And behind those eyes as I imagined them was the thought of me.

CHAPTER 8

I DID NOT take the Metro, but decided to walk to Gottwaldova instead. The snow was settling in the streets and the silence was broken only by the occasional squeal of a tram. I walked down, with wet shoes and a light heart, into Malá Strana, the Little Side, hemmed in between the hill and the river. This part of our city was not ours at all: created by Italians for our Habsburg masters, it had been carefully dropped onto our soil like a fairyland of icing onto a battered old cake. The Church of St. Nicholas took 150 years to build and was to testify to the Jesuit Order as spiritual owner of the land beneath it and of the soul and the soil all around. Just two years after the church was completed, the Order and its claim to ownership were both dissolved. Yet from the scaffolding erected by such dead ambitions, the worn façades still hung, glinting with their jewels of snow like dew-spangled cobwebs. I looked on it all with a new wonder, as though this place that belonged to no one belonged in another way to me.

Each building seemed to embrace its neighbor, gable touching gable, curlicue wrapped in curlicue, roof sloping into roof. The lines of window frames and moldings were picked out by the snow; cornices and stringcourses seemed to shoot sideways, rush together like hectic streams, and lose themselves in foreign windowsills. Turrets and pediments poked through the white blanket, and the crumbling wall of a palace, propped on scaffolding, was like the face of a dying person, desperately sucking the snowflakes in his thirst. The wedge-capped towers of gates and bridges, the spikes of onion domes, the gesticulating statues on the parapets, barely arrested in the architectural whirlwind, like flimsy ballerinas on a surging sea of stucco—this superfluity of form and detail was thrown into drastic relief by the snow and the decay. Things seemed to be standing only by a miracle, each building propped against its neighbor, reduced to a flaking shell. One breath and the whole contraption would collapse, and I felt the quiet streets vibrating to either side of me as my wet shoes shoveled through the slush.

I crossed the river at the Střelecký Island and made my way towards Nusle. Everything appeared to me as though newly revealed, as though I came from some distant land and was seeing the truth that was hidden from those who lived in the untended graveyard of my city. At one point, I passed an Agitation Center, the place where some local branch of the Party rehearsed its immutable decrees. Behind glass that had never been cleaned, in a window that had never been dusted, a sloping board of posters proclaimed the socialist cause: Nazi-faced American GIs thrust their bayonets into Vietnamese babies, fat capitalists with bulging cigars stood on the heads of helpless workers, and huge missiles, decorated with the stars and stripes, flew in regimented flocks over the cowering cities of Europe. Dusty photographs showed weary communist potentates in grey alpaca suits, signing with fat old hands the bits of paper set before them on modernist desks, while Marx and Lenin stared across their porcine bodies into the future. Notices were pinned to a screen of cork behind the window: more slogans, written in a shaky old hand, composed in the same impersonal syntax, and with the same impenetrable vagueness: "Forward with the Party to a Socialist Future!!" "Long live our Friendship with the Soviet People!!" Strange, I reflected, that some frail old person should have taken the trouble to copy out those empty words, to etch them round with quotation marks, and to place them in this dusty shrine. I sensed the pathos of the Agitation Center: the pathos of an agitation that has dwindled to a palsy. The message of the Center was that you are not to hope or plan or strive, that everything has been fixed eternally, and that nothing remains for each successive generation but to append its signature to the senseless decree of Progress. Looking through that dirty window, I saw something for which I found words only here, in America, in a poem by T.S. Eliot, another exile from modernity: I saw 'fear in a handful of dust'. I had lived with that fear all around me, and now I was fighting it, not on my own behalf but on behalf of my city, my country, and my friends. It scarcely seemed to matter at that moment that I had no friends, nor did I see that I was striding into solitude. But I will come to that.

It was at the railway line beneath the Nusle Bridge that I knew I was being followed. The barrier was down at the crossing and I had to wait as a local train carrying a few huddled forms clanked through the darkness towards the river. From the corner of my eye, I noticed the figure moving quickly out of sight into a doorway. I crossed the railway and hid for a moment in the bushes that lined the path. I saw him hesitate and turn back. Then, when I began to walk, my footsteps echoed faintly below me as he resumed his pursuit. I had not seen his face, and his form was hidden beneath a heavy black coat. But there was something intimate in his way of moving, as though he already knew me.

There was a police car parked in front of our block. I did not turn round, but I knew from his steps that my companion had suddenly veered away, like a sparrow at the sight of a hawk. Whoever it was, therefore, he was not working for them. This thought troubled me, since it suggested that his motives were personal. And who, besides Betka, could possibly have a personal interest in me?

The wood had splintered away from the hinges of our door, which hung from its lock at an angle. I stepped across the wreckage and pressed the light switch, but nothing happened. The dim light from the stairwell went out, and for a moment I groped in darkness among broken glass and overturned furniture, until finding the bent metal lamp that Mother kept on the table beside her bed. I pressed the little button in its base, and felt a sudden stab of grief, remembering her presence in this room, and her hand reaching out to this button, which was the last thing that happened each night at home, when she had put aside her book and settled down to sleep. She touched this little button in order to wrap the day's troubles in a parcel of darkness, and I recalled her way of arranging our penury in neat and compact shapes, so that the trouble of our life was both controlled and stored. When the lamp came on, showing the smashed remains of her dominion, with the shards of glass from the ceiling light scattered across the upturned chairs and shelves torn down in cascades of plaster, I could not retain my tears.

After a while, however, I began to look on the disaster in another way—a way that showed that it was not a disaster at all, but a challenge. My life underground had been possible only because everything else was predictable. Although we lived in poverty and had no worldly hopes, we had our routine. Food appeared on the table; wages were paid; Dad's books were at hand, and Mother was busy each evening with the typewriter. I was free to invent my world, and that is what I had done, leaving Mother to pay the cost of it. Now, however, the fictions had been swept aside and another landscape appeared. *You must change your life.* Yes, and I could; because of Betka I could live in truth. That was the thought with which I went across broken crockery to the kitchen window, and looked down in defiance at the street.

The police were driving away, having no doubt reported my return. It was pointless to complain of a crime to those who had committed it, so I had no choice but to return to my changed life, restoring our little cupboard as best I could and planning for a long-lasting program of intimidation. I pushed the door back into place, and cleared away the debris. And the next morning, because it was a Saturday, I devoted myself to repairs, using the box of Dad's old tools that we kept in a cupboard in the kitchen. I sawed up one of the broken chairs, and used the pieces to secure the splintered door on its hinges. I took down the shattered light and fixed a bare bulb to the wires with insulating tape. And I hung the shelves in such a way as to hide the holes in the plaster where their brackets had been torn away. I returned Dad's paintings to the wall, and shelved the books that had been thrown in a corner. I made the place look like a home, to which Mother might one day return and where Betka, too, could visit. A queer feeling of apprehension came over me when I thought of Betka sitting here on Mother's bed. And I quickly closed the door of the apartment and set off into town.

The snow had settled in scattered precincts and there was no traffic on the roads. A chill yellow sunlight fell on the castle, which shone above the river mist like a mirage. Everything was beautiful and full of hope, and the sight of Betka, sitting amid untrodden snow on the Střelecký Island, her head wrapped in a woolen scarf, her gloved hands gripping a book, opened a door in my soul through which light streamed in. She looked up and fixed me with a smile, not moving or speaking but winding me in along her eyebeams, until we were face to face. Then she jumped up, kissed me on the cheek, pushed the book into her pocket and said, "Honzo! Let's go."

"Go where?"

"You'll see."

She took my arm, steering me towards the steps, which wound on themselves, making a little alcove with a curved seat of stone. She stopped for a moment, looked at me silently, and then with a sigh and a shake of the head led me across the bridge to Smíchov. She was silent, trembling, and pressed against me as though fearing something. We walked along the Újezd to an old arch between stucco façades, where a metal panel opened in a wooden carriage door. The panel slammed shut behind us, excluding the world. Before us was a long courtyard. On one side there were buildings with a functional appearance, like warehouses, one of them belching steam from a pipe that pierced the roof tiles. On the other side, casement windows, neatly framed in stucco, faced the courtyard, and in the middle of them a door opened onto some old wooden steps. We went up a flight. Two more doors bordered a flagstone landing.

Betka took an iron key from her pocket and let us into a room with an antique desk, a bed, some shelves full of books and papers, and a glazed partition leading to a kitchen. On one wall, above the bed, was an oil painting—a still life of fruit in the manner of Cézanne, whose paintings I knew from one of Mother's books. Above the desk was a window through which I could see the roof of the building opposite. Against the wall stood the case of a large musical instrument. It was warm in the room and everything within it was neat, harmonious, arranged with a kind of visual competence that I could not explain, for taste had been absent from our life at home. Betka took off her coat and hung it carefully in an old-fashioned cupboard that stood against the wall behind the door.

"But where are we, Betka?"

"This is where I live, silly."

"But I thought..." I stopped myself.

"What did you think?"

[ROGER SCRUTON]

"Oh, I imagined you living, you know, in some old family farmhouse, somewhere on the edge of town."

She turned to me with a serious face.

"The person you imagined, Honza, is not the one you see. Look at me."

I looked at her and with eyes fixed on mine, her hands shaking, she began to take off her clothes. Her soft skin, her breasts tight and firm, with a kind of gooseberry translucence, the trembling flesh of her neck as she steadied her eyes on me, these excited such desire and tenderness that I, too, began to tremble.

"So?" she said.

The softly-spoken word, half-question, half-command, still sounds in my memory. *Takže?* I say it to myself as I look down at the autumn leaves blown here and there on the street below my window, three thousand miles and twenty-three years from that place and time. And I hear again the sweet sad anguish of Janáček's "A Blown-Away Leaf"—the piece that Betka put on the record player, when she got up later from the bed where we had lain.

In the afternoon, we walked in the Strahov orchard. The snow, which had thawed in the sun, was freezing again as the short day ended. It was like walking in a virgin place, the ground crunching beneath us as though receiving its first human imprint. No figure moved in the shadows, and the mist from the river drew the horizon close around us, so that we moved in a space of our own. I asked her again what she did and how she lived.

"Oh," she replied, "I work in the evenings sometimes. In a hospital for sick children in Hradčany."

"And what do you do there?"

"Medical things. I qualified as a nurse."

"But you are studying, too?"

"It's my hobby," she replied, "the unofficial culture. One day I'll write a book about it."

"So I'm a hobby of yours?"

"Oh, Honzo," she said, taking my hand. "You are a mistake of mine. A big mistake."

"How come?"

She did not reply, but pulled me to a standstill and pressed her cold face to mine. It seemed to me that her cheeks were wet. But when I drew back to look at her, she hid her face and walked on.

I recounted what had passed on the previous evening: the footsteps behind me, the shattered door of the apartment, and the chaos inside. She listened in silence, sometimes shaking her head, and at one point stamping her foot as though in anger.

"I wonder why he followed you," she said at last. It was a strange remark, and I asked her whom she meant.

"Whoever it was," she replied, and then fell silent. We had left the orchard and were walking in the dusk through Malá Strana. We lived then in a world of enigmas. Each person was a secret to the other, and also to himself, and it did not trouble me, but on the contrary enhanced my love, that I walked beside a mystery. To every side were secrets: silent buildings, doors quietly closing, lights that shone dimly behind curtains furtively drawn.

I am writing of an experience that has disappeared from the world, and am writing in America. The American city never sleeps as Prague slept then in its mortuary silence. All night long in Washington, the noise, the light, and the commotion continue; for the American city has taken leave of its residents and functions like a machine. It has been programmed to work, to speak, to sing, and to riot on its own, almost without human company; to enter such a city is to be taken up by it, to be swept along into a rhythm that is more relentless than a monologue and more exhausting than a dance.

But you could stand in the squares and streets of Prague and listen to the quiet noises of a city settling down: the lifting of a latch, the turning of a key in a lock; a window opening; the flapping of curtains in a sudden breeze: the noises made by strangers as they retire, divided by thin partitions, and melt into a shifting silence. Those people sitting side by side in that ancient city probably never spoke to one another by day, or did so only in the cautious way that the Party required of them. At night, however, in the side-by-sideness of domesticity and of sleep, they seemed unconsciously to acknowledge their need, and to repair in secret ways the social bond that the machine tore apart each day. Betka and I stood for an hour or more in a street beside the Maltese church, listening to those noises, clinging to each other, each of us lost in secrets and in dreams. And when we reached the Malostranská Metro station, and she looked up to say that she would leave me there, I saw in her eyes not only anxiety, but also longing, and that longing was for me.

CHAPTER 9

DURING THOSE WEEKS that led from winter into spring, everything changed for me. I walked in the streets and parks as though belonging there, my eyes and mind now open to the world. I did not invent the lives of passersby, but allowed them to live with their secrets. I knew their fear and their resentment, and I sympathized. As I traveled underground I took no pleasure in exploring their weary faces and felt no need to prolong my daily journey. I turned up for work as before, and helped Mr. Krutský write his reports. But I did this with a lightness of heart, as though I were soon to be free of all such sublunary matters, lifted to the orbit where Rudolf and Betka circled among the stars.

Each Friday I attended the seminar, taking notes and asking questions. Rudolf had read *Rumors*, and when Betka explained their authorship, he began to treat me with a special regard. I was admitted to the privileged group of "pupils" who could borrow books from his library, signing for them in a notebook that was tied to a shelf by the door. I was allowed to call on him in the hour after *oběd*—the meal that divides the Czech day in two—and which he kept for his special visitors. I would go there each Wednesday with my private questions and my little attempts at essays. I devoured the literature of the Austrian twilight: Rilke, Musil, Roth, and von Hofmannsthal. I dipped into the philosophers: Husserl, Heidegger, Sartre and the revered Patočka, trying to extract from them, though without much success, the messages that could guide me more firmly into the orbit that was Rudolf's. I read works of history, studied the controversy between Palacký and Pekař, when they fought over the meaning of Czech history, in those days when our collective soul hung above us like a vision in the clouds. I read Zdeněk Kalista, who had spent many years in prison after the war, and whose writings were no longer published in our country. His posthumously collected essays on the *Face of The Baroque*, describing the twofold art that lifts time to eternity and summons eternity back into time, had just been published in Germany by an exile press. Rudolf had obtained a copy and generously lent it to me, along with his most precious possession, a samizdat journal—*Střední Evropa*, Central Europe—devoted to exploring the history and culture of our country and to showing that we are not what Mr. Chamberlain had said we were at the time of Munich, a far-away country of which the British know nothing, but the very heart of Europe.

I was amazed by what I read, for although I had sneered at our official history lessons in school, I had no knowledge of an alternative. To think of the baroque city not as a foreign incrustation, a veneer sprayed onto our Czech obstinacy from an aristocratic scent-bottle, but as the essence of what we are, to think of this fragile cake of crumbling stucco as the realized form of eternal meanings, to think of our folksy national revival as simply one manifestation of a central European consciousness that is rooted as much in Germany as in the territories settled by Hungarians and Slavs—to think such things caused an upheaval all the greater in that it reminded me guiltily of Dad. For all his hatred of what the Communists had done, Dad believed the official myth concerning the Battle of the White Mountain. He believed that we had been enslaved in 1620 by a decadent aristocratic culture, and not been fully liberated from the German yoke until the defeat of the Nazis in 1945. And those old-fashioned beliefs, which I was discovering to be so much propaganda, endowed Dad's image with a special poignancy, since they were proof, in their own way, of his innocence. I shared my thoughts with Betka, who listened to my tales of Dad with a kindness that was something more than the kindness of a lover. In all her words to me she sought to lift me free from the darkness, to open my eyes to better and clearer things. And, in time, I understood what she meant when she said she was seeing how I blinked.

I began to explore my city, visiting the National Museum, the Castle Gallery, and the few churches that were open, studying maps and learning the names of the palaces and the stories of the great families—Lobkowicz, Sternberg, Wallenstein, Schwarzenberg—who had lived in them. And I began to identify with another Rudolf, the Emperor Rudolf II, who reigned from 1576 until 1611, and who had vainly attempted to conciliate the religious passions that would soon drag us into that Battle of the White Mountain and so replace one civilization with another. The Prague of Rudolf II was a place of religious tension; but it was home to art, science, and the patronage that supported them; it was a place where alchemists and chemists pursued their uneasy rivalry; where philosophy and magic, religion and sorcery, fed from each other's extravagances. Something of that time still lived in the city, seeping down into our catacombs across centuries of repudiation, even bypassing through some hidden capillaries the concrete barrier called Progress. Rudolf's empire was stolen from him; and his remedy was the very one that we had rediscovered, which was the life of the mind. And the world of spells over which he presided was with us still, handed down like the elixir that promised eternal life to Elena Makropoulos, and from which she turned, at last, when she understood that it is the quality and not the quantity of life that counts.

During all this excitement, I felt the watchful presence of Betka in my life. Because she was, in her mysterious way, a part of me, I felt that I could not be harmed. Whatever they did, whatever went wrong for me, for Rudolf, for Mother—and we were all massively threatened, there could be no doubt of it—Betka's love would redeem it. That *this* had happened to *me* was enough. When she permitted, I would visit the little room in Smíchov and enter the enchanted world that we shared. I say "when she permitted," for Betka lived, spiderlike, on a web of imperatives woven by herself. All our meetings began and ended with a command or a permission, and never could I presume at the end of one day that it was up to me to initiate the next. She was in control of everything; and yet, when I came to her, she welcomed me as her mistake, *moje chyba*, as though this very regime of commands had been torn asunder, and she had given up trying to repair it.

She would be waiting for me—not impatiently, since impatience was not her style, but with a heightened appetite for life. In some way I had rescued her from a routine that she could not confess to. She would open the door and immediately stand back from it, one foot slightly to one side like a ballerina, reaching behind me to close the door before swinging me into her arms. And she would repeat the words, *moje chyba*, adding some gentle explanation such as *dech podsvětí*—breath of the underworld—which was not an explanation at all but a delicate way of avoiding it. This delicacy was something that I loved in her: once admitted to her presence, I could be wholly myself, and nothing in her manner condemned me. Her gentle laugh, her beautiful glances and turns of phrase, all of which seemed directed to the corners of the room as though taking me in obliquely, so that I loomed at the edge of everything she saw, her fastidious way of arranging the desk or smoothing the bed, putting herself so perfectly on display that often my desire for her could not be contained beyond the first few moments of greeting—all this so drove from my mind the old sense of isolation that I lived those hours in her room as though returning in triumph from an ordeal for which she and all her beauty were the reward.

We lay on that bed for whole afternoons, Betka rising from time to time to make tea in the little kitchen that lay tucked away behind the glazed partition at the back of the room, and I sometimes reading the books that I took from her shelves—exile press editions, some clumsily-bound copies of samizdat, and philosophical works in German and English. She showed me that it was possible to talk without fear of everything, to praise and condemn with total freedom, to explore in words all that was locked away and forbidden in reality—like those flies that dance on the crest of moving waters and are never wet. And always there was music: the heart-breaking quartets of Janáček, the songs and sonatas of Schubert, and also Betka's music, to which she devoted much of her time.

Since Dad's death, the only music I had encountered was that contained in his record collection—long-playing Supraphon records of the classics, with Smetana, Dvořák, Fibich, and Janáček added as a sinful excess—sinful because personal to Dad and a distillation of his dreams. The records enhanced my apartness. The Czech masters in particular spoke of another world, a natural world, in which human beings rose from the soil like plants and, dying, left their fossilized traces. The art and music of our national revival spoke of homecoming and mother's love, because those things were more fully longed-for then, when they were being shaped not as disappointments but as promises. But there was no consolation in this music: to connect to that vanished world was impossible, just as it was impossible, now, to disappear. The young man in Janáček's *Diary of One Who Disappeared* enjoyed a freedom that we lacked, the freedom to go about the world unobserved. You could not disappear;

you could only hide, as I had hidden belowground. And then, when I was brought suddenly to the light by Betka, I appreciated all that old music in another way, not as mine but as Dad's.

Music was Betka's first love, the only one of her loves that she ingenuously displayed to me. And her music was curiously interwoven with her life, in a way that I had not imagined to be possible. The musical instrument that leaned in its black morocco case against the wall was a theorbo, a kind of bass lute, and Betka described the ensemble to which she belonged with a peculiar sweetness, as though unwrapping something precious. For her, the music of the sixteenth century, of the Prague of Rudolf II and the England of Elizabeth, had a purity that cleaned her spirit as she played. She sang Moravian folk songs too, and her own poignant melodies, accompanying herself on the theorbo with a few simple chords. Her voice was thin and clear, and seemed to sound somewhere inside me like a memory of childhood. She promised to take me to one of her private concerts, and to introduce me to the leader of her little ensemble, the very Vilém whose name I already knew, for whom she was collecting music, and who, she one day confided to me, though with a peculiar hesitation as though confessing to something illicit, was the true owner of the room where we met.

"Then you are lovers?" I cried, as the blade touched my heart.

"Foolish man!"

"Well?"

"Have you not heard of friendship?"

And she turned her head from me and would not speak until I had asked her to forgive me. It crossed my mind that I had never asked forgiveness of anyone in my whole life before, and I was troubled by this. And then she kissed me and changed the subject.

She spoke slowly to me, as though to a child. Once, she said, "You cannot hurry with words, otherwise you drop them and they break." Her language was correct, almost old-fashioned, as though she had learned it from books and not from people. And it is true that, while she was surrounded by people, far more people than I had believed it was possible to know without arousing suspicion, they all occurred on the edge of her life, as though held back by an invisible barrier, where they stood waiting like patients in a surgery or litigants in a court of law. And they were unusual people, too, each with a key to some inner room in Kafka's castle. One of them is important in what follows, and I must describe him now.

Pavel Havránek was an ordained priest of the Catholic Church, who had been banned by the Ministry of Culture's Religious Affairs Department on account of an article he had written, published abroad, about Pacem in Terris, the organization of disloyal and compromised priests through which the Party controlled the Catholic Church. Pacem in Terris had been proscribed by the Vatican in 1982, three years before the events that I am describing. It was Father Pavel who had sat next to Betka on my first visit to Rudolf's seminar, wearing the smudged clothes from his day-time job as a mechanic, and also the cross of his vocation. He came each week, and Betka would smile at him and stroke his arm, though without making any effort to introduce us. It was on my third visit to the seminar, when for some reason Betka had left early, indicating with a silent glance that I was not to follow her, that I fell in with Father Pavel. I was walking away from Rudolf's apartment towards the Vltavská Metro station when he came up beside me and began to talk. He spoke softly and slowly, with a Moravian accent.

"Rudolf tells me that you are Soudruh Androš," he said. I replied with a nod.

"The book meant a lot to me. It was like a door into the under-world, where the silent bodies lie. It gave me such hope."

"Why hope?"

To me, looking back on it, my stories sprang from despair, though a despair that I had now miraculously discarded.

"They are not dead, you see, only sleeping. And all of them are purified by grief."

I was intrigued by his words and because we were walking past a pub, I suggested we enter. We found ourselves in a dark corner, two tall glasses of beer on the table between us, and no other company apart from three workmen at the bar who from time to time broke the silence with loud shouts about football.

"There is something very Christian in your vision," Father Pavel said. "I assume you were brought up in the faith?"

"No," I replied. "Ours was a modern family. We had no faith, only doubts."

"But doubt can be faith. You knock on doors, and at last someone opens. To your surprise, you already know his face."

His words touched something in me and I asked him to explain. He leaned back and studied me for a moment. A lock of dark hair fell across his brow, and he swept it aside with his hand, which was large, rough, and blackened with grease. His brown eyes fixed me with a calm, even gaze. The taut lower folds of his cheeks stretched across the edges of his mouth like the flanges of a helmet, and his nose was strong, slightly arched, with a notch dividing the gaze. I had seen faces like that carved from limewood in a book about German altarpieces that stood on the shelf over Mother's bed. Father Pavel drew in his breath before speaking, like a child repeating something from memory.

"Mine was a modern family, too. My father was a Party member, manager of a collective farm near Olomouc and also big in the local committee; my mother was raised as a believing communist in a family of peasants. They had a fit when I converted, but that was back in 1968, in the days of 'socialism with a human face,' and they couldn't stop me entering the seminary. I pray for them now each day."

"Then they are dead?"

"No: you can pray for the living, too. But for them I am dead, because I have changed my life. I have learned to accept the void without throwing myself into it as they did."

"But isn't it hard for you now, to be a priest, when nobody believes?"

"You really think that nobody believes?"

I hesitated. His eyes seemed to reach into me, shining their light on unacknowledged regions of my soul.

"Well, *I* don't believe. Nor can I."

"You are wrong about that. The gift is offered to everyone. I read your stories and they are like a question, forever repeated. Simone Weil writes that when we cry out for an answer and it is not given to us, it is then that we touch the silence of God. I find that silence in your stories. And I know it in my life."

"But if there is no God?"

"God has withdrawn from the world: that we know, and we Czechs perhaps know it more vividly than others. Our world contains an absence, and we must love that absence, for that is the way to love God."

"But how can you love an absence?"

He gave me a look of indescribable sweetness, as though I had touched on what was dearest in his life.

"I was called to this love, and at first I did not find it. During my early years as a priest, I felt powerless to help. People came to me as a refuge from the system, laying their problems at my door, asking for the proofs of another and a better world than this one. And I had no proofs. As a refuge from the system I was also part of the system, an improved version of the slavery they knew. I thought all the time of my failure to be what they wanted, which was an alternative. And if you spend your days obsessed with your powerlessness, then every good and beautiful thing is like an insult. It was only when I was thrown out of the official church that I understood what was being asked of me. I was abandoned among the abandoned, and I had to love them for what they lacked. Quite suddenly, my life as a priest was full of joy. My flock still came to me, for they had witnessed the cloven hoof under my successor's cassock. But they did not come for refuge. They came for prayer, for stillness, for the life of the imagination to which the gospel so beautifully speaks. I would kneel beside them and we would become nothing together, because in our nothingness we could encounter the love of God. Perhaps that sounds strange to you?"

It did not sound strange at all. Father Pavel's words came from a place that I had never known and that I was suddenly eager to enter. His liquid accent sounded in my ears like a pure stream in a dark gully, welling up from some underground region unpolluted by the poison in the air above. His soft brown eyes, moving slowly from side to side as he spoke, seemed to take in his surroundings with a look that was both blessing and forgiveness. And his shabby cotton clothes, stained with the oil and grease of the garage, were like the rags of a pilgrim, worn thin on a journey that stretched from shrine to shrine the whole length of a life.

He talked to me in this vein for an hour or more, pausing every now and then to sweep back the lock of dark hair that fell across his brow, and for a moment looking at me quietly before resuming his narrative. I asked him how it was to be in holy orders secretly.

"Oh, there is no secret about it," he responded, holding out the cross at his neck. "I am there for whoever needs me, and I have nothing to hide. They sent me to prison for a while, so now they can assume that my case is closed."

At that moment, however, one of the workmen who had been leaning against the bar with his companions turned in our direction, and Father Pavel lowered his voice.

"If you want to know how it is," he went on, "then come to me at the garage after work, and I will show you."

He told me the address of the garage, near the Olšanský cemetery, and we arranged to meet on the following Tuesday. I rode the Metro to Gottwaldova in a state of high excitement. To have met, in the space of weeks, three people such as Betka, Rudolf, and Father Pavel, to have acquired in one bewildering sequence a capacity for love, a need for friendship, an awareness of the mystery in which we lived, and a glimpse of the key that would unlock that mystery—all this went to my head, and caused me to look forward impatiently to the next day, a Saturday, when Betka and I were to spend the afternoon together.

On the shelf above Mother's bed, where she had kept her small collection of art books and which I had put back together as best I could, there was an old Kralice Bible which I had never seen her read. Late on that Friday night, arriving in our vandalized cupboard, I took it down. It was full of pencil marks—underlinings, multiple exclamation marks, marginal notes—in a hand that was clearly hers. On the flyleaf was written, "To Helena Košková, from her parents, Easter 1952." Košková was Mother's maiden name, and this book, given to her when she was ten years old, at the height of the communist terror, and with the reference to a forbidden festival, told me much. I knew that she had been brought up in the Protestant church; but I assumed that faith had never been more than skin-deep in her, and that she, like Dad, had accepted agnosticism as the best way to negotiate our life—certainly the best way to bring up children. Reading her cramped marginalia, however, I knew that I was observing another personality, one that she had hidden not because she was ashamed of it but because she knew that to reveal things did no good. Her pencil marks spoke to me now of feelings that had been locked within her, and of a hundred silent sacrifices. I saw that I must make her part of the new life that was to be mine, and so pay the debt that I owed for all that she had suffered, on Dad's account, and on mine. For she, too, had glimpsed this "life in truth," and tried, at some period long past, to follow it.

Some of her marginalia referred to a "he" whom they did not name. At first I assumed this to be Christ. Verse 8 of the first epistle of John reads, "If we have no sin, we deceive ourselves, and the truth is not in us." She had underlined the last phrase twice: *a pravda v nás není*. And next to it she had written "but it *is in him*." And the words of Christ to Thomas in St, John's gospel, so famous that even I, even in those days of official atheism, had heard them spoken—"I am the Way, the Truth and the Life"—had been given three underscorings, with the words "truth" linked to the margin, in which she had written "Your truth *is in him*—let him believe!!" I knew then that she was not referring to Christ and closed the book sadly; for I had uncovered her love for Dad, still warm and bleeding in the place where she had hidden it. And it is especially significant to me now that she had hidden her love in a book.

CHAPTER 10

FATHER PAVEL'S GARAGE lay on a backstreet among featureless buildings of concrete. It consisted of a courtyard that was also a scrap heap and a sheltered area at the back where two or three vehicles stood awaiting repair, official vehicles with Hlavní Město Praha— the capital city of Prague—stenciled on their doors. Behind them was a workshop with a line of windows in wooden frames. Father Pavel was the only person there when I called, and I found him standing by a blue Avia truck that had been squeezed into the recess, notwithstanding a broken rear axle. He was wiping his hands on a cloth and staring at the damaged vehicle with his mild expression, as though he pitied it. Only when I greeted him did he acknowledge that I was there.

"Jan, thank you," he said, "I am so glad you came."

"But how would I not?"

He brushed the hair from his eyes and looked at me.

"I spoke about intimate things, and those things hurt."

I dismissed his worry with a wave of the hand.

We walked through the Olšanský cemetery, where the once proud families of our nation lay interred, though not at rest. The doors of their ornate sepulchres had been wrenched from their hinges, the vaults pried open, and pieces of broken marble scattered across the floors. "No full stop is allowed under communism," Father Pavel said, "for even among the dead the wheel of Progress turns." He seemed to me like a child, describing things as though encountering them for the first time. A little pile of phalanges and metacarpals had been thrown, stripped of their rings, by the ransacked tomb of the Bradatý family. "But one ring remains," Father Pavel said, "which is the ring of truth." And he made a sign over the bones that I took to be a blessing.

He led me through the streets of Žižkov, where crumbling apartment buildings, crammed side by side during the nineteenth century, propped each other up behind their scaffolds. In a little alley a long wall of brick, pierced by white-framed windows, led to an arch of stone, under which a heavy wooden door swung on creaking hinges. This, Father Pavel told me, was the church of St. Elizabeth, Svatá Alžběta, whose name to me was the sweetest in the Roman calendar, but whose story I did not know. In the dark interior I discerned rows of battered chairs, a lectern and a plain wooden altar. Above the altar there was a large nineteenth-century painting in pastel shades, bordered by a simple wooden frame fixed with screws to the wall. It showed St. Elizabeth, mother of John the Baptist, welcoming the Virgin Mary to her house and garden.

Father Pavel explained that the church lacked a parish priest, and had remained open by neglect when plans to use it as a nursery fell through. It was here that Father Pavel came to say Mass, and where he would meet members of his old congregation. As he led me around that dark and somehow purified interior, with its dim bulbs hanging from the wooden slats of the ceiling, and its penitential smell of dust and damp and snuffed-out candles, I felt the power of Father Pavel's presence, as though I walked with a spiritual being whose feet touched the earth more lightly than mine ever could. When he turned his eyes on a thing, and made that now familiar gesture of sweeping back his unruly forelock, the thing, however insignificant—a chair, a piece of rough cloth on which to kneel, a cracked porcelain cup which served as a chalice—was as though turned upon itself in some imaginary space, so as to disappear from the host of fallen things and reappear among the saved. Religion, for Father Pavel, involved no escape from the natural into the supernatural, no repudiation of this world for the sake of a better one whose unreality made it more malleable to our wishes. In his perspective, the natural and the supernatural were one and the same: the world became transparent, with the light of eternity shining from the other side.

Under one of the chairs a canvas bag was strapped out of sight, and Father Pavel reached down to it, extracting a small sheaf of carbon copies.

"Remember this chair," he said. "You will always find the latest edition here. But please put it back."

He handed me the roughly stapled journal—*Informace o církvi*, information about the church. It described the activities of forbidden priests, announced times of Mass and calls to prayer, and explained the Gospel in naïve terms that reminded me of the words with which Jan Hus had described the pious old woman who added her bundle of sticks to the flames that martyred him: *sancta simplicitas*. Was I wrong to harbor those skeptical thoughts, as cheap in their way as an editorial from *Rudé právo*? I don't know: religion was new to me, and I had discovered an unusual guide to it, who seemed to change whatever he touched into its own eternal version. Turning the coarse pages, I encountered a list of people who needed our prayers, and there was Mother's name—Helena Reichlová, accused under Article 98 of the criminal code, and awaiting trial in Prague.

"So you knew about Mother?"

"Of course, we all knew. And if you want to talk about her, there is no better place than here."

I looked at him for a moment, as he swept the hair from his brow and steadied his eyes on me. Of course I should talk to him, and no doubt he had brought me here for that purpose. I needed to confess, to atone, to be reconciled, and what better place than the Church of Saint Alžběta, with Father Pavel as my confessor? But something in me said "no." I was recovering my mother in fragments from the well of guilt, and what Father Pavel wanted was to show her entire. He would tell me how to reassemble her, not as she was in the world of lies, but as she would be and will be in the world of truth, the world that Mother herself had been striving to conjure in those sad annotations to her Bible. But I postponed the moment. Instead I told him that I had already spoken of the matter to Alžběta Palková, who was giving me very useful advice.

He looked at me for a moment, and then said, "Ah, Betka. Yes, she knows about these things."

And he promptly changed the subject, describing his own time in prison, the difficulty of celebrating Mass, and how, for the Eucharist, it had been necessary to beg a few raisins from the cook, to steep them in water, and to offer tiny sips of the turbid bubbling mixture to the communicants. Mass took place in a corner of the workshop where the prisoners spent their days making wooden pallets. He described how it was, to raise the cracked cup in hands swollen with splinters, to pronounce the sacred words, and then to minister to the bowed-down forms of his fellow criminals.

"And yet, you see, miracles were our daily diet, and especially in this place did we know that we were drinking the blood of our Redeemer."

The Church had been wrong, Father Pavel said, to condemn Jan Hus for offering the sacrament in both kinds—*sub utraque specie*—and the persecution of the Utraquists should be forever remembered as a crime. The sacramental wine, he said, was the right of every sinner who prepared for it: "for the Lamb was slain from the foundation of the world." Even in this consecrated space, those words (which I later discovered in the Book of Revelation) sounded extravagant. They would be heard in the street outside only as the mutterings of a madman.

Living now in a country of religious maniacs, I hold onto my Czech skepticism as a badge of sanity. But I spontaneously resonated to Father Pavel's message. He described the supernatural as an everyday presence, folded into the scheme of things like the lining of a coat. The Christian religion, he said, is not refuted by suffering, but uses suffering to make sense of the world. And he added a thought that surprised me, not because it was at odds with what I knew, but because it fitted my experience so exactly. God, he said, could be present among us only if He first divests himself of power. To enter this world dressed in the power that created it would be to threaten us all with destruction. Hence God enters in secret. He is the truly powerless one, whose role is to suffer and forgive. That is the meaning of the sacrifice, in which the body and blood of the Redeemer are shared among his killers.

Those thoughts astonished me, not because they led me to adopt Father Pavel's faith, but because they wrapped all that had happened to me—Dad, Mother, my life underground, and Betka too—in a single idea, the very idea that Mother had chosen as the name of her press. And it is this that I appreciated most in Father Pavel—that his religion was not an escape from suffering but a way of accepting it. The supermarket heavens of my new neighbors, which draw a veil over suffering and therefore make no sense of it or of anything else, take me back to those beautiful, terrible days, when our dear city turned in its sleep and its dreams were dreams of a crucified God.

As we left the little church, I asked Father Pavel whether he had suffered much in prison.

"Oh no," he said, "those were happy times. When you lose your worldly power you gain power of another kind. Those who have only worldly power are truly the powerless ones."

I shrugged my shoulders at this but, as we walked away from the church towards the Main Station, where he had a train to catch, Father Pavel spoke about his time in prison. His conversation moved quietly and with great calm strides above the mountaintops, touching on faith, sacrifice, and freedom, never mentioning those great things by name, but simply lifting my eyes to them, as they are lifted by the dawn. In prison he had lived among common criminals; but he had also found himself working side by side with a few of our nation's best, people who had been placed there for their virtues and not for their sins. It had been a university of the heart, and around him were people who had been seeking what he had found, and who had the knowledge and will to convey it. I came away from this conversation in a state of astonishment, and each evening thereafter I would read in Mother's Bible, trying to reconstruct the person who had written in its margins.

Apart from the Psalms and the book of Proverbs, Mother had left the Old Testament alone, and I did not blame her. The genealogies, sieges, and slaughters, the unforgiving genocides, the piling of bones upon bones, reminded me of our old Jewish cemetery, a compressed nugget of memory whose only message was death. My eyes could not rest on those pages for long.

Of course, our Jews had suffered terribly, far more than the rest of us. But what credibility did that bestow on these life-negating chapters, in which savages hacked each other to death for the sake of a God who seemed bent on nothing save revenge against his own creation? What had this to do with the hopes of Mother or with the powerless God of Father Pavel? Each evening, however, in the Epistles or the Gospels, I would find some marked passage that opened a little more of Mother's soul to me, and brought a kind of comfort. And when I came across these words of St. Paul, underscored and commented with an emphatic "yes!" I felt that Mother had walked the path that I was walking and perhaps seen, as I did, that it led always back to the present: "Look not at the things which are seen, but at the things which are not seen: for the things which are seen are temporal; but the things which are not seen are eternal."

I would often call on Father Pavel at the end of his day, to take him to the Hospoda na vandru, where he was welcomed by the pious manager, a large man with a neatly tonsured beard and sideburns. In the manager's watery grey eyes there swam a kind of fearful compassion as he greeted the person who I realized must be his priest. Father Pavel's thoughts always began from some paradox, and he would frequently quote Kierkegaard's remark, that a thinker without a paradox is like a lover without feeling: a paltry mediocrity. But, he added, we must love what doesn't exist: nothing else is worthy of love. He frequently referred to the absence of God: the world, as he put it, is empty of God, and that *is* God. The purpose of these paradoxes was not to tie me in intellectual knots, but to persuade me to see the world in another way, or rather to see through to its other side, on which the light of eternity was shining. I had to practice what he called "a gymnastics of attention," always detaching things from their circumstances so as to overcome their randomness. The tree, the bowl, the desk; the car, the book, the window—all ask, he said, to be rescued, to be pried free from the flow of mere events and raised to the dignity of being. He confided in me that this was his spiritual exercise, and that by means of it he had driven from his soul all resentment at what *they* had done—not to him only, but to our country, to those woods and fields that smile in the music of Dvořák, to those garlands of wildflowers woven into words by Erben, to the old legends of what we are, which are not legends at all but ideals to live up to.

"Purity," he once said, "is the power to contemplate defilement. Our world must be redeemed from its circumstances piece by piece, place by place, time by time. It is up to us to lift things from the muck, and to polish off the taint of their misuse."

Those words seemed to describe my new way of living, and I was grateful for them, as I was grateful for our walks and drinks together during those months of happiness. Father Pavel introduced me to the spiritual literature that had strengthened him through his trials—to St. Teresa of Avila and St. John of the Cross, as well as Pascal, Kierkegaard, and Simone Weil. It was a remark of Pascal's that he applied to my situation: "You would not have looked for me, if you had not already found me." And he asked me to reflect on those words, which had guided him in times of darkness.

He would bring the books that he wished me to read, wrapped in coarse paper, to the garage, and he allowed me to take them away, provided I surrendered at the same time the last ones I had borrowed. He had a keen enjoyment of our conversations, which offered him the rare opportunity to pass on his knowledge and experience to a young person whose mind had not been polluted by the thing called education. Of course, his knowledge was one-sided and incomplete, since he had retained only those fragments that were needed for survival in the threatened regions where he roamed. But it was a knowledge full of beauties, decked out with ornaments lifted from the wayside, as he made his pilgrimage through.

He knew every church, every palace, and every garden in our city, and walking with him I felt the veil of negation being lifted from the things we passed. I had known the city only as a kind of figment, the stage-set for a drama that had finished long ago, a place where people fled underground and were observable only as they hugged the walls of their private catacombs. In truth, however, as Father Pavel taught me, Prague was the spiritual center of Europe and the only city to have rescued itself from those sacrificial wars invoked by

Patočka; it was not a remnant, but a place where religion, culture, style, and manners had triumphed over the innate disorder of mankind. We entered the churches, and stood side by side in wonder at the wrestling pulpits and aspiring saints that had been lowered into our city from regions long since obscured by the rising mist of apprehension. We walked through the orchards below the Strahov Monastery and behind the Lobkowicz Palace, which housed the West German embassy; we got to know all the paths on the Petřín hill, and the unvisited corners and mysterious cul-de-sacs which are the edges of real history.

One such cul-de-sac encloses the West façade of St. Thomas in Malá Strana. We stood there on one wet afternoon, Father Pavel holding an umbrella high above me and tracing with outstretched finger the dripping protrusions on Dientzenhofer's façade. His voice trembled slightly as he spoke. I was not to see this church as a creamy concoction in stucco, a fanciful attempt to build a dream in the clouds. I was to see it as a visitation from a sphere where the forms imagined by people are transfigured into their eternal replicas. Those swelling cornices, broken pediments, and whirling scrolls are not some Catholic veneer sprayed onto Protestant stone by Mr. Dientzenhofer. They are representations in eternity of the attempt to build here and now. To make a home, Father Pavel said, we must settle among eternal things, and therefore we must bring the eternal to earth. Those moldings which swell around the pilasters as though drawing them together in a dance are not made of stucco or stone but of light, and in the shade of their chiseled parallels angels are always resting, even on a day like this when the light is pale and the shadows weary. In such façades we find the meaning of our twofold city: every building wears a face, and looks down on us from the elsewhere of salvation.

Father Pavel's words enchanted our city, but only by forbidding the present tense. His vision was tenseless, like logic or mathematics or theology. The power that haunted our streets would have been unimaginable to Mr. Dientzenhofer, and the lovely invocations that I read in Zdeněk Kalista were of a city that had since been captured and hollowed out by fear.

I asked Father Pavel where he lived, and he replied that he would take me there one day. Like Betka, he did not wish to be entirely known, not even to those he trusted. And I respected this, for it conveyed an experience of the world that had the authenticity of suffering.

I had another reason to be glad of those walks around our city, besides the poignant glimpses that they afforded. For Betka often hesitated to be seen with me, so that I could not walk with her placidly and easily in the land of truth.

CHAPTER 11

ON THE SATURDAY after that first meeting with Father Pavel, I called, as we had agreed, at Betka's room. I was thinking of Mother, and of the religion that she had cast like a lifeline into the sea of lies, hoping to rescue Dad but instead landing his corpse in a tangle of driftwood. I did not despair of Mother's case; side by side with Betka, I would surely make headway against *them*. And when she opened the door with that ballerina flourish, shone her eyes on me, and took me silently to bed, my resolve grew strong and firm.

The days were longer now, and it was still light in the little courtyard when we began to talk. I poured out to Betka all my newfound interest in the world aboveground—in the history and culture of our homeland, in the architecture of our city, in the hidden meaning of that literature of the Austrian twilight that I had unearthed from Dad's trunk, which was all that we had for him by way of a tomb. She corrected me from time to time, with careful didactic remarks that both revealed and concealed her store of knowledge. And, with quiet words, mentally holding me by the hand, she brought the topic back to Mother.

It was like this with Betka: I walked beside her in a landscape strewn with flowers. And beneath the flowers, concealed by their very abundance, were chasms that I saw only when they opened beneath my feet, and her hand reached out to protect me. She who led me could also save me, and so it was now, when she mentioned Mother. I leaned forward at her desk and dropped my head into my hands. Through my spread fingers I could catch the pure look of interrogation from those steady eyes, and the glow of young life from that naked body. And I was overwhelmed by a sense of mystery—the inexplicable fact of being there, in that room which belonged to no one, beneath the searing light of truth, while somewhere below-ground the shy sad author of *Rumors* still shunted his futile guilt along rails leading nowhere.

Betka told me of someone she knew at the American Embassy, Bob Heilbronn, who was charged with relations with the press. He would ensure that Mother's case became a *cause célèbre* in the West, so raising her status from ordinary person who stumbled to dissident who dared. Betka's tone was ironical. For she never ceased to remind me that the world of marginal people had its rewards and its charms; that there were ways of playing the cards of dissidence that brought more benefits than costs. Sure, there were the real heroes like Havel, Kantůrková, Vaculík, people who had lost the arena in which they could have shone as public figures. But such people belonged to the heroic past, and now we had to deal with the remainders, the failed writers, failed philosophers, failed artists, journalists, composers, and performers who, by donning the mantle of dissent, dressed up in the borrowed costumes of the heroes. Real people should be carefully distinguished from fakes, she argued, and the difference between them is as great as that between the line of verse that changes the world and the sprawl of words on a sheet of paper.

I accepted her cynical reflections. After all, she was twenty-six, four years older than me, and she had been moving in these dangerous circles for long enough to be aware of the pitfalls. Still, I was not sure that she was really convinced by the course she recommended, or that this person from the American Embassy was not someone more to be avoided than sought.

"How come you know people like that?" I asked her.

"How come I know someone like you?"

"That's no answer to my question."

"Yours is no question to be asked," she said, and with a quick movement rolled off the bed and came across to me. And when she sat like that in my lap, her arms wrapped around my neck, her naked body pressed against me and her kisses exploring my neck like the games of a kitten, I accepted everything she said as a revelation. I would understand this revelation eventually even if its purpose was obscure to me now.

Two days later she told me that Mr. Heilbronn would meet me the following afternoon. I was to go to the Vrtbovská Garden in Malá Strana, and sit on a stone bench at the end of the second flight of stairs at 2:30. He would come to sit beside me.

The Vrtbovská Garden is all that remains of the great baroque palace built in the early eighteenth century for Count Jan Josef of Vrtba. It is composed of terraces set in the hillside, joined by elegant flights of steps and embellished with the energetic statues of Matyáš Braun. Terrace rests on terrace like the voices in music, ascending to a little grotto from which you can see across the rooftops of Malá Strana to St. Nicholas, whose cupola and tower, green with verdigris, dominate the skyline. In my days underground it would never have occurred to me to visit such a place, which was trapped in our mournful city like a thought in scare quotes. But I assumed that Betka had chosen it deliberately, to remind me that I could live on terms of my own. This garden was good; Mr. Heilbronn was good; and my being here on a cold stone seat on a cold March day was good, so long as I did as she did, and always looked forward to the exit.

The man who came to sit beside me was small, dark haired, with heavy black eyebrows behind thick-rimmed glasses that stuck out above sunken cheeks. Nothing showed him to be American apart from a smart pink tie of some silky stuff visible beneath his fur-lined jacket. He sat for a moment without speaking, staring straight ahead, and with his gloved hands resting on the seat to either side of him. Then he spoke quietly in English.

"You can assume I wasn't followed," he said, "and I know for a fact that this place is safe."

"Thank you," I said. "But we may need to explain ourselves."

It was my first attempt at speaking English, and the words came slowly.

"Here is the spiel," he replied. "I am writing a book about baroque gardens; as luck would have it, I bumped into someone who spoke English, and helped me find my way around."

"But I don't know my way around."

"Then that's your homework," he said. "In case you need it."

He had an abrupt way of talking, as though pushing out each sentence fully formed and stopping in the wake of it. It made me think of him as a solitary person, who had no private life of his own. I asked him how he knew Betka.

"Liz?" he replied. "I met her at the embassy. She came with a little group, to perform old music in the garden. She's some kid. Speaks good English. Knows everyone. At least, everyone *I* need to know. You, for instance."

"Why me?"

"She said you'd tell me why."

"And do you trust her?" I asked. He smiled ironically.

"In my profession, trust is not allowed. Certainly not here. But we make distinctions."

I wondered how well he knew her and by what means they communicated. And did I have the right to talk of the girl I loved to this agent of Imperial and Zionist forces, which is undoubtedly how he would be described in a *Rudé právo* editorial when Mother's case was publicized abroad? I had the image of myself standing on the edge of a precipice, Betka holding me back; and below me, at the bottom, another Betka beckoning. A wave of fear swept over me, and it was a moment before I could speak.

I told Mr. Heilbronn what I knew. Mother was being held in Ruzyně prison, and would be tried in the coming weeks under Paragraphs 98 and 100 of the criminal code: subversion of the Republic in collaboration with foreign powers, together with incitement and illegal commerce. I gave him the facts of the case, emphasizing that I was not allowed to visit her and that her defense lawyer had been appointed by her accusers from the list of advocates who could be relied upon not to disturb the verdict.

While I spoke, Mr. Heilbronn made little whistling noises, as though he had never encountered injustice in his life before. The punishment prepared for Mother mattered to me; but his blurted interventions, invoking Jan Masaryk, Miláda Horáková, and all the others who had been done to death by the criminal who had given his name to our Metro station, made me squirm with embarrassment, as though I were engaging in false heroics for the sake of some personal gain. I wanted to play down the facts, even to accuse Mother of her own mistakes—like taking the typewriter from the factory, and retaining copies of the things she produced. I wanted to "normalize" her crime, to remove it from the great game of shadowboxing in which Mr. Heilbronn was engaged, fighting for human rights against the machine of communist repression.

"Let's walk," he said, of a sudden. He got to his feet and began to descend the steps to the lower terrace. He walked with jerky steps, swiveling his head from side to side like the turret of a tank. I tried to guess at his inner life, at the motives that had drawn him into this strange career on the edge of diplomacy. But nothing emerged from him save jargon. He was one machine in conflict with another. He rattled out the provisions of the Helsinki Accords, proved in a hundred ways that Mother was protected by international treaties and by the unwritten law of human rights, and in general remade that poor defeated woman as an American citizen who had somehow strayed into the no man's land between the warring machines. As he spoke, I fixed my eyes on Braun's statue of Minerva. The serene grey-stone face spoke of a place where conflicts were the business of gods, and men's souls were clear of ideology. Perhaps, through the door that Betka had opened, I would enter that place, and stand before the thrones of the immortals, released from the squabbles of machines.

At one point, I interrupted him.

"You see," I said, "my mother's case is not really about human rights at all."

I wanted to say that it was about our country, about the loved and imagined thing that had spawned Dad's collection of records, about the books under the plank from which Mother and I ate, about the little paradise of statuary that surrounded Mr. Heilbronn and which he seemed not to notice, about the twofold city that hemmed us in. Those precious things were not abstractions like treaties and rights, but realities, reimagined over centuries and constantly loved. And it was Mother, not her accusers, who represented them. Thoughts like those poured through my mind in a confused moment of protest; but I was young, shy, uneducated, and could find no words to utter them.

Mr. Heilbronn swiveled his glasses round to me.

"Trust me. It is about human rights."

We stopped in the alley that led from the garden to the street. Mr. Heilbronn plunged a gloved hand into his pocket and took out a small business card, containing the legend Robert Heilbronn, Ph.D, Art Historian, and underneath it a London address. As I took it, I noticed a figure in a leather jacket who emerged from a laurel bush and walked past us, his dark eyes fixed on a distant vision of angels. I indicated his retreating form and, like Betka, said "You go that way, I go this." I left him standing with a puzzled look on his face, as though he were waking from a dream.

CHAPTER 12

OVER THE WEEKS that followed I got used to the figure in the leather jacket, who was always passing me and never looking at me. His jug-handle ears and staring eyes hardly suited him to his calling, but why waste the precious gift of invisibility on a pointless case like mine? The fact is that Heilbronn did what was expected, and Helena Reichlová had soon assumed a worldwide significance. One evening I stood with Father Pavel at the back of his workshop, listening to a program about Mother on Radio Free Europe, in which she was portrayed as something vast, pure, truth-telling, a self-sacrificing creature who was fighting for the liberation of her country. Our mother, the timid, worn-down, grieving figure who would cook pancakes in our tiny kitchen, wash clothes in the sink, and spread out her ironing on the board where we would also eat and work. Our mother, who had done only one heroic thing, so far as I could tell, in her whole sad life, which was to condemn herself to prison for the sake of the under-manager of a failed paper factory, a man whom I had never met, and whose traces in Mother's life were so faint as to be barely observable. Her lined face with its blue-black shadows around the eyes, her pursed lips and frail neck, her long slender hands always at work, and her patched old clothes which she seldom changed and which served as a kind of camouflage of mustard yellow and brown—all these struck me then as signs that she belonged not with the heroes but with our everydayness, our *každodennost*. The radio program infuriated me. I wanted to call out that this woman was not Joan of Arc or Princess Libuše but a routine product of the system, one who had gotten mixed up with another routine product—the dissident, the intellectual who had found the way to disguise his failure as an inner success, and who had found a niche in which the view from Olympus was painted on the wall.

Later, when he was called as a witness in her trial (which I was allowed to attend only as an observer), the under-manager revealed himself to be a disheveled, grey-faced creature with a lopsided mustache and a nervous tic that continually dented his left cheek as though another person were hidden behind it, anxiously tugging it like a sleeve. He expressed his outrage at the way in which Mother had abused his trust and her position, and the shock with which he had learned that his precious stores of socialist paper were being used to distribute such filth. It was inconceivable that there could have been love between them, and Mother resolutely refused to look at him across the courtroom. Instead, she turned her eyes to me, silently begging my forgiveness for this folly. By then, I had come to see Mother in another way, as the owner of that Bible above her bed, who had lived in the tiny corner assigned to her, nurturing a kind of soul-music that at last was audible to me. Her drab clothes and rimmed Picasso eyes, her knitting-needle fingers and taut unsmiling mouth all bore witness to the inner determination that governed her. Meeting her glance across the courtroom I no longer saw an ordinary victim. Those evening sorties from which she returned with a secret look on her face were no longer the pathetic refuge of someone whom life had passed by. And I looked back on my underground years with a revised conception of their meaning. It was not I but she who had tunneled beneath the castle of illusions, who had packed the cellars with explosives, and who had been arrested too late. It was true what she said to the StB officer at the time of her arrest. She had done what she did for love: not for some abstract idea, but for Dad. Freedom could not be won through the war of machines, or the trading of abstractions. Nor did it come from that drastic solidarity of which Patočka wrote. Freedom was won through love: the love that pays the price of its own lastingness. Mother had paid that price, and the foundations of the system shook above her deed.

All that became clear to me in time. But already I knew from Betka that the way out from underground was not political but personal. We created in that little room a space apart, where the writ of everydayness did not run. In that space I could breathe and I could love. It was the place of my redemption, the place where I wanted to be entirely open and entirely known. Yet for that very reason it also troubled me. Betka was with me only there, in the room that she borrowed, the room that was removed from the real life that she softly but firmly prevented me from entering. In Rudolf's seminar she would sit apart from me. She told me that she worked in the evenings and only her days were free. I asked if I could come to one of her concerts, which tended to occur on Saturday afternoons, and she screwed up her face and said, "wait awhile." And then I began to doubt her.

"What do you know about me, Betka?" I asked one afternoon.

"Oh, everything!"

"Am I so easy to decipher?"

"Yes, or you wouldn't use that word."

"What word?"

"*Dešifrovat*. Most people would say *rozluštit*, which is at least Czech and not Latin. You make yourself into a secret. And secrets can be pried apart. It is only when people live openly that they are hard to know."

"Is that why I know so little about you?"

"That's one reason."

"But you hide so much from me."

"That's where you are wrong, Honza. I hide nothing that you need to know, and would answer any question, if you knew how to ask it."

Her clever reply left me tongue-tied.

"But you see," she went on, "I made a decision, not just to live in the open, but to unlock other people's secrets, yours for instance. And the secret is that there is no secret. Just as in Kafka. Rudolf makes a big thing about Kafka. In those days Kafka was the prophet, the one who had foreseen it all."

She had a particular way of referring to "those days"—*v té době*—when the dissidents, who had yet to use that word to describe themselves, emerged from the rubble and lit their pale candles in the dark. She wanted me to admire those people, and also to suspect them.

"Kafka imagined the corridors leading nowhere, the doors painted on the walls, the floors that were thin ceilings over some other person's life. He was the guide to the labyrinth, and you paid him with sighs. But he told us nothing, nothing at all. It was all literature."

She spoke with unusual vehemence, as though from some personal hurt. I searched my mind for a reply. But I found only the image of Dad, poring over Kafka's *Castle*, in preparation for one of his weekly meetings. The images of Dad's finger on the page, of his knitted brow and of the pencil held between his teeth, were objects now of an unbearable tenderness, and I could not speak. Betka was sitting on the edge of the bed, her arms stretched along her thighs, her eyes fixed on the floor.

"Actually," she went on, "nothingness has its attractions. You can buy it cheaply, and sell it at a high price. Sometimes I think that's what goes on in Rudolf's seminar. All this solidarity of the shattered, for instance. What does it mean?"

I was shocked by her words, which seemed like a denial of everything we shared.

"So why do you go there?" I asked.

"I wish I knew. Oh, but I do know. I go there because I love those people too. And yes, I want to learn. I want to see our situation as a whole, to complete it, to rescue it."

In such a way she would always undo the effect of her cynical words, bringing me back to what mattered, which was the love that had its home in that room—the room where she didn't belong.

CHAPTER 13

LOOKING BACK ACROSS nearly a quarter of a century to those never-to-be recovered days of beauty and fear, I find no ready words to convey her way of being. Americans divided our people into three classes: the oppressors, the dissidents, and the silent majority. From this simple typology, which was all that Bob Heilbronn knew of our national fate, the reams of simplifying journalism flowed. But we were like people everywhere: we refused to be categorized. Each of us had his own way of breathing our poisoned air, so as to minimize its impact on his body. It was through reading and teaching that Dad had made the space in which to pass a form of human life to his children. For others it was music, poetry, country walks, or sport. From Betka I learned about the dissidents. But I also learned that she was not one. She had been a teenager during the years of normalization, and had watched with sympathetic detachment as her contemporaries joined the underground, singing and playing in the style of Frank Zappa or Paul McCartney, gathering in smoke-filled rooms to read poems, plays, and novels that were passed excitedly from hand to hand not for their merits but because they were forbidden. It was the ambition of many young people then to defy the world with the stomping sound called *Bigboš*. But rock music had no appeal for her, and when, with the trial in 1976 of the Plastic People of the Universe, the regime issued its warning to the youth, Betka's life remained unaffected. For her there was only classical music, and, with a few carefully pondered exceptions such as the amateur bluegrass band in which she had once played the bass, and some smuggled records of the Beatles and Pink Floyd that she kept hidden under her desk, popular music was an offense to her ear. True, she had joined the Jazz Section of the Musicians' Union, through which the regime extended its protection to a "proletarian" art form associated, in earlier times, with communist ideas. But the Jazz Section had branched out, had expanded beyond its permitted maximum of 3,000 to 7,000 members, and had begun to publish texts that could never be issued by our official publishing houses, including the speech given by our national poet Jaroslav Seifert on receipt of the Nobel Prize for Literature in 1984. It had even issued Nietzsche's writings on Wagner that lay, stuffed with paper slips, beside Betka's bed. The regime had begun to move against the Jazz Section; and at the time I am describing, its leader, Karel Srp, was on trial for having kept the thing going as a clandestine network. Needless to say, Betka was part of that network; and also not part of it at all.

In those days of our love, the poet known as Magor, the madman, who had managed the Plastic People, was rolling his "swan songs" into cigarettes and smuggling them from his prison in Ostrov nad Ohří. The poems made their way to the West, and then back again in tiny cyclostyled editions. Betka obtained a copy, as she obtained her share of all things beautiful and good. She would set the verses to weeping melodies, in a kind of caricature of Dowland. When I first read those words in the tiny book, smuggled from Germany with its own magnifying glass inserted in the spine, they seemed slight:

How long, O God, must I still bear
To live in this unshifting care?

However long you wish to last
This old frustration, never past,

I'll patiently endure my fears
And humbly ask you in my prayers

At least that, when the whole thing's done
You'll place a poem on my tongue.

Yet, when Betka in her thin sweet voice sang the poem to a plangent tune of her own, and let her strange soul shine through the cracks between the words, I was overwhelmed. I heard the voice of my homeland. I was called to a primal experience of belonging, of which Betka was a part. The Plastic People too had sung words by Magor, but it was as though Betka had lifted these verses from the seedy frontier, where the long-haired youth of the seventies had staked its territory, and placed them in the very center of our nation as the common property of our people, the voice of their sufferings then and now and always. She taught me that the life of the dissidents was one small fragment of our world, and that things were changing too fast to remain locked in the griefs and conflicts of our parents. Our concern was to learn, to know the possibilities, and to seek out and destroy every kind of phoniness, including the excusable phoniness that had grown around the harsh privations of dissent.

Magor's real name was Ivan Martin Jirous, and he was an art historian by training. It was from his encounter with Václav Havel, Betka told me, that the movement to compose Charter 77 had begun. As a schoolgirl, Betka had been excited by the Charter, and by the fate of those few of her classmates whose parents had signed it, who in consequence had lost, as I had lost, the chance of an education. Our faces had been brushed at that moment by the air from other planets, so she said. But then was then and now is now. Jirous, with his long hair, rude language, and belligerent hippie manner, was, for his contemporaries, the voice of youth. He wanted the Charter to have the impact that John Lennon had. He saw it as two fingers thrust in the face of the establishment. And yet it was not that at all. The Charter was, in Betka's view, a piece of half-baked philosophy, composed in the same Newspeak as the official protocols of the ruling Party, with its invocation of "progressive forces," "human development," *pokrok, vývoj,* and a hundred other dead words meaning progress and therefore nothing at all, like a speech on May Day. I nodded sadly, and thought of Dad.

"But you see," she went on, "that was not Magor's idiom at all. He is not the kind to swap one lie for another, even if it took prison to wake him up to this. His swan songs are prayers, filled with the love of God and with contrition and repentance."

I longed for the opportunity to discuss Mother's Bible, and the strange world of Father Pavel. Until now I had not dared, but she had made an opening and I took it.

"Do you believe?" I asked.

"Believe? In what?"

"In whatever it is that Christians hold sacred."

"Oh yes, Honza, I hold many things sacred, like Magor. But I don't believe that God is a person, who watches over us, loves us, and is angry at our sins. I don't believe in the afterlife—one life is enough for me. When you hold something to be sacred then, as Sidonius says, there is a kind of faith that comes with it—a sense of infinite freedom, as though myriad worlds opened before you in the here and now. That's how I live, and it's how you should live too."

"Show me how," I begged.

"It can't be shown—you must discover it."

"Where?"

"Here, silly. And now. What do you think is happening between us?"

"And who is this Sidonius?"

She took from her bag a volume written in Czech, entitled *An Invitation to Transcendence*. It was edited by Václav Havel and published by an exile press in England. She opened it to a chapter by Sidonius.

"That's not his real name, of course. He lives here in Prague. He might even have an official job, as an engineer or something. I'm not sure."

I looked at her, aghast. It was as though she had been waiting for my enquiry, and come fully equipped with the things needed to deflect it: an illegal book, a pseudonymous author, an invitation to join in a life that had no explanation save Betka.

"How did you get hold of such a book?" I asked.

She shrugged her shoulders and made a puffing noise with her lips. "Don't ask."

She handed it across, and I turned the pages. They were dense with religious ideas: God, Eternity, Transcendence, Being; the door that opens, when love appears, onto the bright garden of the present. And on the horizon, so many miraculous worlds! The words were Czech. But I could not understand them. I had asked her a simple question. And her answer had led me into labyrinths where I was lost without her guidance.

"Is this what you believe, Betka?"

"Half and half. Take away the Christian metaphysics, and the rest is truth. We live now or never. And God is another dimension in the now."

So what, I asked, did she think of Father Pavel. She looked at me for a while before replying.

"Listen, Honza, there is a lot to learn from Pavel. But just be careful what you say to him."

"Why? You're not implying…"

"Of course you can trust him. But just remember, he's a priest. He will want you to confess to him. That's his way of exerting power."

"And why shouldn't I confess to him?"

She seized me by the wrists and looked hard into my eyes.

"Because your confessions are mine."

Only later did I see the chasm from which she was holding me back.

CHAPTER 14

THE FIRST WEEKS of my new life moved fast. Sometimes I had the impression that they were happening to someone else, that I was sitting in a cinema, watching the adventures of a man caught up in events that lay beyond his comprehension. I went with Father Pavel to places that I had never imagined to exist; I met with people whom I believed to have been removed from history; I listened to music that could never be openly performed, and read books that could never be published. I sat in churches whose priests emerged from underground to whisper old and forbidden messages, and who disappeared at the end of the Mass like gnomes into hidden crevices. Father Pavel, like Betka, knew people with the keys to secret places. One member of his congregation was a builder, working on the apartment once owned by Kafka's parents, with a window set in the wall of the Church of our Lady before Týn. I stood at the place from which the young Kafka had watched Christians assemble and depart as though herded by spells, and a strange shiver of isolation came over me, as though I were peering into my tomb.

Father Pavel took me to other seminars—to those on Czech history by the bald and fussy František in his house on Kampa, and to those on theology in a dingy apartment in Nusle, where Igor Novák lived with his wife and six children. Igor was a grim, portly figure, with a wispy beard and a face obscured by lamp-like spectacles. He stood in the midst of the assembled listeners like a king among his courtiers, sometimes acknowledging their questions, more often pursuing long, slow rambling thoughts of his own. Everyone deferred to him, and no one more than his wife, who was always present and who would begin timid sentences with a smile, only to hand them over to him for their grim didactic conclusion. For Igor believed himself to be the voice of the nation. He referred often to the myth of Přemysl, the plowman summoned to marry the princess Libuše and thereby to found the first dynasty of our kings. He compared his role as a dissident to that of the simple plowman, who brought the natural world and its truth into the castle of illusions. Igor and Přemysl were both avatars of a higher purpose, sent to reprove us for our faults. We had not confessed to our history. We had denied our inheritance as the heart of Europe.

The Czechoslovak State, he told us, was a kind of mask worn by Czech society, and onto it was projected, as onto a movie screen, an entirely fictitious story, concocted elsewhere and without reference to the life behind the mask. That life was not the secular, materialistic routine that we were told to believe in, but a moral struggle imbued with the Holy Spirit, according to the hidden law of Europe, which was the law of the Gospel, embodied in a national idea. We must be true to that law, we must establish the alternative customs, laws, institutions, and social networks—and here he gestured widely to the room, while seeming only partly conscious of the people actually contained in it—in order to live as we should behind the mask.

As he pronounced his implacable verdicts, he stared fixedly into infinity. And I could not help noticing, since Betka had schooled me in this vital matter, that nothing in Igor's surroundings matched anything else. The brown leather chairs clashed with the pea green nylon cushions that sat on them; a dirty grey carpet with a zig-zag modern design supported an ornate Jugendstil desk edged with nickel. On top of the desk a grotesque modern lamp mounted on a slab of bottle-green glass stood beside a kitsch sculpture of the Virgin and Child. It was as though everything around Igor had washed up there, like garbage at the feet of some howling prophet on the shore. Yet this, too, was life. Looking round at the audience, several of them young like me, and all of them fixing the prophet with intent, expectant eyes, I felt a surge of amused joy. The parallel polis was built from garbage; but it was built by the imagination, and you could assemble it however you liked.

Afterwards I wanted to share the thought with Father Pavel, and suggested we go for a beer. But he looked serious and preoccupied, refusing my invitation and looking askance at my laughter. After a while I began to understand that amusement did not have much meaning for those who were living in truth. Betka was satirical, yes. But she was a thing apart, more an observer than a participant, and she kept her amusement for me. If I made a joke in Rudolf's seminar, he would stare at me for a moment, from that place behind his eyes where the machine was kept, and then emit a sudden jagged laugh, like the high-pitched clatter of a xylophone. Only one of my new acquaintances saw what was truly risible in communism, and he kept away from the seminars in a secret world of his own.

Betka and I had been reading a samizdat journal—*Literární sborník*—which she was allowed to keep only for a couple of days. She sat at her desk taking notes, and then handed it to me, saying "read this article." The author wrote under the name of Petr Pius, and his theme was the language of communism. He gave a hundred examples, from Marx and Lenin to the editorials of *Rudé právo* and the speeches of Comrade Husák, showing the deep syntax of our torment. Substantives were demoted to verbs, and verbs made fluid and directionless; concrete realities were vaporized into abstractions, and the whole set into a kind of demonic motion, with "historical forces" and "progressive elements" swirling one way, and "reactionary elements" and "ideological forces" swirling the other. The writer showed that the torment of Czech society was not imposed by the Evil Empire but by language. We lived under a regime of nonsense, and our sufferings were concocted in the looking glass by the faces that stared at us from there.

"Who is this man?" I asked.

"You will meet him," she replied. "Today."

"Oh?"

"I have to go to work now, so I want you to return this to Petr Pius. You will find him in the boiler room of the Na Františku hospital. I was due to be there at five o'clock prompt. That is when you must knock on his door. Don't speak, but give him this note from me."

She described the door at the bottom of some steps that led down from the street, and handed me the note of introduction. I set off in a state of high excitement, not just because I was to meet the man who had made sudden sense of things for me, but also because Betka was trusting me as a go-between, and allowing me for the first time on equal terms into the life that she kept to herself.

"By the way," she said as I left. "His name is not Petr Pius but Ivan Pospíchal, and you should call him Karel."

In reality I had no opportunity to call him anything. The person who came to the metal door in answer to my knocking was tall, slightly stooped, with a thick beard in which he twined his fingers. He stared at me for a moment, and then took the note that I held out to him. When he raised his eyes to me again it was with an amused but distant look. The high collar of his white shirt framed his face like a ruff, giving the impression of a seventeenth-century portrait. In his hand was a cigar, and throughout our meeting he smoked, taking a new cigar from his pocket whenever the old one faltered. From the effect of this habit, his teeth were black and scaly like old tombstones.

He looked left and right along the street to see whether I was being followed. Then he ushered me quickly across the threshold into an antechamber containing a broom and a few buckets, and from there into fairyland, which took the form of a large square room, the walls of which were covered in pictures. There were wilting ladies in florid hats; saccharine Madonnas with pneumatic breasts; amorous hussars winking suggestively; doe-eyed children with bare bottoms and pom-poms in their hair. Buxom mermaids offered glasses of frothy beer, fey Rusalkas emerged from their lakes in carefully-ironed crinoline, merry gnomes sang around their tavern tables with tankards raised in salutation, Red Army soldiers thrust their bayonets into the future blessed by the ghost of Stalin in the clouds. I was surrounded by every possible form of kitsch lovingly mounted in gilded frames. Against one wall stood an upright piano, on which were sepia-toned photographs of once-loved people, mounted in padded silk. In a display cabinet fixed to the wall was an array of plaster-cast gnomes and pixies in lurid purples and greens, beside a busty milkmaid in Mucha-style gold and brown.

There were a few slits of glass set high up in the walls at street level. But most of the thick, curdled light in the room came from table lamps, with gold shades mounted on the heads of pink porcelain poodles, and a flame of glass held aloft by a *Rosenkavalier* negro. One of the poodles stood on a desk upon which lay a neat pile of papers beside an old-fashioned fountain pen, of the kind that I had seen on that fateful day. Next to the desk was a bookcase containing the bound volumes of a serious scholar's library. For Karel had been a professor of philology before his expulsion from the university, and regarded his present employment as affording an ideal refuge for his "editorial work." He was making a study of falsehood: false theories, false opinions, false sentiments, false loves, and false hatreds, all of which had the capacity to colonize the human soul and turn it into the mocking mirror by which he was surrounded. There are things, he explained, which in their true form cannot be bought and sold: love, honor, duty, sacrifice. But if we wish to buy and sell them nevertheless, we have to construct soft fairyland versions of them. That, he said, is the meaning of kitsch: it is the representation, in a world of falsehood, of ideals that we once had in the world of truth. All this culminates in communism, which is kitsch of a new kind: kitsch with teeth. And with that judgment, he held the cigar away from his mouth and laughed a conclusive laugh, as though there were nothing more to be said.

It was strange and flattering to be spoken to by such an exotic character, although I put his loquacity down to his isolation in this Aladdin's cave, rather than to any feature of myself that could have sparked his interest. He responded to all my questions with a kind of scholarly precision, offering his judgments of our society and culture as though they were the judgments of some visiting anthropologist, testing his theories against the strangest of facts. He had an expert knowledge of what he called the First Church of Marx Scientist— by which he meant the post-war years when we Czechs were told that we were "building socialism." The main thing we built, he said, was kitsch monuments, while our national assets were being forcibly transferred to the Soviet Union.

For Karel, no sign of the cultural degradation of those times was more eloquent than its music and, at my request, he sat at the piano to play some of the Red Army marches that he had heard as a schoolchild during the 1950s: "White Army, Black Baron," "The March of Stalin's Artillery," and "The Battle Is On Again." Every once in a while he would put his cigar in the ashtray on his desk, take a pair of grey overalls from the hook beside an inner door, cover himself with these, and then go through to an adjoining room to feed coke into the boiler that was housed there.

Karel clearly regarded all clothes as provisional, to be changed at once as the situation evolved. At one point, he paused to take a long redingote in dark blue velvet from a closet set in the wall. Dressed in this music-hall costume, he accompanied himself in the song composed by Radim Drejsl for the First Church of Marx Scientist, Czechoslovak branch: *Za Gottwalda vpřed*, "Forward with Gottwald," which he sang in a high caressing tenor. The effect was so ludicrous that I found myself curled up in laughter on a broken-springed sofa, clutching in my merriment the batting-eyed doll in frilly underwear that occupied one of its corners.

I asked Karel why I never saw him at Rudolf's seminar. Surely he could make an important contribution, of which we all stood in need?

"Seminars are good," he replied, leaning his head sideways towards his cupped right hand, as if to decant his eyes into it. "Good too are the protests and petitions, the exile presses. *Et cetera*. But I work in another way. I look for the right words, which are also the wrong words. The forbidden words: words with the shape of the things they describe. I must work in my own way, in my own space."

"But when you have discovered those words, what do you do with them?"

"I shake them, ferment them, distill them. And sometimes, when they have lain on the desk long enough and taken on the aroma of old maplewood, I publish them."

"How is that possible?"

He looked at me in an amused way and pointed to the volume of *Literární sborník*.

"Like that," he said. "Though it's not so easy now. My contact at the paper factory was arrested."

I almost resented Mother, that her image and her fate came always like a cloud across my new excitements, reminding me that I was entitled to nothing until the debt of guilt was paid. But I decided to conceal the connection and asked Karel instead how he had got to know Betka.

"Alžběta? I know her hardly at all. Only once she came here, with her friend Vilém. I asked him round to tune the piano. An odd character, and not to be trusted, I should say. Are you to be trusted?"

He shot me a mock-accusing look, and then went back to the piano, sitting down to leaf through the old volume of Drejsl's *Budovatelské písně*—songs for the building of socialism.

"Whom do you mean," I asked anxiously. "Vilém or Alžběta?"

"Distrust was built in to the system from the beginning," he said, ignoring my question. "The first axiom of Marx Scientist is that everything they tell you is a lie. The second axiom is that it doesn't matter, since you are lying too. The third axiom is 'Kill all liars!' That's what they did to this guy, Radim Drejsl, who came back from the Soviet Union with an odd desire to tell unofficial lies of his own. He ended up on the pavement, five floors below his apartment. In those days you went forward with Gottwald through the nearest window."

And with a cheerful laugh he put down the cigar and launched himself again into song.

Karel's way of conversing was to package each topic in precise satirical sentences and then move on. So I never learned whether it was Vilém or Betka whom he judged to be untrustworthy. At the same time, in all his talk and actions, something eminently human beaconed from Karel's eye. In this he was totally unlike Rudolf or Igor, or the people whom I met at their seminars, all of whom, when challenged by some pleasantry, greeted it with a hunted look, as though some secret part of themselves must be at once protected.

When, during the days of that never-to-be-forgotten spring, I visited Karel, it was at an appointed hour, and only, at his insistence, after walking twice around the block to see that I was not being followed. Sometimes I would bring a copy of *Rudé právo* so that he could analyze the editorial Newspeak, and always I would hope for a recital of those songs which told me that "Lenin is young again, and a new October comes," or that "From the wild forests to the British seas, Red Army is best!" Karel regarded all political opinions with irony and all political actions with disdain. He belonged to no dissident circle but enjoyed an ordinary life at home with his wife and son as well as a magic life of kitsch in the world that he had created underground.

One day I discovered a framed poster showing the profile of Gottwald emerging from those of Marx, Lenin, and Stalin in the sky over Prague. Someone had thrown it into my bin at the Husovy sady. I cleaned it and took it as a gift to Karel, who greeted it with a rendition of *Za Gottwalda vpřed* and hung it delightedly above his desk. I felt as though I had passed the highest test in discrimination, and could now address him as an equal.

It was not only because he amused me that I spent time with Karel—though God knows amusement was welcome then. He taught me to understand things in a new way. Words, for Karel, were not the servants of things but their masters: they arrange and rearrange the world. In Orwell's *Nineteen Eighty-Four*, language had been doctored so that only the official opinions could be expressed in it. Something like this, Karel argued, had happened to us. The official literature, the official press, even the news on television, deployed a small vocabulary of reliable words, and a syntax permitting only their reliable combinations. People appeared in this discourse not as freely-choosing individuals but as abstractions, through which impersonal forces "struggle" for domination. The forces of progress were bound to win, and the forces of reaction to be defeated. Meanwhile, it was important to fuse the permitted words into bundles, so as to block the doors through which reality might enter. Hence "reactionary" went always with "bourgeois," "imperialist" and "Zionist," the last allowing a permitted note of anti-Semitism; "progressive" was invariably tied up with "proletarian," "fraternal," and "internationalist." Our "society" was "building socialism," and meanwhile living in a condition of "actual socialism" that in some way anticipated the heroic goal. And what, Karel asked, did this word "actual" mean? Just the sediment that sinks to the bottom, when the jar of possibilities has been stirred.

The abuse of words upon which our official doctrine depended was already prefigured in the sacred texts of Marx, Engels, and Lenin. The goal, Karel said, was not to tell explicit lies but to destroy the distinction between the true and the false, so that lying becomes neither necessary nor possible. And he compared Newspeak to kitsch, the purpose of which is to destroy the distinction between true and false sentiment, so as to remove emotion from reality and invest it in a world of fantasy, where nothing has a value, though everything has a price.

Karel, I came to see, was one of those finely tuned people—Václav Havel was another—who vibrate just to the moment of history when they happen to exist. Ours was the last gasp of the written word—the last time when reality bowed in obedience to our way of describing it. And he stood vigil over language, allowing only the cleanest, the clearest, the most transparent words to pass onto the paper. Betka read his articles with delight. For she, like him, was fastidious with words. But the official words of our rulers interested her less than the words leveled against them, fired in those sparse samizdat editions like precious eggs thrown as a last resort against the advancing tanks.

One afternoon she sat me down with a samizdat text by the philosopher Egon Bondy, whose real name was Zbyněk Fišer, and who was then living in Slovakia. Everybody loved Bondy, in the semi-official way that they loved Magor, John Lennon, and the Plastic

People, for whom he had provided words. He was a prodigious talent, a writer of poems, novels, science fiction, and philosophy, in all of which he promised the truth of our condition. As she ran her finger along the lines of his text, hovering above the words signifying movement, progress, development, technology, all moving in a line towards something called *ontovládnost*—ontological self-government—I saw the whole puddle of abstractions evaporate into nothingness. These, she said, were words without thought, words to prevent thought.

She proved the point not by argument, but by placing herself squarely in front of the text and forcing it to face up to her. She did not discuss things but confronted them, as she confronted me, and her very being was a challenge and a revelation. Her careful use of language, her suspicion of popular culture, her deep love of baroque music and of those heart-wrenching chords and phrases in Janáček—all these were signs that, by some miraculous process of self-discipline and spiritual knowledge, she had lifted herself free from our polluted world, and learned to live in another way. And by the same miracle, she was determined to lift me after her. How could I not love the woman who did such a thing for me?

CHAPTER 15

LITTLE BY LITTLE I came to understand that it was for each of us to sift the garbage in search of knowledge, freedom, and hope, and that there was no single formula, no set of rules or heroic postures, that would guarantee the outcome. Such was also Betka's message to me, and she constantly guided me to experiences that would confirm it. She had entered my life as a liberating angel: more, she *was* my life, which had begun with her, and my underground days were like a chrysalis which had fallen away at her touch.

Of course, I had paid a price for this. Mother was constantly in my thoughts, and I several times took the bus to Ruzyně, in the days when she was on remand awaiting trial, in the hope of being admitted to her presence, only to be told that her case was in preparation and that I would be called to give evidence if either the prosecution or the defense required it. In fact I was never called. But, as I wrote, Bob Heilbronn did what was expected; Mother's case was taken up by the "human rights machine," as Betka called it. This poor dingy woman whom I loved and pitied became a symbol of the nation that had ignored her. So frequent were the mentions of her case, on Radio Free Europe and Voice of America, on the BBC World Service and Deutsche Welle, that she at last received the accolade of an editorial in *Rudé právo*, referring to the reactionary elements and Zionist conspiracies that had chosen her as their tool. I studied the editorial with Karel, to whom I had finally confessed my connection with his former publisher. He pointed to the word "tool"—*nástroj*. In Newspeak, he said, this indicated a part of the enemy machine that was not truly dangerous. And so it was. When the charge was finally laid it was not one of subversion in collaboration with foreign powers but the far lesser one of misuse of socialist property for private gain. Mother pleaded innocent, but her defense counsel confirmed her guilt and asked only that she be treated leniently on account of her confused state of mind, as proved by her crazy belief that she, who knew nothing of books, could turn herself into a publisher. She got nine months, with a five-year ban on the use of a typewriter. She smiled at me as they led her away, and there was, in that smile, a kind of triumph, as though she had at last done her duty to Dad. Like me, she had come up from underground to live in another way. And even if she had lost a life on my account, she wanted to tell me that she had also gained one. I tried my best to convince myself of this, but the image of Mother was now at the back of my mind, even in the intensest moments of my newfound happiness.

The seminars, visits to Igor and Karel, walks with Father Pavel, and the never-ending flow of books and music—all this had its center and its meaning in that room where I was side by side with Betka. I came there after work, always with her permission. She would open the door and stand back from it with her familiar gesture, before embracing me. Those first moments of silence were, for me, the most important. She was not fighting me with words, not putting me in my place, not warning, teaching or dramatizing, but simply acknowledging, in every trembling part of her body, that she

[ROGER SCRUTON]

wanted me and needed me. All the long grey hours apart from her were redeemed in those moments, and never have I been happy as I was then.

In that room, I practiced Father Pavel's "gymnastics of attention." I studied each object, not so as to dissolve it in some narrative of my own, but so as to allow it to speak for itself. Objects around Betka lent themselves to this exercise. For she displayed them with a natural and easy-going grace that gave them the character of heirlooms, things that were there because they were there. I saw her framed at her desk between an old-fashioned lamp of brass, its bulb shaded by a bowl of frosted crystal, and an equally old-fashioned telephone in black Bakelite, which she had found in a junk-shop and never sought to have connected. She kept the telephone, she said, because it was a symbol of our country, begging speech but not transmitting it. For me, however, it had a voice. I thought of those telephones in plays and operas—in the *Makropulos Case,* for instance, which Betka especially loved. This thing contained the congealed remains of human dialogue; it was the tomb in which speech had been buried. Its black sheen was dignified, sepulchral, and addressed to our collective memory. Not since Dad's arrest had there been a telephone at home: we were too criminal to have a right to one, and not criminal enough that they should need one to keep track of us. Betka's telephone therefore addressed me directly. It was like a sculpture of a telephone, one of those pop art objects that seem to have suffered a metamorphosis from concrete object to abstract idea, while still remaining the same. In that black tomb was contained a history, a society, a pathos, and I lay on the bed communing with it as though hearing the voices within.

So it was with the other objects in that room: the two rococo candlesticks on the bookcase beneath the other window; the still life oil painting above the bed, in which a misshapen pear wrestled with two green apples for possession of a plate; the old Russian icon of the

Virgin and Child in an ebony frame, which hung on the opposite wall between the desk and the bookcase. I would watch these things until conscious that they were watching me. And the quiet rustle of Betka at her desk, as she took notes on the latest piece of samizdat, or wrote in the black-bound folder that I was forbidden to touch, was like a summer breeze, filling my heart with hopes for the future and inspiring in me a kind of confidence that I was really living.

But the fountain at which I drank sometimes had a bitter after-taste. Even if I could keep the thought of Mother out of mind, it was evident that I, too, was in trouble. I was puzzled, indeed, by my freedom. The creature with staring eyes and jug-handle ears whom I occasionally glimpsed in my wake must surely be acting under instructions. The vandalizing of the apartment at Gottwaldova must surely have been a warning. The contemptuous dismissal with which I had been greeted at Bartolomějská must surely indicate that my case was in hand and that there would be no escaping it. And yet nothing happened. I was free to come and go, to pursue my new life as though with official sanction, gaining the education that I had fruitlessly petitioned for, just as if the Minister himself had suddenly put his rubber stamp on the typewritten permit. Yet above me, still and intent in every changing breeze, the hawk was motionlessly watching.

More troubling still was the source of my happiness, Betka. It mattered that she was four years older than me. She had a life behind her already, one that she would not reveal. We had been lovers for three months, and still I had no idea what she did when not with me. Since discovering that the little room that was our only sanctuary was not hers, and since asking myself why she said nothing of that house at Divoká Šárka where she was so evidently at home, I ceased to trust her entirely. At the same time my distrust belonged to the world I had left behind, the world of lies, fears, and betrayals, and I strove to banish it. I was side by side with Betka, and her candid eyes addressed me sorrowfully if ever I hinted that she was withholding some part of herself.

"Sometimes," she said, "there is a short circuit between Heaven and Hell and the lights go out everywhere. That's what it's like when you question me." In such a way she strove to set me again on the path that I called living in truth.

Then everything changed. It began on a Wednesday in April. It was late afternoon and I had just returned from Ruzyně, where I had been allowed to visit Mother for the first time. In the minutes allowed to us, she had said very little, only that she shared her cell with five other women, and that boredom was the hardest part of it. But I could see from her weary face that the moment of courage was past, and that her days were days of suffering. Betka did her best to comfort me, and we lay still for a while on that bed like fugitives. Evening sunlight stretched across the desk like a reaching hand, almost touching her thigh. Two voices in the yard exchanged inaudible words. A tram squealed distantly. Then footsteps sounded on the stairs, and I felt Betka freeze beside me.

There was only one door at the top of the stairs apart from Betka's, and that opened onto her tiny bathroom. The footsteps were those of a man, and the knock, tentative at first, but then loud and insistent, had a tone of accusation. Betka put her hand over my mouth and lay still. The intruder was now turning the handle of the door, and it struck me that Betka always locked the door when we were together, and left the big key in the mortise, so that nobody could unlock it from outside. Was the intruder expected, then? Did he have a claim on her that was earlier, better, and more urgent than my own? I waited for him to speak, to call out her name, to explain the nature of his connection. But after a few seconds of rattling and muttering, he retraced his steps, and we heard the clang of the metal door as he left the courtyard.

"So who was that, Betka?"

She had jumped from the bed and was putting on her clothes.

"How should I know? Maybe someone who had this room before."

The explanation didn't satisfy me, but she was rushing now, telling me that she was late for work and I must go. I did not see her until the following Friday, when we were both at Rudolf's seminar. But there was something evasive in her manner, and afterwards, as we met on the stairway, she said that she could not see me on the Saturday, since her group was performing at one of the embassies and she had a rehearsal in the morning. In fact, she could not see me until Monday afternoon. Looking me in the eyes, she said only "Honzo!" and turned away. I did not know whether it was a reproach or a confession, and all that weekend I lay on Mother's bed in a state of distress.

Father Pavel had lent me a samizdat copy of Eva Kantůrková's *My Companions in the House of Sadness*, describing life in Ruzyně prison. He was reluctant at first, but I told him that I needed to prepare myself, so that I could confess to my part in Mother's suffering. He looked at me with a kind of tenderness as he handed over the book. But as I read the sad stories of those imprisoned women, it was not Mother I thought of but Betka, who had taught me to follow truth and then concealed it.

CHAPTER 16

SUNDAYS IN OUR block were a torment. Our neighbors to either side were builders from Slovakia, brought to Prague to work on a housing project in Žižkov. On Sundays they stayed at home, drinking and quarreling, so that our little cupboard was filled with the sound of their shouts and blows. By the early afternoon the noise was intolerable, and on that Sunday especially so, since it echoed in the void inside me. I went down into the valley, to the Chapel of the Holy Family which I had haunted in my days underground. I had found consolation in this abandoned place. Like me, it had no use and belonged to no one. It was always there, waiting for me, as a blank sheet of paper awaits the pen. But I found no comfort in it now. This place had been frequented by another, simpler person: one who had adopted the clean untroubled discipline of loneliness. I was no longer that person.

I walked up the Nusle steps into the Nové Město, and took the Metro to Leninova. A girl with a pale pretty face wrapped in a pink scarf sat opposite. She was looking at me, and her mouth fluttered as I returned her gaze, as though she were enquiring into my sadness. I was glad when she got out at Malostranská. I took the bus to Divoká Šárka, and went in search of Betka's house. It was only a few hundred meters from the bus stop, down a little lane that branched off the street named after Lenin, across an old railway line, and then branching away between blocks of colored concrete panels. My image of the little farmhouse was so complete that I could count the number of casement windows in the old stucco façade—six—and the number of trees in the little orchard—eight. I remembered exactly how the tall trashcans were arranged along the alley beside the apartment block, and how it all looked from this angle—although it had been dark then, and I had had no clear impression of the house's depth.

For two hours I patrolled the streets, among housing complexes with their Sunday noises and Sunday smells, along dusty tracks pitted by bulldozers and lined by the unfilled concrete frames of new constructions. I found no farmhouse, and nothing resembling the little street in which it had stood. An uncanny feeling came over me. It crossed my mind that Betka did not exist. Her image had appeared in another element like Rusalka at the water's lip, trembling on the edge of things, and then vanishing. My glimpses of her were mirages, reflections in the mirror of my anxiety of a figure that bore no relation to the one I had invented, and to which I clung as a woman clings to her stillborn baby, refusing to believe that there is nothing there.

I took this thought with me into the gorge beyond the road, to wander beside the stream that flowed in those days clear and strong beneath the cliffs. The bent saplings of birch and maple struggled for life on the steep slopes of stone; birds darted from cranny to cranny in the shadows, and at one point a mangy dog appeared above me at the edge of the gorge, his square head thrust fearlessly through a screen of couch grass. All around was the sound of the stream, and above it the bare branches of ash trees tied down the sky. A screen of cloud touched the grey cliffs at the horizon's rim and fluttered like a skirt. The world had closed around me, and for a long time I listened to the stream, and to the cliffs honeycombed with voices. I heard the voice of Dad in the role of Prince Ctirad, and of Mother telling him to sing more quietly lest the neighbors complain. And the hollow feeling grew within, as though a great hand had scooped out the living matter. I was a dead person, and the tears on my cheeks were tears of glass. This feeling lasted until Monday afternoon. When she opened the door and stepped back from it, I half-expected to find no one there. I walked towards the desk, eyes averted, seeking emptiness. Then she seized me from behind, her hands around my chest.

"Honzo!"

"No," I replied, "not Honza, just a mistake of yours."

She jumped round to face me.

"You mean I'm a mistake of yours."

I looked at those eyes that looked into me. Their silver sheen lay over deep waters. And there was something moving below the surface—something that was seeking me, preparing to emerge from its element and to cast off its invulnerability in order to be at my side. I had the sense that Betka had done this for no one else, that I was—despite my youth and maybe because of my youth—the recipient of a peculiar privilege. In a moment my jealousy vanished, and I stood before her in a state of helpless apology.

"Betka, I am sorry. Something upset me, something quite unimportant."

"Not unimportant at all," she said, and putting her hands on my shoulders, pressed me down gently so that I sat at the desk. Next to her notebook lay the copy of *Rumors*, in Mother's blue pasteboard binding, and I noticed many slips of paper between the pages.

"You have every right to complain," she went on. "Of course I should have said more about my work, my family, where I come from, and where I'm going. You have told me everything, and I have only told you what you need to know."

"What *you* think I need to know."

"Yes, if you like. So what do *you* think you need to know?"

"What you do when you are not with me. And where you are when you are not in this room. And yes: who it was came to the door on Wednesday last. And why."

"Is that it?"

"For the time being, yes."

"When I am not with you, I am often at the children's hospital. Sometimes I stay there, for they run a residential school, an *internát*, and I make myself useful as a teacher. Or, if I am not there, maybe I am playing in our little group. Because there are posh parties even in Prague, where people who pride themselves on their taste sit in antique chairs and listen to ancient music. And the person who came to the door was possibly Vilém, whose room this is, and if he didn't mention it when I saw him on Saturday, it was because I had forbidden him ever to invade my private space, and there, I suppose, is the story you need to know."

While she spoke, Betka was looking at me with a tender and half-smiling expression, as though talking to a child. I nodded meekly and, drawing up the bedside chair, she sat down beside me and took my hand.

"I was a student in the school of nursing and Vilém was teaching in the Academy of Music. He sent a notice around the university proposing a baroque ensemble. The early music movement was big in the West back then, and I was always envious when I read about it or heard things on the radio. One of the last things my dad had done for me, before the divorce, was to buy a theorbo. So when Vilém sent round his appeal I was ready and willing to join. I had to think a bit. The Solidarity Union was taking off in Poland, and the government was nervous. The Party has its own version of Christ's saying: when two or three are gathered in any name but ours, there shall we be among them. But I decided there was no risk. Although the Party was down on rock music, a baroque ensemble, led by an official professor, could hardly stir things up as the Plastic People had done.

"I was sharing a room in a student house in Nusle with a girl from North Bohemia who spent her evenings playing with the radio, hoping to hear some scraps of Western pop. I rescued myself through our early music group. I liked it that Vilém was attracted to me, liked it that he enjoyed my voice and wanted to give me the star role in our performances, liked it that he found excuses to detain me after rehearsals and talk to me. We became close, and for a while I didn't care that he was married with kids of his own. I wasn't going to fall in love with him, in any case. Interesting people are rare; rarer still are those who trouble to impart their knowledge. Vilém, you see, opened a door for me. He knew what I wanted to know; he had connections; he was an insider, a Party member, a smooth operator who could get things done. For me, he was a means to self-improvement, the ladder to get up on top. And I expect that disappoints you."

I shook my head. This much I had guessed. And had she gone on to tell me of a farmhouse in Divoká Šárka, where Vilém maintained her as his mistress, that too would not have surprised me. But the next thing she said was truly surprising.

"Vilém let me borrow this room: he had kept it from his own student days, and had no use for it since getting married. After a few attempts, he stopped trying to seduce me and sought cooperation of a different sort. Early music scores can be obtained only from the West, since our archives here are chaotic and largely forbidden. This provided an excuse to visit embassies, and in the course of the visits, to obtain invitations to play. Vilém insisted that I should do the negotiations, presenting myself as the leader: he did not want to be noticed. Once inside, however, he made a point of getting to know the diplomats and their guests. Vilém speaks good English and

German, and has an easy charm that comes across as sincerity. He would come away from our concerts with more invitations, as well as with information about Czech musicians living abroad, about Czech musicians who had sought to emigrate, and other things that I could only guess at. I didn't like what he was doing, but who was I to complain about it? I was getting a lot from the experience: not only the pleasure of playing and singing and learning a real craft—one that will help me in all kinds of ways if this country finally enters the modern world. I was making useful friends, like Bob Heilbronn. I was seeing the world, and getting to places that only those with Party protection can be trusted to get to. And you see, I treated myself to the excuse that many who move on the edge make use of. I told myself that, when the time came to act against the system, I would be better placed on account of being to this tiny extent inside it. And I think you know what I mean."

I was staring in a shocked way at the desk, and could only just manage a nod.

"What I did for him was innocent enough—for instance, collecting those old editions of Fibich, Janáček, and Martinů, which he adds to his collection and also sometimes barters at the West German Embassy for the music we need. But he began to snoop and pry in ways that troubled me. He found out somehow that I attended Rudolf's seminar, and asked me to take him along. I refused. He found out that I was part of a samizdat circulating library and wanted to join. Again, I refused. He came here once or twice in my absence and let himself in with the spare key he had kept, so as to look through the books I was reading. And he asked me where I obtained them and to whom I passed them on. All this was done with utmost good humor, of course, and he said that he had only one motive, which was his love and concern for me, which could take no other form since he respected my inability to reciprocate. And, you see, it was half true. Vilém enjoys Party privileges of a middling sort;

he is bound to make reports, and he is entrusted with tasks that only he can perform and which touch on things I don't want to know about. If I need anything that he can give, he will rush to provide it. He loves his wife and children and works for their well-being as my mother worked for mine. He is a good listener, and his Party card does not prevent him from feeling a keen sympathy for the dissidents, for condemning their imprisonment and especially the harsh treatment of Magor, who had been his teenage idol. Without Vilém I could not have achieved what I have managed, including the little I have managed for you.

"Then one day, it all changed. Have you not noticed how it is with us? A kind of soporific compromise, a set of tacit agreements that keep everything on an even keel until suddenly, quite unexpectedly, there comes a great wave, and all that was secure and certain is swept away? Dear Honza, this has happened to me many times, and who am I to make a fuss about it? My case is not exceptional, nor is Vilém's.

"Well, he had discovered in me an asset, and that asset was Hans, a minor attaché at the West German embassy, who fell in love with me. Vilém's vigilant jealousy took instant note of the fact, and his self-interest likewise. I hesitate to say this, because Vilém is fundamentally decent. Of course he had made compromises. Of course he was reporting on the people he met. But he recognized the limit beyond which it was morally impossible to go. And one evening, he reached that limit and transgressed it.

"You don't want the details. You don't want to hear about that hour in a car parked in the woods above Karlštejn, Vilém's car, of course, which was never followed, and Hans beside me in the back of it, grasping my hand, watching me with beseeching eyes. Vilém wanted an invitation to Germany, one fixed at the highest level, but with a secure job secretly promised so that he could defect with his family. Hans was offering such an invitation with his eyes—but to me, and an invitation that needed no diplomacy to complete it. Did I love Hans? I told you: I don't make that mistake, haven't made it for years, even if I have made it now. But yes, I was at peace with him; yes, I could have followed him; yes, I could have said to him everything he wanted to hear, save 'yes.' One day you'll understand, Honza.

"That was when Vilém dropped out of my life. He promised Hans that he would make it possible for me to follow: he offered me as bait. And of course he *wanted* me to follow, wanted to continue in some comfortable Western university the erotic games he had tried to play in Prague. I was young, Honza, confused, and lonely too. But I was not merchandise, and I had my reasons for staying here. Hans told Vilém he would do what he could, and I said 'count me out,' and not another word as we drove back to Prague. Next day, Vilém came knocking here, pleading, and threatening too, reminding me of the danger I had been courting in my affair—yes, that is what he called it—with Hans. For it was Hans who placed in my hands those little cyclostyled texts with the magnifying glass in the spine, which he smuggled in the diplomatic bag from Germany. Vilém stood there, on the threshold of the room that is his, and I let him rave and plead and weep. What was I to do? I needed Vilém's protection. I wanted to learn, to live freely, to read and think and be. With Vilém's group, I was earning money, and I could do as I wished without incurring a charge of parasitism. To be outside the system as I was, and yet wholly unprotected, was to be like you—that cheerless underground creature who came up blinking into the light but who blinked so beautifully that I couldn't stop myself from loving him, alas. You mustn't blame me, Honza. Think of your mother. One way or another, she too found protection and used it to lift a little corner of the blanket that was smothering her."

"So what did you do?"

"I did nothing. Hans was recalled to Germany without an explanation. And Vilém and I agreed to go on as before, with no reproaches, provided he left me alone in this place until the day when he would ask me to leave. That day will come, and I must be ready for it."

In everything she said and did, Betka withheld as much as she revealed. But what she revealed was so full of the distinctive life and ambition that shone from her that I could only accept it as the truth—a partial truth, but the truth all the same.

This story was unlike the others, however, in a crucial respect. Although it was the truth, it was the truth about a lie. In order to live in truth, Betka had lived a lie, pretending to herself that she was not tainted by whatever deals Vilém had made in order to protect himself and her. This was the paradox that had magnetized me from the beginning. Her social competence, so far from the diffidence of my contemporaries, her firm melodious voice, so unlike the cagey whisperings at Rudolf's and Igor's seminars, her habit of querying, dismissing, and even laughing at the sterile solemnities of the dissidents—these were exactly the qualities that enabled her to stand outside our world, looking down into the catacombs and up towards the stars. But only a protected person could have acquired them.

I sat in silence for a while, Betka stroking my hand and trying to capture my eyes. When I looked up, it was with the question that had troubled me from the first.

"Where do you live, Betka?"

"Here, as you know."

"I mean, where do you *really* live? Where do you go, for instance, when you leave your work?"

"Usually I come back here. In the early hours. Why?"

"I don't say that there's *someone* else. But there's *somewhere* else, I am sure of it."

She gave me a quizzical look, and then suddenly dropped my hand.

"OK, there *is* somewhere else, the place where I *really* am, and I'm going to take you there. Satisfied?"

"Where is it?"

"A long way from here."

She looked at me reproachfully and got up. Her way of changing shape, from standing to sitting or sitting to standing, had a fluidity and expertise that seemed to condemn my awkwardness. It was as though she were saying, "see, I belong to the real world; and you are just a boy." The tears sprang to my eyes as I watched her.

"Don't you see that I belong to you?" I said.

The blood drained from her face as though my words had frightened her. And she dropped down again beside me and buried her head in my breast.

"Oh Honza, my Honza, you are mine; entirely mine. Entirely my mistake."

And my shirt was damp with her tears.

CHAPTER 17

IT WAS AFTER this exchange that she decided to reward my love. It was spring, the May Day Parade was about to take place in Prague, a lugubrious time when the people of the city are displayed in all their disgrace, like a conquered army paraded in chains. I had permission for a few days off work, and Betka proposed that she take me to the place where she *really* lived, about which I was to ask no questions until the moment when we arrived there.

Anticipating this event, we were quiet and meek together. I came and went as she instructed; I brought my questions, my reading, and my love to her; and I learned from everything she did. I had received a parcel permit from Ruzyně, and Betka bought and packaged everything as though already familiar with the task. She insisted that Mother, who did not smoke, would nevertheless need cigarettes to barter, that toilet paper, hand cream, soap, and shampoo were essential, that chocolates filled with strong liqueurs were a hundred times better than the plain variety, that smoked ham and sausage were more precious than sweets. And she had a tender way of wrapping these things and folding them into the cardboard box, as though she were remembering someone dear for whom she had once performed this service.

The day came for our excursion. Betka had arranged to meet me at the main station, where we were to take a train to Pardubice, and then another to Česká Třebová, where we would change again. I awoke that morning in a state of high excitement like a child at Christmas. I even looked in our little wardrobe for a suit of clothes that would be smarter than my usual green canvas jacket and cotton trousers, as though I were to be presented as a fiancé. I found the old suit of Dad's that we had been keeping for the day of his release, and which was crumpled now and moth-eaten. I put it on, along with a clean shirt and tie, and packed my rough clothes in a hold-all that had also been his.

Betka was standing by the ticket office, fresh and beautiful in a pair of white slacks and a pale green woolen coat. She came to me, rubbed my upper arm affectionately, and pressed a ticket into my hand. She did not speak as she led me to the platform and installed me on the train. Her movements and gestures were imbued with an unusual gravity, as though she were performing a ceremony, a rite of passage into another mode of being.

I have often tried, and always in vain, to explain to Americans what a real train journey is. Although the tracks of our railways had hardly been repaired since they were first laid during the Austro-Hungarian Empire, none had been destroyed by war, and all were used in a country where rail was still the most important form of transport. Our trains were dirty and smelled of diesel oil. They moved slowly and cautiously along tracks that were often buckled, or perched on adverse bends. They crept beside winding rivers and along the edges of cliffs; they groaned up steep inclines and sang out metaled chords in the valleys. They dropped and took up their passengers in every conceivable place: among the concrete towers of industrial suburbs and in the overgrown parks of ancient castles; in sore red villages amid collective farms and in the centers of cathedral cities; in hectic junctions among mineworks and factories, and by lonely forresters cottages shrouded by trees. There was hardly a human habitation in our country that could not be reached by rail and, as you changed down from branch-line to branch-line, the journey became steadily slower, more intimate, more interspersed with domestic glimpses and confidential scenes.

I write that now. But it was not what I felt on that day twenty years ago. Mother and I had sometimes taken the train to Brandýs, to visit Ivana. But that had happened in my underground days, when I was seeing only masks and striving to fill them from the sterile source inside. Now I sat opposite the silent Betka, whose grave eyes sometimes crossed mine with a solemn look, and who sat perfectly still, with her hands folded on the little *tele*—the wanderer's rucksack of those days—that contained, I discovered, only her nightdress, some papers, and a book of Erben's folk-tales.

There was no one else in the carriage, but we did not talk. The train crossed the river and slid through the first suburbs. There followed a ring of weekend gardens, and the scattered factories on the edge of Prague. I peered intently from the window. I was seeing a country that I had never known, a place outside time, outside the reach of the will, an unowned place from which the indigenous gods had retreated. The fields had no edges, and the bald patches among the green stalks of corn were like wounds inflicted by some giant hand. The crops changed from corn to beans and back again without any barrier, and wherever the fields were planted nothing relieved the green save the occasional cluster of poppies, which stained it like a hemorrhage. There were no animals, no people, and the distant villages with their red roofs piled up against the onion-domed churches had an abandoned look, as though killed off by plague. At one point we passed a small town of tower blocks, with pastel-colored slabs set into their sides, and a cemetery of black sculpted marble: nothing else—not even a church or a street. And in the background were bare hills, without trees or grass or bushes, the soil scraped from their surface, leaving only a greyish-white scree.

Every now and then a factory stood amid the fields, motionless, unvisited, forlorn, and bearing some slogan in giant letters on its roof. Unfinished blocks of concrete stood fixed in their final postures, the rusting cranes poised above them in the interrupted gesture of their death. I recall a modernist structure of tubular steel, with broken windows hanging from its metal limbs, and along its flat roof a sign in yellow letters on a red background: "A peaceful life, the socialist program!" Here and there were piles of hay and silage, shoveled up anyhow, rotting and black beneath their dirty yellow crowns. And long lines of trellises had been installed on the crests of the hills, in an effort to retain the soil against the wind and the rain. It was a landscape whose face had been eaten away, which turned its eyeless contours to the sun like a burnt out leper on his deathbed.

After Pardubice, however, the country began to change. The patches of woodland grew larger, the hills struggled free from the valleys, and the villages that rose on their sides were more compact and self-contained, as though growing from the churches in their midst. Only the grey concrete blocks, dropped at random and smashing the narrow alleyways, told of the power forbidding the old way of life that had here been inscribed in stucco and stone.

From Česká Třebová we took a local train, following the path of rivers and gorges, stopping at tiny hamlets where chickens ran in the yards, and snaking through dark woods like a predator stalking its quarry. The still-silent Betka took a packet of sandwiches from her rucksack and spread them on the table that we shared. It was the first meal that she had prepared for me, and she had taken care over it, including what were at the time rare delicacies: smoked carp, bantams' eggs, and fine Spanish ham. She watched me as I ate, with a motherly smile that seemed to match the intimate scenes that passed our window—scenes of settlement and belonging that I had not imagined, in our dispossessed world, to be possible. And when the train stopped at a little place called Lukavice on the Morava, Betka, who had packed everything away in her rucksack, reached across the table to take my hand and guide me like a child onto the platform.

From Lukavice we took a bus to the village of Krchleby, from where we were to walk to our destination. All my suspicions had been blown away by our journey. Now I trusted Betka completely—trusted her to lead me in the way of truth, which was to unite us in this moment and forever. She held my hand as we walked through the village. We passed a chapel of ochre-colored stucco, where a rococo angel spread its wings over a belfry above the porch. Betka tried the door, but it was locked. And then, to my surprise, she crossed herself before walking on. She led me to a single story house at the edge of the forest, and held me back as the door opened to her knock to reveal a little old woman dressed in a voluminous collection of potato-colored skirts, the lappets of a pale blue cap hanging on either shoulder like the headdress of a sphinx. Her small blue eyes sparkled as she cried out with delight.

"*Bětuško! Moje milá, miloučká, dušinečko moje...*"

The endearments emerged from one another like Russian matryoshka dolls, each more diminutive, more tender than the last. Betka kissed the old woman on her smooth pink cheeks and introduced her as Mrs. Němcová, and me as Jan Reichl, a friend from Prague. We were made to sit down in a tiny parlor on a pair of low wooden chairs piled with woven cushions. A low ceiling of yellowing whitewash crowned the smoke-smeared walls. Photographs of weddings and children cluttered the shallow mantelpiece above an iron stove, and older photographs hung in ornate frames on the walls, showing bearded men in uniform, and women with starched collars and widow's weeds. Mrs. Němcová went to and fro through a low paneled door, bringing coffee, apple juice, and sweet plum dumplings, talking of the pig who had died in February, of the chickens that had been eaten by a fox last Thursday, of the marrows that still had not flowered, and the local council's decision to exclude her from the half acre that she "borrowed" from the collective farm. Every now and then she would interrupt her flow of words to bestow a kiss on Betka and to compliment her on her health or looks. And a kind of wonder spread through me, that I, Comrade Underground, could fall like this into a nineteenth-century fairy tale.

I sat in that darkened room, practicing Father Pavel's gymnastics of attention, focusing on the armchairs—squat little goblins bursting with horsehair—on the heavy sideboard of oak with its bronze-edged top and, through its glass doors, on the carefully arranged china, as precious to Mrs. Němcová as it was surely worthless to the world. The hum of soft words was the soundtrack of a film, and I was the camera that shot out meanings like an archer. Betka had said nothing to explain Mrs. Němcová, or to put this little cottage in any other context than the one that it declared. But it was enough for me that I stood near the source of Betka's life, sending arrows of attention into the pool that had produced her.

The bond between Betka and Mrs. Němcová was not one of affection only. In exchange for fifty crowns, the old woman provided us with bread, cheese, eggs, and sausage, and sent us on our way with a smiling sense of benefits received as well as given. We took a stony track along the forest rim. To our right, the collective farm spread to the near horizon, and under the wrinkled fields were the little bumps of vanished buildings, like crumbs beneath a tablecloth. Fences stood rotting among the weeds, and every hundred yards or so we would come across a stable, a sheep pen, a pigsty, crumbling to a heap and overgrown with nettles. At one point we passed a dilapidated farmhouse standing among broken-down sheds. The windows were hanging from their frames and a beech tree, rooted somewhere within its walls, rose with outspread arms like an escaping ghost above the roof tiles.

We came to a fork in the track, marked by a cross of stone, on which the dying Jesus hung above a jar of dried flowers. His face was long, thin, lined by suffering, and the pointed chin seemed to bury itself in his chest like an axe. It was not a work of art; but the sculptor had portrayed in Christ the human archetype as he knew it. And that archetype was German. On a tablet of stone at the foot of the cross was written in Gothic letters: *Vater, vergib ihnen. Sie wissen nicht, was sie tun,* "Father, forgive them, for they know not what they do"—words from St. Luke's gospel, spoken over fusty guitar chords by Magor, at one of those village concerts by the Plastic People of which Betka possessed the tapes.

"Look," she said, and nodded towards the landscape before us. We stood on a hillock, the horizon rimmed by forest. Here and there a ruined farmhouse stood in an apron of trees, and the fields bore wide scars where the banks had been flattened and plowed. Those old boundaries of earth and piled-up stone, which divided owner from owner, had protected both the people and the land that they had settled; facing this skull-like vista of mud and clay, I could not escape the feeling that the communist war on property and on the *škůdci*—the pests—who owned it had been, in every sense, a war on the soil. The hills were crisscrossed by tracks like the one on which we stood and a few stone crosses still punctuated the fields, spreading long afternoon shadows like defensive hands. But those crosses, I saw, were rooted in another ground, which lay below the surface, packed with the God-fearing dead.

"Do you understand?" she asked. She turned to me with the serious expression that summoned my discipleship.

"Perhaps I do," I replied, and we walked on. The path took us through weed-filled orchards where apples and plums ran wild. To our left stood abandoned houses, their whitewash stained to grey, scabs of brickwork showing through the fallen stucco. Here and there were broken pedestals, on which stone saints bore witness to vanished joys.

She began to speak to me, for the first time that day, in a voice both urgent and tender, as though imparting a vital lesson to a child.

"You see," she said, "God laid his hand on these fields, and it lies there invisibly. No human being has been able to lift that hand. All we can do is cover it with rubbish. For these fields are not ours. Those who consecrated them were driven out, but without relinquishing their spiritual claim. Some, when the witch-hunts began, preferred to kill themselves rather than abandon the place that God had given them. This place is home to me. But it is a home that was stolen from the people who made it. That is the story of my life, and the story, too, of yours, if you don't mind me saying."

She took my arm and pressed against me as we walked. Her words troubled me. I knew about the Czech Germans, about Gottwald's call for retribution against them—not just for the Nazi occupation, but for the Battle of the White Mountain, when the old Czech nation was destroyed—and about their expulsion from their homes. But now I was glimpsing, beneath the willful desecration, the consecrated place that they had made. Those people, who clung in bad times to their inherited way of life, and who were punished for their mistake in doing so, had made a place in which tranquillity and piety achieved such concrete and visible form that not even Gottwald and his thugs had been able to wipe them entirely away. Betka showed me chapels hidden among weeds and creepers, carved milestones along forest paths, and in one place stations of the cross, leading through impassable bushes to some hidden place of pilgrimage. Her words, at once so precise and so gentle, seemed not to describe but to address the things they touched, like invocations of the dead. Somehow, she made this devastated country speak more directly to those old longings for the homeland, for the *domov mŭj* of our national anthem, than any landscape made by Czechs.

Of course, as Karel would remind me, the *domov* had been hidden under socialist kitsch; for him, this landscape would be part of the never-ending black joke of communism. But for Betka it was not so. For the first time since Dad's arrest, I had a vision of home, and it was a home that she conjured from a ruined way of life and a pillaged countryside.

We came to a place where small fields had been allocated to individual families by the collective farm. The fences had been mended and the meadows kept for hay. Wildflowers grew amid the grass, and their many-colored heads waved in the evening breeze. Betka told me their names—*kokrhel, chrpa, šťovík,* yellow rattle, knapweed, sorrel dock, as my dictionary tells me—and another, with rose-pink serrated petals, *slzičky panenky Marie,* "tears of Our Lady Mary," for which I can find no English name. She pointed to some cottages, recounting the story of those who lived there—people who had kept their heads down, and enjoyed for whatever reason the gift of stolen property. And then we came to a copse of trees beside the track. A steep path rose towards double doors, set in an arch flanked by walls of stone. A stone medallion had been carved into the arch: it showed the Virgin and Child, with the words *bitte für Uns* in Gothic script beneath it. "Pray for us sinners, now and at the hour of our death."

I recalled a conversation with Father Pavel. You don't have to believe in life after death, he said, in order to utter that prayer with conviction. Watching Betka as she took a big iron key from her rucksack and turned it in the lock of the double door, I knew what he meant. All time is now; and where there is love both life and death move in love's shadow.

"This," she said, turning to me, "is my home. And you are the first man I have brought here. The only man I shall ever bring here."

She kissed me gravely and took me by the hand. We entered a horseshoe-shaped courtyard enclosed by sheds of stone. On one side were low stalls fronted by an earthenware trough; this, Betka told me, was where the pigs had lived. On the other side was a stable with a divided door, and a large stall for cows with partitions and mangers. Inside the doors, and to either side of them, were huts for ducks and chickens, and in the center, surrounded by a walkway of flagstones, was a deep pit—the dung-heap that had warmed the farm in winter and which was spread on the land each spring. At the back, overlooking this autarkic kingdom, was the house, a single story of rubble and plaster, from which a chimney reached skywards above a roof of tiles.

We entered through a low door and were immediately in the central parlor. The room was built around a tiled woodstove, surmounted by a platform on which the family had slept in winter. To one side of the stove stood an old-fashioned kitchen dresser. To the other side were a table and chairs of oak. The facing corners harbored two low beds under cheerful cushions, and above them mullioned windows set in deep white-washed walls. The panes were framed by old gingham curtains, giving the appearance of a girl's bonnet around an unblemished face. The light that entered was filtered and uncertain, strangely reminiscent of the damp smells of the forest, not picking things out but settling everywhere like a mist. Oil lamps stood on bedside tables, and against one wall was a roughly carved cabinet with cloth-bound books in German and Czech. A nineteenth-century painting hung above it, showing a woman with rosy cheeks framed by a high starched collar above a buttoned dress. Opposite stood an upright piano against the wall. Janáček's collection of Moravian folk songs was propped open above the keys and on the wall behind it was a plaster Calvary on a carved wooden mount. The dresser contained bowls and platters, tureens and skillets, instruments of brass and iron from another more diligent, more penurious, and more pious age, when every object had a precise function that explained it, and every function was organically linked to the business of survival. These things, once valued as means, lived on as ends, basking in their own once-functional nature. The whole effect of the room was of a shrine maintained, with impeccable taste, to a life that had gone.

My eyes were caught by an old desk beneath one of the windows. It was of plain brown wood, with a blotter and a grey marble inkwell. Next to the inkwell was a cast iron bottle opener, an old matchbox full of paper clips, and a neat row of fountain pens with brass levers for filling the rubber tubes within. I recalled another fountain pen in a white hand, the same hand that had clutched the leather strap on the bus to Divoká Šárka. But none of the pens that lay unused and collected on the desk had the distinctive navy blue marbling that I remembered. A kind of mist descended on my thoughts. For a moment I did not know who it was that shared this room with me.

I turned to look at her. She had taken off her jacket. Her sky blue shirt and slacks, her medallion profile, her long neck from which the brown hair was raised in a bun, and her pale and peaceful hands as they took possession of the things around, all added to the stillness. She was an exhibit, neat, self-contained, and beautiful as the place where she stood.

She told me to sit while she made the room ready for our presence. I watched her unpack Mrs. Němcová's provisions, and stow them in a gauze-fronted cabinet beside the dresser. I watched her take matches from the cabinet and light the oil lamps in the room. I watched her take sheets from a chest between the beds and make up the larger of them. I watched her rehearse, as though in tribute to it, the life of everyday economies that had once filled this house. And her gestures told me more than any words could have done, that this place was Betka's source, the pool of meaning from which she had come like Rusalka into the world of human beings, never to lose the wonder that it had implanted in her soul.

She took one of the lamps to show me around, leading me through rust-red doors beneath the lintels of which we both had to stoop. In a corridor behind the parlor was a still for slivovitz and a second chimney, with spits for roasting and hooks for the smoking of sausage and ham. Beside the chimney was a coal scuttle of tin with a cast iron shovel, and I felt a kind of tenderness for this object which spoke so eloquently of its former function. Betka's refuge had been built from the uselessness of once-useful things; you could belong here only as Betka belonged, by not belonging. Nearby, in a corner of the corridor, was a large stone vat, in which plums, Betka told me, would be slowly simmered into jam. Containers, bottles, and jars all spoke of the vanished economy of the plum, which had been the source of wine, spirits, jam, sweetener, and relish. One end of the corridor opened into a shed full of tools, with an earth closet and a neat stack of logs ready for burning. At the other end was a cascade of stone steps down to a cellar where the food was stored.

"Whose food?" I asked.

"Ours."

"And who are we?"

"Me, my uncle. And sometimes, though he has drifted away now, my cousin Jakub."

The cellar had been hewn in rock, with ledges in the walls supporting gherkins and apricots in large sealed jars. Unlabeled bottles of wine, both white and red, lay in a rack at the cellar's end, while on the floor, in every available space, were vegetables—carrots, turnips, potatoes, kohlrabi, onions—lying in beds of sand. Drops of clear water were condensed on their skins, and against the pale green flesh of a kohlrabi, a large black spider trembled on frozen legs. Old farm accessories were laid out in a recess—chains, catches, and the heavy hinges of a gate, the only reminder here of the uselessness that reigned above. It was like a place on the frontier, a home provisioned in the teeth of adversity. I recalled a verse of the book of Proverbs that Mother had underlined three times in her Bible: "Better a dish of herbs where love is, than a stalled ox and hatred withal." And I wondered the more about Betka, that she should have acquired such a home in the time of our nation's homelessness.

CHAPTER 18

THAT EVENING, SHE told me. We were sitting at the oak table, warmed by the woodstove, a half-empty bottle of red wine between us, and beside it the oil lamp, whose light stuck to the wall like bits of white paper. Betka had cleared away the remains of our supper of eggs, sausage, and potatoes, which she had cooked with a quiet competence that seemed to belong not to her, but to the space in which she moved. She had diverted all my questions, some- times with a kiss or a caress, once with Janáček's beautiful setting of "Zpěvulenka," in which her right hand on the piano descanted above the voice like a shadow moving on the air. And now she sat across from me holding my hand on the table. Outside in the twilight a nightingale carried its bubbling song from tree to tree. Inside we were secured against the world, self-sufficient and com- forted. Everything was arranged with that unassuming good taste that marked Betka out as someone who had never belonged and never would belong among the dispossessed. It was as though she had made an arch in time across the world of the proletariat and its vanguard party, that grey world of queues and slabs and shortages, of an enforced and joyless equality in which every smiling eye was an act of treason. The aristocrat in her had reached to the peasant life of this farmstead and joined forces with it against the ruin in between. I sat in silence, awestruck by her presence, and successively catching and avoiding those still, soft, moonlight-colored eyes. At last I found my voice.

"Can I tell you something, Betka?"

"Yes, but I already know."

"What is it you know?"

"You."

"And how?"

"I wanted to show you how to live openly in the space they allowed, how to forget all those imagined secrets and to live for yourself. And when you teach you learn. You taught me to want you. So I let you into my life, and here you are, in the citadel, and I am glad, because I love you."

She drank from her glass before returning her hand to mine.

"My grandfather came to this place at the end of the war. He came with the Red Army, a member of a scratched-together battalion of partisans who were really nothing of the kind, but scavengers and avengers, with an eye for whom they could punish and what they could steal. They forced the locals to wear white armbands, with the letter N for Nazi; they took away their land and their crops, their tools and their animals; they turned a blind eye when people were murdered, and laughed when they committed suicide. And then they took possession of the houses. Oh, of course, it was all done correctly, with documents, committees, and rubber stamps—that is how communism works. Poor Jan Molnar—whom his neighbors knew as Hans Müller, and for whom the plaque dedicating his dwelling to the *heilige Jungfrau* expressed the sum total of his philosophy—lived the kind of blameless life that you see inscribed on every single object in this house. He prayed to the Virgin mother and she answered in his mother tongue. When his wife was raped and killed by our fraternal allies, he fled, with the few things that he could stack into his cart, and his two babies balanced on top of it. But he didn't get far. The Russians stopped him on the road and took the horse. He carried the children for a mile or two, and then sought sanctuary under a Calvary. Whoever shot him had the kindness to spare the children. They were taken into care and packed off to Germany—two among the hundreds of thousands expelled under the Potsdam Agreement and the Beneš Decrees. What the world would be without rubber stamps!"

Betka's eyes filled with tears. But she spoke calmly, as though relaying an official story.

"One day, when this nightmare is over and people can travel freely between East and West, those children or their children or their children's children will be back, seeking their inheritance. I am keeping it for them, and this place that is home to me is not my home at all, but somewhere entrusted to me by suffering."

"But how did you come here?"

She made a sardonic grimace.

"The house was given to my grandfather by the Party, which has always been generous with other people's property. His brief pretense at being a partisan had paid off; he was a commissar in Prague, working in the housing department, and of course he needed a second home. His son, my father, inherited it in the early sixties, just after I was born. And when my parents divorced eleven years ago, it was decided that my father would stay in Prague, while my mother and I would be banished to this place that he didn't care for since nothing ever happens here save peace. That suited everybody very well. After all, Dad was doing fine in the export business, he had a smart young girlfriend who was moving up in Party circles, and Mum had discovered dissident tendencies that made her an embarrassment to her husband. The last service Dad did for her was to fix things when she applied for a job teaching English in Moravská Třebová. The last thing he did for me was to give me a theorbo for my fifteenth birthday, the day before he left for Prague. We never heard from him again, though of course you can read from time to time in *Rudé právo* of the heroic exploits of Comrade Palek, the well-known expert in international trade.

"Then, when I was nineteen, with my heart set on studies in Prague, Mum married again. She moved to Brno, where her husband was a professor of English in the Purkyně University. He was a quiet, nervous man, who had grabbed Mum at a conference on English language teaching. She was the person he had always needed to look after him. After that time, I hardly saw her: Mum's husband resented my visits, and she would rarely come here to see me. Her brother, my uncle Štěpán, would plant vegetables in the spring, harvest them in summer, and chop the wood in the autumn; and sometimes Jakub, his son, would come with him. Otherwise, I had no one save Mrs. Němcová, whose daughters had moved away to Ostrava and Prague, and who loved me with the remainders of her love, just as I love her. For a year I was alone with my thoughts, and my only desire was to study at the Music Academy in Prague. But there was no way to reach such a destination from a high school in Moravská Třebová. Finally I was admitted to the Secondary School of Nursing in Vinohrady, which was the only place in Prague that would look at my application. That was the beginning of many adventures, you included."

I learned many things about Betka on that evening, as her soft, clear, sometimes tearful voice supplied the meaning to the nightingale's sweet song beyond the window. She told me of her time, aged eleven, in America, when her father was a junior trade attaché at the embassy, and she learned American English and American confidence in a Washington school. She told me of Lukáš, her first boyfriend, whom she had met in Prague, where he was a student of medicine. She told me of her sense of betrayal when he escaped to the West one day in the boot of a diplomat's car, having kept his plans secret, even from her. She told me of the great change that came into her life through books, and then through the underground, which she had entered bit by bit, until it became a home—a home like this one, taken from others who had the better claim to it, since the sacrifices had been theirs—but a home all the same, in a country where everything was stolen. From time to time she would look at me sadly, as though to say that this elusive, ambitious, world-defying woman could never be tied to a boy whom she had dragged from the sewers. She had come from a place that was hers because it was not hers, to which she was attached without attachment, which would be a home to her forever because it was not a home but a dream. And she would leave me, of that I was sure, just as soon as her ambition required it, and with a tender regret that I could already hear in her voice and see in her beloved eyes.

That night we lay close. Betka's tears on the pillow were mingled with mine and from time to time I felt the moth-soft touch of her fingers on my face. In our sweet sadness we were man and wife. All our gestures in the days that followed affirmed this. We walked together in the woods and fields, gathering kindling for the stove and wildflowers for the table. Betka cooked and cleaned, assigned definite hours to reading, walking, singing, and telling stories of our past, of which she had many and I just a few. She read to me the fairy tales of Erben, and the letters of St. Paul, telling me how much she had taken strength from them in her times of near-despair. We studied the local map, showing ancient villages with names that stitched them to the land: Květí (the place of flowers), Řepová (the place of beets), Nebíčko (Little Heaven), Bezpráví (Lawless). And we took two bicycles from the outhouse, wheeled them along the track to the nearby village, and roamed the quiet lanes around Veselí, where the tales of the Cunning Little Vixen once were told. From time to time we stopped in the silent forests to kiss. The sad joy of those days remains with me. It is my most precious memory, and the only known reason for my life.

CHAPTER 19

ON THE THIRD day she set off on her bicycle with a certain determination, along a road that branched off into the forest, signposted to Nebíčko. I cycled beside her. The morning sunlight was scattered by the arms of the trees, like balls of fire thrown back and forth above us by the gods. Betka surprised me with her strength and fitness: while I puffed and sweated, she talked calmly, hardly panting from the exercise. She told me the names of trees and birds; she stopped to read the old German milestones, and drew my attention to stone walls, to the enclosures built for animals and to a broken shrine to the Virgin above a spring of fresh water. All these things were precious to her, and seemed to reach to her from the ground where they were half-interred like the supplicating fingers of the dead.

We reached a fork, where a path of old flagstones diverged from the metaled road. Here we left our bicycles by the road and followed the paved path to a chapel, surrounded by cottages and consisting of a single large room with stucco walls, crowned by a bell gable of brick from which the stucco had crumbled away. This, Betka told me, was her church, Our Lady of Sorrows, closed now for five years, but still a place of prayer for those who knew how to enter it. The west porch had been boarded up, but a side door had escaped the attention of the Department of Religious Affairs, and a local carpenter had removed the old lock and replaced it with another. Nailed to a nearby tree was a bird box, from which Betka took a mortise key that let us into the aisle. As she closed the door behind her an alarmed blackbird flew off, shrieking like chalk on a board. For a second we stood still.

Then I watched with astonishment as she first knelt and then crossed herself at the threshold. Touching my hand, she detached herself and walked on tiptoe to one of a line of chairs in the center of the Church. She sat for a long moment with her hands pressed over her eyes. I could not see her lips, but her cheeks moved as though in prayer. She was surrounded by emptiness: the church furnishings were gone, and although the large stone altar remained, nothing stood on it apart from a simple cross of wood. There was no lectern, no pulpit, no pictures on the damp-stained ochre walls. Here and there an altar or a monument had been prized away, leaving patches of rough brick like exposed wounds in the plaster. The tall windows divided the chapel into lozenges of light and dark. In a thin slice of sunlight, the face of Betka shone like a vision, and shone more brightly from the tears on her cheeks. I stood by the door, troubled by the transformation that had come over her, not daring to approach for fear of precipitating the decision that I knew to be imminent, whether I was to be part of her life. And when she turned in my direction, I avoided her eyes, looking up into the barrel vault of the nave where faded pictures of rococo saints gestured absurdly into the vacant space beneath them. She and the chapel enfolded each other in a shared form of defiance, disregarding all that had forbidden them. She had arisen from nowhere, with a hunger to possess the world. And these abandoned things responded to Betka's need as the sleeping castle to the awaited kiss.

She came across to me and took my hand.

"Don't be afraid of me," she said. "I am weak too."

She led me to one of the chairs and we sat in silence. Doves were cooing on the chapel roof, and their soft voices bubbled in the vault like hidden children. I conjured in my mind the vanished congregation, the priest at the altar, the mumbled words, and the teenage Betka, the sheath of childhood just fallen from her body, kneeling to receive the faith that had left this indelible trace in her. I turned to her.

"Is it because you are weak that you believe?"

She looked at me with a slight smile.

"God found me here and he lost me here. I am no more a believer in my daily life than you are. But this is not my daily life. And anyway, we all need to pray, you as much as anyone."

"But I don't know how."

"The important thing, *miláčku*, is not to ask but to give: to give thanks, since it is all that we have."

She had never addressed me as "darling" before. It was as though I were entirely hers, but only in this special place, where the God of love was briefly, at her bidding, resurrected. She leaned against me, pressed her cheek to mine, and we sat in silence. We had reached the turning point. She had brought me here, to store me among her treasures. And soon she would return to that daily life, from which I was always banished to the periphery. For this, she implied, I was to give thanks. And yes, I did so, not knowing to whom or why.

From my window I look down on the sunlit suburb of Friendship Heights, where overweight people in summer costumes walk with cell phones pressed to their ears. Across from my block of rented apartments is the local nursery school, where cartoon animals project their vapid grins from the windows, and stickers in primary colors tell me that today is Shirlene's birthday. Before my mind is the image of two figures, clinging to each other in a chancel light, around them a quiet like falling ashes, and it is a tableau in some hidden passageway, an altar kept by a secret devotee. The world that then surrounded us has no equivalent now. We were not strung on wires of communication across a warm sea of comforts, grinning from puppet faces and mouthing trivial words. We came to each other out of vast and fearful silences, using what tools were available to make ourselves known. Nothing protected us, save the friendships we had made, and the knowledge, so carefully and painfully acquired, that enabled us to rise above our situation. We were the last romantics. Our words were poetry, and our deeds were crime. And because we lived in hiding, every touch had the force of a revelation. Looking at that tableau now, I see the workings of necessity. It was necessary that we came to that place, necessary that we sat in silence, fused into a single substance, necessary that Betka should recite those famous lines from our first romantic poet, Karel Hynek Mácha, which Dad had taught me and which she had learned in school.

> For those sweet years, my childhood years
> The fury of wild Time has borne away;
> Far is that dream, that vanished shade:
> A vision of white towns in the water's womb...

It was necessary that we should look for long minutes into each other's eyes, necessary that we should depart from that place on tiptoe, as though leaving our marriage there, in the place where it had been made.

This sense of necessity, which haunted all that happened from that moment, is disappearing from the world. I live here in the aftermath of unalterable things; and from those things I learned the lesson of Spinoza, that freedom is the consciousness of necessity. Here, in the land of the free, all can be altered and freedom is never achieved. Willingly would I abandon this life of multiple choices, if I could return to that brief moment of freedom in the Moravian forest, and experience again the necessity that tied love and loss in a single knot, and which led us hand in hand and speechless away from the chapel towards our fate.

We cycled slowly home, pausing sometimes to look at each other, once silently making love beside a stream. We stood for a while by the clear water. In the depths, minnows faced the current, their tails flicking them into place. From the distance came the cry of an animal, a deer perhaps, like a lid being prized from a coffin. She took my hand and said, "Let's go."

We lit the stove, and cooked the last of Mrs. Němcová's sausage, with that strange vegetable—*kedlubna*, or kohlrabi—which Americans never eat. After supper she sang to me from Janáček's settings of Moravian folk songs. In one song, a girl wanders through the meadow, plucking flowers with which to conjure love, and the names of the flowers are like spells, *kúkolí, polajka, dobromysel, navratnička*—think-well-of-me, forget-me-not, come-back-to-me. The names and the melody haunt me still, bound together in a garland around the face of Betka, which was never again to turn to me as it did on that evening in the unowned place that she owned.

CHAPTER 20

WE ROSE EARLY the next morning, and Betka said almost nothing as she prepared the house for our departure. Everything was cleaned and stowed away, and there was an intensity in her way of accomplishing this that drove me once again to the perimeter of her life. When she turned the key in the double doors, looked up at the *heilige Jungfrau*, and quickly crossed herself, I felt as though I had been hastily ushered out from a place that I had compromised by my presence. We walked in silence past the hay fields, the ruined farms, and the calvaries, and at Krchleby stood side by side in anxiety as we awaited the bus.

We said goodbye at the Main Station in Prague, since she was hurrying to work. We were to meet in two days' time at Rudolf's seminar, Betka having indicated that she could not be free until then. For two days I wandered the streets in a state of distraction, hardly knowing where I was. I called on Karel in his boiler room, hoping that he would cheer me; but he was busy editing a manuscript and asked me to come back at the end of the day. I looked for Father Pavel in his garage and, not finding him, tracked him to the church of Svatá Alžběta, where he was being whispered at in a corner by a young man in jeans. I quickly ducked out, in the hope that he had not seen me.

A police car had again taken up residence in the street below our apartment. Whenever I passed it, the occupants—usually there were two of them—looked busily in some other direction. Once or twice I thought I was being followed, though the impression occurred only in moments when it could not be verified. Two policemen had been posted outside the building where Igor lived, and demanded identity cards before allowing visitors to pass. Igor was giving weekly classes on St. John's gospel, in which he argued that the communist order would soon be overthrown, not by violence, but by a sudden self-emptying, as the servants of the system quietly departed from their posts, leaving them undefended. I listened to Igor, not to relish this nonsense, but to glimpse through his words the vision of St. John, who had been commanded to comfort the Mother of Christ, who had once been a comfort to Mother, and who would surely, if I could find the path to him, be a comfort also to me. But I could not focus on holy things without encountering the image of that house in the Moravian Sudetenland, where the door beneath the *heilige Jungfrau* had been closed against my return.

Whether it was on account of my state of mind, or whether there had been some real change in the workings of power, I do not know; but Prague in those days seemed wrapped in a cloud of danger. The police were in evidence everywhere; the streets seemed more than normally deserted. And when I walked at night, as I did since I could bear to return to our cupboard only when all other options had been exhausted, I sensed the footsteps close behind me, which stopped and resumed when I did. The day after his seminar, I learned, Igor was taken into custody—a frequent occurrence, but one that I took for a warning. Shortly afterwards, encountering Karel in the street, I watched in astonishment as he stared right through me and walked past without a greeting. Later, answering my knock on the boiler room door, he handed me a note. "You are being followed," it said. "Don't come here again." I went to Rudolf's apartment that Friday carrying toiletries and Mother's Bible, in a briefcase that had belonged to Dad.

There was another reason to be cautious. Two weeks earlier, Rudolf had announced that we were to receive a visitor from America, a distinguished professor of philosophy who would be talking to us that Friday about the concept of human rights. His name was Martin Gunther, and he had written two books on the subject, one of which had been passed round at our seminar. It was full of references and footnotes, and suggested an academic industry devoted to this matter which, for us, had been crammed into a manifesto and then pressed like an icon to the heart. Apparently, Professor Gunther had taken a personal interest in our doings, was anxious to set up a network to assist us in our studies, and would do his best to provide us, through the channels available under the Helsinki Accords, with the visitors and materials that would advance our studies. I had concluded from this that Professor Gunther was either naïve or stupid. Either way, however, he was leading us into unpredictable territory, and I wondered why Rudolf had agreed to this.

CHAPTER 21

I ARRIVED EARLY to find Betka waiting at the bottom of the stairs. She came across to me with a darting movement like a swallow. Her manner was strangely excited. She neither greeted me nor looked at me, but seized me by the arm and pulled me into the recess at the back of the stairwell.

"After the class," she said, "we go separate ways—OK?"

"Forever?"

She made a pert face and turned away.

"Don't be stupid. Just do as I say. Come to my place after work on Monday and I'll explain."

She didn't wait for a response but went quickly to the stairs and climbed them two at a time. I next caught sight of her in Rudolf's living room, half-hidden in a corner behind Mr. and Mrs. Černý, two frail old lecturers in philosophy, who had refused to sign the official denunciation of Charter 77 and as a result had been dismissed from the university. She made no effort to catch my eye as I sat down on the floor beside Father Pavel.

Professor Gunther was already installed at Rudolf's desk. Since arriving in America and becoming acquainted with the template used to create the type, I can no longer be surprised by the individual instance of Professor Gunther. Then, however, I looked on him as a creature belonging to another form of life, about as relevant to our situation as a migrating bird to the branch she sits on. He was young, with pale skin and freckles, and wore thick-rimmed glasses that stuck out beyond the edges of his narrow face like the bars of a cage. His was a mobile face, of a kind that we Czechs, in our attempts to go unnoticed, had long since discarded. His nose made a neat right angle with his thin straight lips and he pushed his head forward on his long neck like a curious rodent exploring the air beyond his territory. He wore a loose green jacket of some expensive material that we never saw in our shops, and a wristwatch of a kind worn in our country only by the Party bigwigs who could freely travel abroad. He shuffled papers on the desk and repeatedly swallowed, so that his prominent Adam's apple moved up and down in his throat like a ball in a fountain. But his serious manner was punctuated by bursts of sociable laughter, as though everything around him could be understood, in the last analysis, as fun. And his lanky good looks gave him the air of a hero in some comedy of university life. I took immediately against him, distrusting him, but distrusting my judgment too.

Rudolf explained that it was Professor Gunther's first visit to our country, that he had come in response to Rudolf's own appeal for academic contacts with the West (the "free world" as Rudolf put it), and that this visit would be the first of many through which we could learn about the latest intellectual developments in places where scholarship was officially permitted. Rudolf's face glowed with self-importance as he spoke, and this too displeased me, since I saw the whole episode as a needless provocation. It was not possible that this visit should have escaped the attention of the police, and all of us were now at risk from Rudolf's act, as I saw it, of heedless self-promotion. But Professor Gunther was enjoying his part in the affair, and stood up to address us with that air of cost-free humility that I have come to know so well in America. His words were translated by Lukáš, a boy of my age, with long hair and slouching manners who, since his expulsion from the university, had become a Lennonist, to use Václav Havel's expression—a devotee of the Beatles, of the easily achieved "outsiderism" of the 1960s, and of the ethic of protest. His English was good, though when it came to philosophical terms he had to improvise, since the works of John Lennon contain so few of them. As a result, Professor Gunther's self-confident presentation of himself, as a person privileged to make contact with the courageous people before him, and humbled by their interest in what he had to say, lost some of its necessary edge. I should not have been so cynical. But my heart was filled with foreboding, and somehow Martin Gunther had become tainted by it.

As Gunther spoke I continually sought Betka with my eyes. But she never emerged from her corner to show her face. There were some twenty of us in that room, bound together not by courage but by a shared experience of defeat. Our visitor stood on the edge of an arena in which the solidarity of the shattered was displayed, as in a zoo. But Betka wasn't part of it, for she too stood on the edge. As I saw it, they were made for each other.

Gunther told us of his deep concern for those who struggle for human rights. The word "struggle" was often on his lips, and it had a rather absurd effect, since Lukáš, who hated communist jargon and refused to use it, translated it not as *boj* or *zápas*, Newspeak words full of belligerence, but as *pokus*, attempt. Gunther expressed his admiration for our part in this attempt, and told us that he would not dream of comparing his situation with ours, he enjoying a secure position in a New York university, and free to travel around the world in pursuit of experience and knowledge. Nevertheless, he felt he could make a small contribution to our endeavors by reflecting on the meaning of human rights, and their fate in his country which, for all its virtues, was by no means the bastion of individual freedom that those oppressed by totalitarian government make it out to be. He paused every now and then to let his eyes flicker across the audience, who leaned forward with eager faces, as captive animals might observe the person who brings them food.

The sounds that filled Rudolf's apartment, whether in Martin Gunther's English or in Lukáš's Czech, were like a distant imitation of our everyday speech. Words like "justice," "oppression," and "power," which we attached to specific situations and specific forms of punishment, were recalled from common use and wrapped in elaborate theories. These theories had no meaning for us, being claims to academic territory in faraway places that we could never visit. I recalled a remark of Wittgenstein, whose words were often on the lips of Father Pavel: if a lion could speak, we would not understand him. Rudolf tried to take notes, but he dropped his pencil after a minute or two and began to stare in amazement at the intruder, who strolled back and forth behind the desk, his eyes often turning to the corner where Betka sat invisible.

Kant, Gunther told us, had subsumed the idea of human rights into the categorical imperative and the moral law; Bentham had dismissed the idea as "nonsense upon stilts;" Hegel had thought one thing, John Stuart Mill another. New thinkers had taken up the question, with a consensus gradually emerging in America, that rights protect groups against their oppressors. Gunther referred to learned American journals, to the traditions of American pragmatism and American liberalism, to philosophers like John Rawls and Ronald Dworkin, whose names we were hearing for the first time, and to the faraway feuds of the American academic class, which seemed as applicable to our position as the tournaments of well-paid mud wrestlers.

At a certain point, Rudolf's apartment detached itself from Prague. We were journeying to the moon like Mr. Brouček in the fantasy novel by Svatopluk Čech, which Betka's beloved Janáček had set to music. We were being carried higher and higher by Gunther's stream of hot air, seeing below us the contours of Absurdistan, to which we must one day return and be punished for our futile attempt to escape from it, but which for a moment had no claim on us since we were protected by a dream.

Below us were the formal gardens of Letná, and the wide street named for the "defenders of the peace" whose patrol car stood at the corner, waiting to defend our peace from foreign philosophy. Dwindling into nothingness was the empty plinth for Stalin's statue, whose sculptor had committed suicide in 1955, shortly before the inauguration of the statue that shamed him before the world; further still was the greasy Vltava, journeying towards freedom with its cargo of waste. Invisible now were the empty streets, the furtive bars, the dirty foyers where men and women passed each other in silence; invisible the dilapidated city of dreams beneath the crust of fear, where harmless old people still cared for the dead and where suspicious lovers lay together in the stolen afternoons. The chains that tied us to our city had been miraculously sundered, and we were floating upwards in a hot-air balloon, powered by Gunther's discourse. Strange rumors hung on the atmosphere, like conversations blown on summer thermals. We were conscripted to the rights of women, homosexuals, minorities, and marginalized groups. We overheard protests against American writers and thinkers who had defied the march of history. We were warned against corrupt and conservative ideas of freedom that were nothing more than disguises for selfishness or pieces of free market ideology. We heard of demonic forces that were ruining the world beyond our borders—corporations, lobbyists, interest groups, obscure conspiracies born of a false idea of freedom. Our small-scale local conflict was absorbed into a "struggle" as vast and all-embracing as that of the Russian Revolution. But the contours of this struggle were unknown to us. Nothing concrete or familiar was suggested by Gunther's words, and for a while we floated in a dream of pure abstractions, liberated from reality and staring in wonder at the visiting lion.

He mentioned Richard Rorty, whose name we were hearing for the first time, and who had changed American scholarship with a new theory of truth. The true belief, we learned, is the useful belief, the one that enables you to affirm the rights of your group, and to gain the illuminated plateau of liberation. Truth means power, just as Nietzsche and Foucault had said. I recalled our official doctrine, according to which the power of the Party and the truth of its theories are one and the same. And by the time Gunther told us that claims to human rights, whenever made by a community in search of liberation, are inherently justified, my head was spinning out of control. Whose side was he on? And on whose side was I?

Then it all changed. Martin Gunther's speciality, he informed us, was "abortion rights," a sphere in which, dare he say it, our country had a better record than his. There was a sudden tension in the room. Of course the topic of abortion had been debated in Czechoslovakia. But the Catholic Church had no public voice, and the matter had been resolved, like every other, to the convenience of the Communist Party, which preferred to address the problem of unwanted children by disposing of them before it arose. Younger people discussed the matter, but we knew that we touched on something fearful and intimate, for which we had no adequate words. Gunther was offering those words, but I felt that his summoning of the "human rights machine" somehow missed the point and that it certainly would not go down well with Betka. Nor was I wrong.

His eyes, which had roamed instinctively in Betka's direction, wavered and then lowered as though sensing a rebuke. Father Pavel leaned forward with a serious expression, waving back his lock of stray hair and looking intently at the speaker. Women, Gunther told us, are an oppressed class, whose reproductive nature has been stolen from them by patriarchal structures installed for the benefit of men. A woman's right to control her own body has been ignored by a system of government that forces her to carry an unwanted fetus and by a culture which encourages violence against doctors who terminate her pregnancy. The discourse had become concrete, and we were plummeting to earth under the weight of a novel kind of Newspeak. A woman, in Gunther's view, should be seen as the victim of her pregnancy; her unborn child not as a human being but as a fetus, a medical condition in search of a remedy. He discussed a famous case before the American Supreme Court, in which it was definitively proven that this fetus has no rights under the Constitution. And so, with a friendly gesture of shared triumph, he concluded his talk, arguing that, however much we Czechs may suffer from the unjust restriction of our human rights, so too did women suffer in America.

It took us a little while to grasp the argument; but one thing was certain: we had landed back with a bump in Absurdistan. Rudolf was stuttering out a commentary, and I felt a stab of pity as he tried to claim familiarity with the works to which Gunther had referred, and to show himself *au fait* with current Western discussions. Father Pavel's face glowed with defiance, and he was leaning forward, ready to speak. But it was Betka's voice, speaking in English from her place of concealment, that captured our visitor's attention.

"I have a question. When you say this to your students in America, do they report on you? Are you putting your life in the balance? And another question. Suppose you were one of us, born here, confined here, unable to move without permission. Would you worry that it was all too easy for you, an intellectual, to speak like you do, knowing that out there somewhere, someone will pick up your signal and broadcast it, and that you would become a celebrity of sorts like our famous dissidents?"

I was taken aback by her tone, which revealed depths of anger and frustration that I had never previously suspected. And there was something personal too, as though she were singling out Martin Gunther as someone who henceforth must be accountable to *her*. He responded at once, confessing to faults that he eagerly described as though each one were a gift for Betka. Yes, he was a comfortable middle-class person, whose defense of human rights was a defense of his own peculiar privilege. Yes, it needed no courage to speak in America as he had spoken in this room. Yes, he belonged to the class that was in any case rewarded for such courage as it showed by the general endorsement of the culture. He thanked the young lady for making this so clear to him, and hoped that it did not adversely affect the reasonableness of what he had said.

"But it does," said Father Pavel, who spoke through the fluttering veil of Lukáš's English. "These rights of which you speak— you admit it yourself—are the privileges of comfortable people. According to you, the professional woman has the right to kill the child who hampers her career, while the child has no right to her protection. Maybe your subtle philosophers and judges have impeccable arguments for thinking that the unborn can be disposed of according to our convenience. But for us the word *právo* means right and also justice, and it is one part of *pravda*, meaning truth. I am the way, the truth, and the life, said our Savior, and he gave his life so that we should live. In the catacombs we make use of this word "right," not because we have those subtle arguments, but because it expresses the thing that they cannot steal from us, which is our humanity. It tells us to protect those who have done no harm and who come into the world without offending it. But you tell us that such people have no rights."

Thus began a collective outburst of a kind that I had never witnessed at Rudolf's seminar. Several people had raised their hands, and Rudolf, whose face wore an unfamiliar expression of bewilderment, allowed them the floor. Two of the girls objected to Father Pavel, arguing that atheists and agnostics also need guidance in this matter, and if we do not invoke the idea of rights, whence could guidance come? The poet Z.D. suggested that the whole question was inappropriate to our discussions, since it concerned individual choices and not our identity as a nation. Mr. and Mrs. Černý, who always advanced a joint opinion assembled from phrases provided separately by each of them, expressed their concern that, in the land of freedom, the unborn are so entirely at the mercy of the living. And Lukáš, citing John Lennon's famous song, invited us to imagine a better world, where children would no longer be unwanted.

What struck me in this was not the vigorous nature of the argument, unusual though that was, but the fact that it really *was* an argument, about a concrete matter concerning which modern people ought surely to make up their minds. And this cast a new and disturbing light on our previous discussions. We had stepped out of the world of ponderous abstractions, metaphysical grievances, and noble ideals to which Rudolf always invited us, and where we had been at one. We had entered a rough terrain of conflict, where we were divided against each other, as individuals making our separate ways. We had been attending the seminar in search of the faith with which to fortify our shared isolation, and our weekly discussions had been bids for agreement. The questions we had been used to considering were questions that could be settled in any way we chose, without altering in one particular how we set about our business next morning, in the cold light of day. Somehow, Gunther had brought the "air from other planets" of which Betka once spoke. We were discussing things as though preparing to make real choices, laying down paths into the future that would be many and divergent when the time for action came.

We were shaping ourselves, for the first time, as the free citizens we would one day need to be.

Of course, the contest was not equal. Father Pavel had no intellectual resources beyond his priestly intuitions and the dogma of his church, while Gunther was full of subtleties, calling on a wealth of experience that was more or less unknown to us—the experience of professional women in the Western city, of the workings of American courts, and of the discussions in academic journals devoted to issues of life and death. My sympathies, however, were with Father Pavel. He lost the argument, but he called upon some personal emotion beyond the tranquil commitment of his faith. He seemed to speak with the authority of suffering, and I knew that this suffering concerned me in ways I could only guess. At one point, Betka intervened. The discussion merely showed, she said, that this idea of human rights is too malleable to settle our deepest moral questions. It is a notion that puts nothing to the test. And Gunther leapt at this opportunity to bring peace to the room.

Yes, you are right, he said, with a sequence of nods. We liberals have a habit of making things too easy for ourselves. We live in a world where we are not put to the test, as you are put to the test. Every expansion of our rights is a cost to someone else, and yes the notion of human rights is not adequate to this problem. His reasoning spiraled away into the stratosphere of concepts: person, freedom, individuality, identity—all of which elicited from Father Pavel only a frown and a shake of the head. Someone mentioned Pope John Paul II, who had inspired our makeshift rebellion; Rudolf formed a question, his dingy wife appeared with *chlebíčky*, and we were back at last with the solidarity of the shattered. Betka came from her corner with intent and inscrutable features, looking at no one in particular but attracting the intermittent gaze of Martin Gunther. At one point she gently touched Father Pavel on the sleeve, but she looked past me as though we had ceased to be lovers. After a while I made an excuse to Rudolf and fled into the street. A police car was parked on the corner, with two dark figures inside. But they made no attempt to intercept me, and I walked on amid clouds of loneliness.

CHAPTER 22

AT FIRST I went towards the metro at Vltavská. But then I veered away, descended to the river and walked west along the embankment. Occasional automobiles tore the silence. The bridge that bore the name of Svatopluk Čech strode on its strong pontoons from road to road, bearing nothing besides a small thin man beneath a crumpled hat. Tucked into the bridge's shoulder by the bank stood the little chapel of the Magdalene, like an octagonal dish cover. Beneath that cover I conjured the breath of the saint. Then I noticed that a group of people were whispering there; a police car, appearing suddenly from under the bridge, stopped to question them. I hurried on, keeping to the river as the road descended into Malá Strana. I saw no one in the street, heard nothing save the creaking of windows and the closing of doors. Then a late tram shrieked in the square, and spots of rain began to tarnish the cobbles.

In the Újezd I recalled Schubert's *Winterreise*, and the song about the road once taken by which none returns. I had put my feet on that road, and they moved forward without my will. Betka had described *Winterreise* as lying beyond enjoyment, beyond music even, in a sacred, untouchable place of its own. Only rarely, she said, could we mortals enter that place, and only through penitence. Everything within me, all memories, images, melodies, and thoughts, led back to her. Behind every word that I inwardly spoke to myself were *her* words, and behind those words her face, her presence, her music, her lovemaking. I stood in the rain by the door of her courtyard, waiting for Betka to appear. The raindrops on my face and in my hair were tears of love and jealousy. Soon I was wet to the skin. And when it became clear to me that she would not be returning, I was seized by a fit of trembling.

It was three o'clock when I arrived home. The next day was Saturday and I lay all day in bed, sometimes reading in Mother's Bible, and once or twice getting up to stare down into the street, where a police car was stationed. I could not understand their game, and in any case regarded it with indifference. Whether they arrested me or merely watched me, what did it matter? My stomach was empty, but with the kind of despairing emptiness that refuses food since it can take comfort in nothing.

On Sunday, I ventured out. I went to Father Pavel's garage, but there was no one there. The Church of Svatá Alžběta was locked, and boards had been nailed to the windows. Notwithstanding Karel's prohibition, I visited his boiler room, but was greeted there by an old man with a clotted beard who smelled of vodka, and who identified himself as Karel's weekend substitute. And then, for long hours, I sat on the Střelecký Island, debating whether to call at Betka's room, and eventually turning for home with no intention of arriving there. How much clearer things had been underground, and for a moment I regretted the steps that I had taken towards a life in truth—steps from the Metro to a bus stop, and from a bus into the realm of Queen Šárka. It seemed then that I had been following some tempting spirit, a will o' the wisp or *bludička*, sent from the lower world to mislead me. It seems now—as I look back across twenty years—that those thoughts belong with the aura of those times, when only books could be trusted, and truth was nowhere to be found, except between their covers.

The next day I went to her after work, as she had commanded. When she opened the door she did not step back with that little flourish. She did not welcome me with a smile as her big mistake and then lead me by the hand to her bed. Instead, she stood before me in silence, tears running down her cheeks and her eyes red from weeping. Then she leaned forward, slowly closing the door behind me and whispering my name. Never before had I seen Betka like this: meek, vulnerable, beseeching. I asked her the cause and she gave no answer save a shake of the head as she pressed against me. Behind her the room seemed to have changed. The pile of samizdat was there beneath the window. The pictures and candlesticks were in their usual place. The theorbo stood in its case by the wall, the briefcase full of music leaning against it. The books were arranged in the bookcase in their usual order, and the notebook lay open on the desk. But it was all just a fraction neater than usual, as though she had lifted each object and flicked off the dust before replacing it.

The blue and brown Ukrainian kilim that covered Betka's bed had been folded back, and the *peřina*, the feather-bed, too was folded. Beneath the bed was a suitcase, which I was seeing for the first time, since the bedclothes normally concealed it. Visible too was a cardboard box, with the name Olga in black marker ink on its side. For some reason the room had acquired a provisional air, and the neatness and good taste with which Betka subdued and ordered her surroundings seemed like a temporary veneer.

"Don't be angry with me, *miláčku*," she said. "I couldn't speak to you on Friday. I couldn't speak to anyone."

"But why?" I asked.

"So many reasons," she replied, "and also none. Didn't you think he was awful?"

"Who?"

"That American, Professor Gunther. Come to see the exotic creatures in their zoo and add another star to his curriculum vitae."

"He certainly was impressed by *you*," I said.

She made a grimace as she pulled away from me. She was no longer crying, but there was a weariness in her features and she made love with a kind of joyless hunger. It was as if she were the victim of her desire and not, as she had always been before, delightedly in charge of it. We lay without speaking until she suddenly rose from the bed and went across to the theorbo and took it from its case. She sang a piece by Dowland:

> *Come again, sweet love doth now invite*
> *Thy graces that refrain*
> *To do me due delight:*
> *To see, to hear, to touch, to kiss, to die*
> *With thee again in sweetest sympathy.*

Her dear voice, those words from a time when life was brief and full of mourning, and the thought of that sweetest sympathy, enjoyed but somehow lost to me, all proved too much. I cried like a child on Betka's bed, and was still crying after she had put away the theorbo, dressed in the pale blue blouse and pleated skirt that she wore to work, and told me that it was time to go. She kissed me tenderly; but there was a determination in the way she guided me to the door. And this determination was there when she opened that door again to me.

CHAPTER 23

IT WAS ON the afternoon of the next day. I stood on the threshold in a state of self-disgust. Yes, I said to myself, I had followed her once before. Out of love and enchantment, I had stepped behind her onto the bus to Divoká Šárka, and then from that bus to the place that may or may not have been her home. But the previous afternoon I had followed her out of jealousy and anger. I had fallen to the level of our rulers, to the level of the person with jug-handle ears who stared past me whenever I discovered him. I had slid from doorways as she passed, ducked behind corners as she turned, watched her every movement as she entered, first a greengrocer to buy some fruit, then a bakery to buy some pastries, then the church of St. Thomas in Malá Strana, where she stood for a moment in the porch, staring at the sealed-off interior. I had followed her up the escarpment named for Jan Neruda, whose tales Dad read to us as children, and who wrote of these jeweled streets as though God himself had shaped them for our uses. And how dirty and diseased I felt as I watched her shrug off a drunk with a walrus mustache, hurry past a young man who turned his beseeching eyes on her, and take the steps up to the castle. She came to the house where the writer Jiří Mucha, son of the painter, had lived, and where, by a miracle, his Scottish wife Geraldine, whom Betka had described as the best of modern composers, was still from time to time in residence. Set within a regular façade of cream and salmon pink stucco panels, beneath a naïve fresco showing St. John Nepomuk risen to glory from the waters of the Vltava, was a door with brass fittings, including a knocker in the shape of a human head. To my surprise, Betka took a piece of paper from her bag, rapped the brass knocker, and stood looking up at the first floor window as though she expected to see a face there. When no one appeared, she replaced the paper in her bag and resumed her journey.

I followed her to the Loretánská, down the hill of U Kasáren to Dientzenhofer's Church of Saint John Nepomuk, Father Pavel's favorite, which had been built for the Ursuline convent next door. Betka strode on, never looking back, and leading me at last to the Nový svět—the New World—a street of crumbling houses facing the high wall of a garden. The street seemed abandoned, with no sound save the song of birds among the birch trees in the garden and a rustle of wind in the leaves. I crouched among the watching dead, catching glimpses of Betka as she walked with even steps on the broken cobbles. Then suddenly she was gone. I discovered an alley of stone steps between two gingerbread houses. It led to a large eighteenth-century house with tall casement windows. A door of modern design bore an official-looking plaque in burnished steel, on which was written *Ústavní nemocnice pro chronicky nemocné děti*—resident hospital for chronically-ill children. From behind the door came the sound of children's voices, and a woman—not Betka—said "quiet please, let Mikin go first." I turned away in shame, and hurried on tiptoe to the Loreta church and the steps down to the escarpment.

Now I stood in her doorway, avoiding her eyes. She said nothing, but stepped back to allow me to enter, and then quietly closed the door. She had been writing. Her notebook was open on the desk, and next to it a volume of samizdat; not one of Mother's, but Vaculík's essays, from the Padlock Press created by those official dissidents. I asked her why she spent so many hours with this literature. Her answer surprised me.

"One day soon," she said, "the mirage will vanish and we will see that we are standing in an empty place. There will be ways of advancing, ways of claiming this unowned land of ours. Someone has to be first in the field of samizdat scholarship: and that person won't be Martin Gunther or Bob Heilbronn or any other of our curious visitors. It will be me."

"Do you really believe that?"

"Why do I live as I do, Honza? I have told you many times. I am not a dissident; I am not an underground person; I want knowledge, scope, a way out of this prison. But I also want to learn from it, to store the experience for future use."

"You frighten me, Betka."

She turned to me suddenly and locked me in a warm embrace.

"Is it the word 'future' that frightens you, Honza?"

"Yes, because you are preparing a future without me."

"And what would a future *with* you be like?"

"I haven't thought about it."

"Maybe you should have thought about it."

She detached herself from me and sat down at the desk.

"By the way, Honza, why did you follow me yesterday?"

The question was like a pistol shot. I staggered onto the bed and sat there in silence.

"No matter," she went on. "You think there are barriers between us. And if I tried to explain that there are no barriers, that would be a barrier."

"You speak in riddles," I said, "and all I want is you. Just you."

"Me? Don't you mean, your idea of me? And isn't that their way of controlling us, to reduce us all to ideas? Isn't that what all this stuff is really about?"

And she waved dismissively at the pile of samizdat.

"But why are you crying, Betka?"

"Oh because…"

She threw herself beside me on the bed, and would say nothing more. Her gestures were clumsy and incomplete. Her body seemed to writhe at my touch, like a wounded thing. It was mid-summer, and the sun had reached over the rooftops into the courtyard. Its rays were exploring the corners of the room, and curling the papers on her desk. Everything in that place was provisional, poised on the edge of things, ready at a moment's notice to let go. I too must be ready, and with that thought I got up from the bed and began to dress. She watched me from far away, with an otherworldly look, like the Venus of Botticelli.

"Listen, Honza," she said. "There is no going back on what has happened between us. You are part of me, and I am part of you. It may be a mistake, but it is also the truth."

"The truth," I began, but the words would not come.

"Can I ask a favor, Honza?"

I nodded.

"Will you come with me to the opera on Friday? I have two tickets: *Rusalka*."

"Are you sure you want to be seen with me in public?"

She looked at me long and hard.

"I think I shall ignore that question," she said at last. "But please come to *Rusalka* on Friday."

We faced each other for a long moment, she not hiding her body but lying motionless on the bed, her eyes shining moonlight into mine.

"What about Rudolf's seminar?" I asked. "Professor Gunther is speaking again."

"Do you think I want to listen to that rubbish? And anyway…"

"Anyway what?"

"We have rehearsals tomorrow. I want to spend time with you on Friday."

"And the hospital?"

"I have the night off. We could be together here."

I had not missed one of Rudolf's seminars since I began to attend them. Nor had Betka ever suggested such a thing. The seminar united our community like a religious observance. Why did she want me to break this sacred routine? After all, the opera in those days was no big deal: the tickets were cheap and the performances vile.

"I think we should go to the seminar," I said.

"Count me out," she responded. But I detected an uneasiness in her manner that gave zest to my refusal. She had, for the first time, given me a chance to hurt her, and I leapt as though at a liberation.

"Fine," I said. "But I intend to go."

She slipped from the bed, came across to me, and flung her arms around my neck.

"Honza, I am asking a special favor. We could be together, as we were in Krchleby. Why do you refuse, just for the sake of an American ghoul who wants to add us to his list of credits?"

"Not for his sake, but for mine," I answered. "On account of that future I should have thought about before."

She detached herself and began to get dressed.

"Well," she said, "if that's the way you feel. You had better go now. And don't follow me, OK?"

She was crying. I looked at her for a moment, in the bittersweet relish that her hurt aroused in me. Then I went quickly into the courtyard and out into the street.

CHAPTER 24

FATHER PAVEL WAS shutting the garage when I arrived. He had been working on an old Jawa motorcycle which had to be locked away in the workshop, lest it be stolen. He smiled gently as he washed his black hands in the enamel sink, and remarked on the beauty of motorcycles, and especially of those old models from before the war, which had been put together with loving respect for detail, and which grew from their parts as a work of music grows from its notes. He described the Jawa as a "mereological miracle," built in the days when people still had eyes for each other and for the things that they used. He added that there was no better way to understand the disaster of communism than to study what happened to this motorcycle when the factory was confiscated in 1948 and thenceforth worked by slaves.

"But of course," he added, "that's not what you have come here to talk about."

I asked him if we could go together to the church of Svatá Alžběta.

"I have been waiting for the moment," he said, and gestured to the door. He bestowed on the motorcycle one last loving glance before leaving, his only indication yet of an earthly attachment. As we walked through the blighted cemetery, he told me that the church had been broken into and vandalized.

"I noticed the windows were boarded up," I said.

"Oh, so you pass by from time to time?" he replied, with a curious glance at me.

I nodded, but said nothing. If anything bore witness to Father Pavel's priestly vocation it was his ability to propagate silence. With Father Pavel, only necessary words had a place, and his unembarrassed face took in the silence like the face of some resting animal.

It was dark in the church on account of the boarded-up windows, and, because the ceiling lights had been disconnected, Father Pavel lit the candles that stood on the altar table. The congregation had done its best to put the place in order: the broken chairs were piled in one corner, the lectern had been repaired with splints made from chair legs, and the few whole chairs remaining had been placed in line before the altar. Liquid of some kind had been thrown at the painting of St. Elizabeth, and a brown stain spread across the face of the saint.

"What happened to *Informace o církvi*?" I asked.

"Oh, that was the chair they were looking for," he said. "But they didn't find it."

"How come?"

He shrugged his shoulders.

"I had a hunch, when they took Igor in for questioning, that we might be due for a visit. It's in the workshop, if you want to read it. And by the way, they released Igor and won't be charging him."

I sat down next to him on one of the chairs. It caused me no surprise that a free-thinking Czech, who considered religion to be a helpless refusal to acknowledge that we are helpless, could stumble again and again on the "moments of truth" that his thinking ruled to be impossible, moments like that of Mother's Bible, like that of the vandalized church of Our Lady of Sorrows, like this in another vandalized church, beside a man who, for whatever reason, had thought it worthwhile to sacrifice the sparse comforts that our regime permitted for the sake of a creed neither believable nor believed. Looking back on those moments now, I know them also as moments of the lie, and know too that, in their intensest and most life-transforming manifestation, the truth and the lie thrive side by side in conflict.

The thought frightens me. It has no place in the world outside my window and forbids me to belong to it. What place in cheerful America for a thought like that? And what instinct was it that led me to confess to Father Pavel, and in the act of confession to invent a life of sin?

I did not look at him as I spoke. His eyes, like mine, rested on the picture of Saint Elizabeth, whose face had bled in a brown stain across the chalky sky. From time to time he brushed the lock of hair from his forehead, as though clearing the way for my words to enter it. I began with Dad, hesitantly at first, but with increasing confidence as I discovered a role for myself, as the one who had never atoned for my own tragic fault in not loving sufficiently that innocent person. Again I imagined Dad's finger, tracing the lines of books haunted by the ghosts that our rulers had wished to exorcise. And I recalled our summer holidays camping in the Krkonoše mountains, our evenings at home with his collection of long-playing records, our Christmases around Ivana's Bethlehem where, amid leaden cows and horses, in the lap of a Virgin made of pipe cleaners, lay the tiny wrapped-up Christ child, in whose existence not one of us believed.

I let the reminiscences come: small things, family things, even my schoolboy misdemeanors, including the theft of Mother's home-made liver sausage, the fight at school with Miroslav Fiala, the attempt for no good reason to run away when I got as far as Chomutov before the police caught up with me and made a phone call to Dad's school, when he came so sadly to collect me without the smallest sign of blame on his dear face, but his eyes turned down and his hand trembling as he reached out to touch me as though to test whether I were real. And as I spoke it occurred to me, maybe for the first time, that I had once been a child, that I had not been born on that day when they took him away forever, and that from that day forth my sins took on another character—no longer misdemeanors but an expanding and soul-subduing fear of other people, a refusal to love or be loved, which was the real engine of those underground journeys and from which I awoke at last only when I followed an unknown girl to Divoká Šárka and in consequence of a Kafkaesque immersion in my own absurdity delivered my mother into the hands of the police and thence to Ruzyně prison.

As the extent of my sinfulness was laid bare, a kind of peace descended on me. I described Mother's life, her hopes, her mute suffering love for her children, her readiness to forgive Ivana who had cut us off for some understandable reason—a lover, perhaps, a fiancé, whose affection would not survive the revelation of our crimes. Bit by bit, my sense of isolation became an old-fashioned family matter, entirely without erotic overtones, so that Betka hovered on the edge of it, harmless and out of reach. Such was the effect of Father Pavel's unspeaking form beside me, enveloping me in a mist of contrition. And, uncanny though it seemed, I sensed that he knew all that I was not telling him, that he was through some telepathic process shifting my feelings away from the girl from Divoká Šárka whose identity I had no need to reveal towards the place from which salvation comes. For what is salvation, if not the ability to confess to your faults, and to open yourself to atonement?

We were silent for a while. The flickering light from the altar candles made a pool of deep shadow beneath him, in which the small movements of his hands and head were recorded. I could not tell if he were praying. When at last he broke the silence, it was in a sibylline whisper.

"Our faults lie in what we hide, not in what we show."

"Yes," I said, "and that is why priests are necessary. We come to you to be taken apart. Even if we don't believe what you believe."

"And what do I believe, Jan?"

"That God exists. And that what I told you was a pack of lies."

"We love God, Jan, through loving his absence. That is to love Him in another way, a better way. And what you told me was the truth. The lie is what you did not tell me: the thing that you have hidden away for safety's sake, the thing that you love more than you should."

"Then you know?" I said, turning to him.

In that moment it was as though his face were lit from behind. His eyes had lost their softness, and the whites shone out with an opalescent glow. The points of stubble on his cheeks seemed like tiny daggers held against me, and his lips were drawn back from his teeth, revealing a crowded heap of pinnacles between shadowy gaps. It was no longer the face of some lime wood saint, but a primeval landscape, shaped by suffering and by the bleak sad sameness of the mortal world. But it was also the face of someone who could fight in self-defense.

"There is another person inside you, Jan, one who lives in imagination, who rejects reality as second best."

"Is that how you read my life?"

"Your life is a fiction. You decided to love fictions, since they couldn't harm you. I am not referring to the girl from Divoká Šárka only, though it is important to learn that you imagined her. Nor are you the only person who lives in this way. This is their greatest achievement, to divide our country in two, on the one hand the cynics who live without morals and who know the price of everything, and on the other hand the pure souls who know the price of nothing and who therefore recoil into the world of the imagination to pursue their beautiful dreams."

"And you," I asked. "Which are you?"

As suddenly as it had vanished, his old face returned, and he looked at me with that indescribable softness, brushing the lock of hair from his forehead and nodding as though in receipt of some undeniable truth.

"I know only that God has withdrawn from the world, and he makes each person feel this in his own way. Oh, I have had my share of phantoms. I have pursued imaginary loves just as you have. But I have learned to consign my life to what is absent and untouchable."

"You talk in riddles, Father."

"No, Jan, it is you who live in riddles. For a long time now you have wanted to talk to me about the thing that really matters in your life, and you have avoided it, as though all change were to come from outside of you—a change in our political system, for instance, another invasion, a strike by the StB."

"So what really matters in my life?"

Was it part of Father Pavel's duty as a priest to be prying in this way? I guessed that it was. For all his sophistication, he believed in that thing called the soul—*duše*—whose name in Czech evokes the disarming softness of his manner. He believed in the other Jan inside me, the one who had never belonged to the world of daylight, and whose eternal destiny was Father Pavel's personal concern. But this too was a fiction, and by believing it, Father Pavel put himself beside me, on a precarious ledge above the abyss of nothingness.

"Let me tell you first what matters to *them*. It is not only that you must live, as Václav Havel says, within the lie. It is also that you must create a life in which truth and falsehood are no longer distinguishable, so that the only thing that counts is your own advantage, to be pursued in whatever way you can. By this means we learn to distrust each other, and every call to love enshrines a summons to betrayal. The precious element from which the soul itself is built, the element of sacrifice, which caused one person once to lay down his life for the rest of us, this precious element is extracted from all our dealings and cast onto the dustheap of history. When I pray, I pray to that person who is the way, the truth, and the life. And at this very moment your mother is praying to him also."

His words were a kind of warning. Whether he was referring to Betka I did not know. But it was suddenly obvious to me that I had never for one moment considered how I might forego some advantage for Betka's sake. Sacrifice had not entered my thoughts of her, and for that very reason my love for her had grown around a core of distrust. And Father Pavel was right to remind me of Mother, whose life had been one continuous sacrifice and who had never distrusted anyone close to her, not even the under-manager of the paper factory, who had condemned her in court as a Zionist agent and an enemy of the Czechoslovak people. I could not pray to that person who called himself the way, the truth, and the life—not through pride, as I clung to my ledge above the abyss, but because I believed Him too to be a fiction, whose power consists only in the quantity of helpless suffering that had been offloaded onto His imaginary shoulders, and fallen through them into the void. But I asked Father Pavel to pray for me and for Mother, and said that I would begin now to live only for her.

"Not only for her, Jan. But for her, at least. For you know, this life of cynical distrust will change, maybe not soon, but nevertheless all of a sudden. She will need you then more than ever."

Of course, I had heard such cheerful prophecies before: always they were on Igor's lips, and several of the older people at Rudolf's seminar gave credence to them. Even Betka seemed to act as though she believed the nightmare would end, preparing herself for a career in another environment than the one we knew. But I shrugged the

prophecies off as part of the great fiction to which Father Pavel subscribed, the fiction of a benign creator who could watch mankind
enslave itself, reduce itself to the condition of mutual antipathy, and
in general make itself loveless and unlovable and still have plans to
rescue us. God, if he existed, was surely not so daft.

CHAPTER 25

THE STRANGE THING is that those skeptical thoughts, which were my normal response to religion, retreated into the background. Sitting with Father Pavel in that ruined church, with the broken chairs piled up in one corner, two candles in cracked cups on the rickety altar, the stained painting of the saint, and the windows smashed and boarded up, I knew that I was in a consecrated space, that all thought and speech had a different meaning here, as music has a different meaning when it is breathed into the silence. Father Pavel's God had withdrawn from the world, but as the sea withdraws, leaving behind it these little pools of clear water in which the spirit still lives. And whatever our condition, however tainted we were by those sordid calculations by which we were forced to live, we could bathe in these secret waters and be refreshed.

Thus it was that, in my journey from Svatá Alžběta to Gottwaldova I felt some of the calm of the confessional: the calm that comes when atonement is at last accepted and begun. For some months now I had avoided the Metro, which belonged to the life that I had left behind. The trams too repelled me, packed as they were with the same silent cargo. I walked everywhere, my eyes turned down to the mosaic pavements that hem the fluttering robes of our buildings and stitch them to the street. Those pavements, made from small cubes of white sandstone and blue granite, were then in poor repair, punctuated by puddles and in places pushed up in heaps. But they were a symbol of our city and of the care that had been expended over centuries to endow this place with a soul. My own soul too had been scuffed and trampled into heaps and hollows, and was in need of reassembling. I followed their pattern, often inventing it where it was broken or obscured, listening to the sound of footsteps on the cobbles. I was conscious that I was often followed, expected always to be stopped and questioned, and was never sure whether it would not be a relief at last, to be taken into custody. What did they hope to gain from my spurious freedom? Did they not have the evidence they needed to remove me and all the others, Betka and Father Pavel too, to the cellar?

I found myself in Wenceslas Square, where tourists gathered in plush hotels, and the young whores, some of them so pretty and enticing that I had to wrench my eyes from them, drifted in and out of the bars. Only foreigners could afford to stay in these places, and I glanced through the plate glass window of the *Zlatá Husa*, the Golden Goose Hotel, knowing that our American visitor would have looked for just such a place in order to complete his experience—perhaps hoping for the orgy described by Philip Roth in a little novella about the Prague of those days, as Americans imagined it.

And yes, there he was, deep in conversation by the window, next to a table lamp held aloft by a naked water nymph in bronze. The girl whom he addressed had her back turned to the street, but she was nodding vigorously—an English speaker and a high-class whore, therefore, one that would cost him not only money but the risk of blackmail. He was even more stupid than I thought, and deserved whatever trap it was that they were leading him into. Of course, it was absurd to think that Betka, my Betka, could be playing this game, and the resemblance of that long neck and gathered hair to my beloved, my ex-beloved, I should say, was surely accidental. I moved away lest she should turn and see me, staring into windows like a madman, like the Doppelgänger in that frightening poem by Heine, which Schubert had made into a yet more frightening song.

The cloud of peace that surrounded me had moved on, and I hurried to catch up with it. Round which corner of our city had it disappeared? Was it lingering in the great porch of the National Museum? Had it waited somewhere along the avenue of Victorious February, date of the Communists' Coup, to rejoin me on my walk to Nusle? Was it there at the corner of Bělehradská, ready to accompany me down into the valley, across the Botič and the railway line and up the steep incline to Gottwaldova, where the police car was still installed, I noticed, at the end of our street? Would it at least wait for me at the bottom of our stairwell, with its broken lift and ill-lit concrete steps, so as to lead me gently at last into the lonely cupboard where Mother and I had once been happy, in our way? Or had it perhaps wafted before me onto the landing and through our broken door, to fold itself away between the pages of Mother's Bible?

I looked for it in vain. All night I lay awake, composing in my head a letter to Mother. I recalled the good things of childhood, thanked her for her devotion, begged forgiveness for my stupid mistake. No such letter could be sent to Ruzyně, and when I fell asleep at last it was with the image of her squeezed into a stinking cell with thieves and fraudsters, listening to them shouting to their imprisoned lovers down the hole of the toilet in the corner of the room. I went to work next morning resolved to contact Bob Heilbronn, and to begin a new campaign for her release.

Arriving to collect my dustpan and broom, I found Mr. Krutský as agitated as I was.

"There was a girl here, and she left a note for you," he said. His watery eyes revolved without addressing me, and his fat hands trembled against the top of his battered old desk.

"Where is it?" I asked

"They took it, see. Almost immediately after she left, their car came squealing against the curb outside, and two of them jumped out, the same ones that used to collect my report. I don't like it, see? Why don't they arrest you instead of playing these games?"

He addressed the grey wall of the cleansing department workshop, on which hung a notice forbidding spitting, smoking, and alcohol. He took comfort from this notice, which forbade only recognized and innocent things. When under pressure, he fixed his eyes on it and reduced his speech to the minimum.

"What did she look like?" I asked.

"The girl? A nice chick, neat, slim, dressed proper in a blue skirt. Said she couldn't wait. Funny thing, though. She said the note was for you. But it didn't have your name on the envelope. Just 'my mistake,' like an apology. I don't know why you have to drag these private things into the workplace. It'll mean trouble for the rest of us, that's for sure."

"And what did they say, when they took it from you?"

"What do they ever say? 'There's a note in your possession that we need to see,' something like that. They looked at the envelope, and one of them, the fat one with the flabby face, he laughed and put it into his pocket."

"Nothing else?"

"They sniffed around a bit. Looked in the pockets of your jacket. Told me to write another report. And then left at full throttle."

I dropped my dustpan and broom and went into the street, ignoring Mr. Krutský's protests. Only when I had knocked in vain on Betka's door for several minutes did I recall that I was wearing the bright orange jacket of my profession. And when, on turning away,

I passed the fellow with the jug-handle ears who was standing at the bottom of the stairs, I said aloud, "a thorough clean-up," and walked stiffly on. Later that day I wrote a report for Mr. Krutský, emphasizing my erratic behavior, describing how I had rushed from the workshop into the street and then returned as though this was all part of the job, and how I had been distracted for many days in any case, as though plotting some interesting initiative that I lacked the courage to embark on. He was very pleased, and as usual failed to notice the spelling mistakes that I always included as proof of his authorship.

CHAPTER 26

I MADE NO further attempt to contact Betka. I assumed that a trap had been laid, for her at least and probably also for me, and that it could not be avoided. I went home to Gottwaldova, began again composing a letter to Mother, and then went down to the *hostinec* for a jug of beer. The police car was no longer at the corner of the street. It was summer now, and the evening peered through the windows of our block as though collecting evidence. A strange feeling came over me. I felt that I did not belong to this place and that all that had happened in the past weeks had in fact happened to someone else, on whose life I had been granted a ringside seat, but whose destiny did not ultimately concern me. I climbed the stairs slowly, pausing on each landing to take a sip from the jug, and listening distractedly to the sounds of families, some broken, some whole, as they settled into their evening routines. Much, I reflected, was permitted, to those who lived within the lie. You could have a family, attend church, take correspondence courses and embark on a fulfilling and interesting career. It was just as possible to live alone, moving from lover to lover, enjoying the abundant food that our masters had provided, watching inane propaganda about tractors and football on the television, and from time to time getting splendidly drunk with your mates. The space within the lie was confined but comfortable; outside its walls, however, a cold wind was constantly blowing, and the effect of it could never be predicted or controlled.

I sat down with this thought and my jug of beer, and returned to the letter to Mother. I had begun writing about Dad's love of music, reflecting on the way in which our national powerlessness finds its way into notes—Suk in the Azrael Symphony, for instance, Janáček's *Diary of One who Disappeared*, Dvořák's *Rusalka*. I wrote in a way that would have been regarded by both of us, only a few months before, as unthinkable and even unseemly. Then the doorbell rang. Through the spy-hole I saw again the girl from Divoká Šárka, the brown hair tied in a bun, the long white neck beneath it, those beautiful silver eyes encased in their rice-paper lids, like diamonds folded in silk.

I opened the door and stared at her. After a moment she turned abruptly and beckoned me to follow. Not until we had emerged from the streets onto the path into the valley did she speak.

"I didn't want them to hear what I have to say," she said.

"Do *I* want to hear it?" I asked, feeling just a pinch of pleasure in the pain that I caused.

"Yes, because you want things to be as they were between us."

"Tell me what was in that note you left for me."

"Didn't you read it?"

"They got there first. It seems they knew you had written it."

"I see," she said, stopping abruptly. And then, after a moment's silence, turned towards me, flung her arms around me and pressed her face to mine, saying, "Honzo, *miláčku*, I can't bear to lose you."

I moved away from her without replying. We walked across the railway and the stream, to the chapel of the Holy Family. I did not mention Professor Gunther, nor did she tell me what she had written in that note. She simply repeated her invitation to *Rusalka*, and expressed the hope that we could spend the night together afterwards. Soon we were facing each other in front of the chapel, the light of the setting sun trapped in the edges of her hair and haloing her face. One thought filled my mind, which was that the woman before me was dangerous.

"So what is it you have to say to me, Betka?"

"I will be away for a few days, a family visit. I want to be with you first. That's all I said in the note."

"Why were they interested in this note?"

"It was bound to happen, however hard we tried. They have made the connection, so now it doesn't matter if we are seen together. Please say yes."

"Maybe when you return from your family visit. Tomorrow I am going to Rudolf's seminar. I want to hear Professor Gunther."

She looked at me with a flash of anger.

"You can't want to hear that man without a soul. What does he have to do with us?"

"Quite a lot I should say. With you at least."

"What makes you think that?"

"For example, your staying behind to talk to him last Friday. And your being deep in conversation with him yesterday in the *Zlatá Husa*."

She paled a little and looked away before replying.

"I have my reasons for meeting people like him, Honza."

There was a pause in which two squirrels chased each other round the trunks of the maple trees, and a train suddenly thundered from the tunnel. Then she took my hands and said,

"Listen, Honza, I am not against truth. But I need something more useful, which is information. Our world is changing fast. I shall end up, maybe you too will end up, in another place, with opportunities that it would be foolish to despise. Why shouldn't I discuss the possibilities now?"

"Is that what you were doing, discussing your future with a man without a soul?"

"As it turns out, yes. Of course he made a pass at me. Influential men are like that. And of course I slapped him down."

She relinquished my hand and took a step back from me. Her head swayed, framed in the guillotine of the present.

"So you will come with me tomorrow?" she asked.

I did not answer. For a long time we looked into each other's eyes in silence, and slowly hers filled with tears.

"Oh, Honza," she said and, turning quickly, bounded up the Nusle steps and was gone. I took a step to follow her, and then sat down in misery on the wall of the chapel precinct. By the time I got up to leave it was dark.

CHAPTER 27

I NEVER FINISHED that letter to Mother. It was still there on the trunk of Dad's books, abandoned halfway through a sentence about Fibich's *Šárka*, when I left the next afternoon for Rudolf's seminar. Rudolf's strict rule was that we should never form a group on his staircase, but contrive to stagger our arrival, so that a minute or two should elapse between each visitor. I was to come at five minutes to six, but I wandered a little on the way and it was already six when I reached Letenská Square, four minutes from Rudolf's building. To my surprise I saw Father Pavel, standing in the way. I greeted him, and he took my arm with an anxious gesture.

"Come with me," he said. "I need a drink."

"But what about the seminar?"

"I was on my way to it," he replied, "and then suddenly I asked myself, do I want to listen to that soulless claptrap about the right to kill the innocent?"

It did not sound to me like a fair summary of Gunther's views. But I was struck by the word "soulless," and remembered the flash of anger in Betka's face, when she had described this "man without a soul." I reasoned with Father Pavel for a while, but he was immovable. And then it struck me that, since I had decided to attend the seminar only as a rebuff to Betka, a few drinks with Father Pavel would be a better use of my time, a commodity which in any case was largely useless.

He led me back the way I had come, across the river, to the great Jugendstil Palace on Republic Square, the Municipal House, built before the suicide of Europe. Here you could sit at brass-bound marble tables beneath lamps that hung from the ceiling like inverted sunflowers, their centers bursting with the ripe seeds of lightbulbs. Here you were surrounded by the symbols of a patriotism that had long ago lost contact with reality: bas-reliefs of saints and heroes, and plush frescoes by Preisler, Mucha, and Švabinský showing buxom women and swelling flowers, narratives of our national emancipation in paint and prose, and the empty space that those things now served, in a country where it was dangerous to sit for too long in a place so visible, and where we now sat with a bottle of Traminer wine.

Father Pavel greeted the bottle with a boyish cheer and seized it from the waitress, promptly filling our glasses to the brim. We had been walking fast, hardly exchanging a word, and now he talked breathlessly, inconsequentially looking from side to side as though expecting to be joined by someone else.

"Thank you," he said. "I had been praying for such an intervention. Of course, Professor Gunther is a decent fellow. We should be grateful that he comes to visit us, to tell us of the wonders that we can never know firsthand. But this philosophy of his, which regards everything in life as negotiable, exchangeable, even life itself, and which is charmed by its own proficiency at finding solutions—it is the philosophy of Mephistopheles."

He drank his wine in deep gulps, all the time looking around him. The café was empty apart from one table in the far corner, where two men in dark suits had just sat down to play cards. Father Pavel did not fit into this place where the spirit of bourgeois Prague still lingered. His green cotton jacket was shiny with grease, his open collar was black at the edges and his strong right hand gripped the wine glass like a spanner. He seemed anxious to prove to me that we were making better use of our time in this public space than in Rudolf's private seminar.

"For Gunther," he said, "there are only two things that we can be: heroic dissidents fighting for the liberation of our people, or weary cynics, sunk in orgies and drunkenness, just as their novelists describe us. It would never occur to him that there is a truth more easily perceivable by us than by him."

"And what is that truth?" I asked. My thoughts turned again to Betka. Had she gone to the opera after all, and if so was it Vilém who had accompanied her or some other man whose existence she had not confessed to? The wine fell on these thoughts and they burst into flames.

"That there are sacred barriers, and that to cross them we must deny what we are."

"But if you don't *know* what you are?"

"That is not your case, Jan. Of course self-knowledge takes time. We become what we are, through contest and opposition. And in the end we understand that we must give everything, our whole life, without remainder. Don't you agree?"

The two men in the corner had got up and packed away their cards. There was a strange light in Father Pavel's eyes, a light of interrogation that burned into me. It was as though he wanted to fix me in that place, surrounded by my troubles.

"But," I said.

I did not know how to continue. Unobserved, the two men in suits had covered the entire space of the café and now stood above us. Father Pavel repeated his question.

"Don't you agree?" he asked, looking at me intently, as though to shut out the intruders. "There are sacred barriers, and only those who deny their own nature can cross them."

The fatal words *občanský průkaz* sounded above us. Father Pavel ignored them, while I fished inside my jacket, finally escaping the grip of Father Pavel's eyes to search the face of the tall young man who took the little red booklet that I held out to him. His face was tight as a clenched fist, and the eyes watched me from behind ridges of flesh. His companion was shorter, balding, with a well-fed look and fleshy lips that were curled in an ironical smile. There was a silence, during which Father Pavel's attention did not shift away from me. And then the tall man reached in his direction. While still looking fixedly at me Father Pavel took his identity card from an inside pocket and placed it in the outstretched hand. Our actions had an air of ritual, as though they had been rehearsed long before to be accomplished according to unalterable instructions. As we were walked towards the door, through that temple to the gods of old Prague, our movements became rigid and robotic. We were wading through a viscous substance that impeded our legs, and our arms were swinging to each side of us as though paddling our bodies along.

Two unmarked cars were waiting outside. Father Pavel smiled and said, "God bless you," as he was pushed out of sight into one of them. I was led to the other.

CHAPTER 28

I FOUND MYSELF in the back of a comfortable Volga. Beside me sat the shorter of the two men who had interrupted our conversation. In front of me were two others, one driving, the other writing in a notebook. All wore suits and ties, as though accompanying some dignitary on an official visit. We were driving fast towards the suburbs, a blue light flashing above us and casting an eerie glow across the road. My neighbor introduced himself politely as Macháček, and informed me that, while he was by no means in charge of my case, he had been given the task of removing me for a while from harm's way, and perhaps using the opportunity to convey a few useful truths about my situation. He spoke rapidly and softly, in an educated accent, opening his lips in a faint smile as though the words were excited children waiting to burst through into the air. The moist, plump flesh of his face wobbled slightly, as though in need of a shell. Occasionally he would turn in my direction, and look at me curiously from slightly bloodshot eyes, assessing the impact of his speech. And then he would resettle himself comfortably and let the flow of words resume. As we left the suburbs of Holešovice, his discourse turned to books.

"One of the things that I like about my job, Mr. Reichl, is that it brings me into contact with books, and especially those books that you enjoy, which for one reason or another have fallen foul of our stupid system. When they decided to open a file on you, I was lucky enough to get hold of a book that you yourself had written—I believe it is you, is it not, this Soudruh Androš who has such harsh things to say about the strangers who surround us on our underground trains? No matter. It is an interesting book—a book about people who are made of books. And of course, this stupid system of which you pretend they are the victims, though I would rather say that they are victims of your bookish way of describing them, this stupid system was itself born between the covers of a book. Nobody now reads that book: *Das Kapital* is the foundation of our curriculum, and foundations remain unknown and unvisited for as long as the building stands. But the demon born between its covers got out, jumped from book to book until finally taking shape as a threat and a cry. You will remember it, of course, since you have been studying how it is that we got into this mess, as you consider it to be. I mean *What is to be done?* by Chernychevsky, which led to another book of the same title by Lenin. That is the moment when books began to take their revenge. Until that moment books had grown from reality, and especially here in Bohemia's woods and fields."

Mr. Macháček interrupted himself to gesture from the window towards a featureless collective farm, vaguely outlined in the darkness like the unlit side of the moon. I recalled the song by Pink Floyd. Betka had purchased the album out of curiosity, from a girl who sold smuggled Western records each Saturday morning in a wood outside Prague. I stared into the darkness, and I recalled Betka's face, screwed up in distaste, as the sound of Pink Floyd burst from the record player under the desk in Smíchov.

"In those days, nobody was threatened by books: the romantic tale of Babička, the stories of Malá Strana, the tales of that observant little court-mouse Ignát Hermann, all the ways in which we Czechs wrapped up our homeland in comforting words—these helped to make it seem as though we belong here, as though this country is ours.

"But we were forgetting the crucial fact, Mr. Reichl. We were forgetting that for us there is no reality outside books. Ours is a nation made by books. We came into being with the Kramerius Publishing House in 1795, designed to shape the new nation as a nation of readers. It was a book, Jungmann's Dictionary, that rescued our language from oblivion. Our national rebirth was planned and accomplished through books and when people decided that we needed a history, Palacký and Pekař rushed to provide us with books, and nobody knows which version to prefer since neither version has any reality beyond the covers that contain it. It was Josef Kajetán Tyl, a literary man and a man of the theater, who wrote our national anthem. And only a man immersed in books would compose a nation's declaration of its right to exist in the form of a question: '*Kde domov můj?*'—where is my homeland? And the answer is obvious: in books.

"Our conflicts have been fought out in books, and our contribution to the wars of the twentieth century has been the books that document their stupidity. Czechoslovakia exists because books had been written to prove that it should, and its first President, who was appointed on account of the books he had written, went on to write more books to prove that the country must go on. The modern Czech, the ordinary man with his dog, his allotment, and his pub, stepped out of the books of Čapek and Hašek. While President Masaryk was churning out his high school philosophy, the communist poets entered the literary scene with their surrealist books about the future. What was it that one of them said? 'I pause before

Prague as before a violin, and gently brush its strings as though to tune it.' Nezval, I think it was. There you have it: a beautiful image, and a fair account of what those early communists intended. Not to change reality but simply to brush it a bit with words. And when at last people made clear that they didn't like being brushed in this way it was because there were books that told them so. Nothing happens in this place save books, and the most influential book ever written here tells us that nothing happens in any case, except the narrative that tells us that nothing happens. That, it seems to me, is how we should interpret Kafka's *Castle*, would you not agree, Mr. Reichl?"

I stuttered a few words and then shrugged my shoulders in embarrassment. He resumed his speech as though I were merely an observer, sometimes rolling his eyes in my direction and once or twice, after some particularly acerbic paradox, settling back with a triumphant smile, striking a studied pose like an actor.

"The dissidents resisted us with books, and we responded by forbidding those books—that is how stupid it has all become. We even started commandeering books and pulping them. And all this culminated in that 'too loud solitude' described by Hrabal, whose hero's one delight in life is to seize from the maw of his hydraulic wastepaper press the books whose fine bindings and fine ideas cry out for rescue and which end up piled to the ceiling on his shelves, with no other use save to remind a powerless person that, whatever power might be, you don't get it from books. Your mother understood the point perfectly when she described her own flirtation with books as the Powerless Press.

"And it is worth pointing out, Mr. Reichl, no, please don't interrupt me, the point is of great importance to you, that Mr. Hrabal owes his success to us. We gave him a challenge. Become an activist, we said, exchange harmless books for futile actions, like Mr. Havel and Mr. Vaculík, and you will become a non-person like them. Stay with your books and your dreams in your forest village, and you will be known and loved all across the world, known precisely as a Czech, a visitor from the land of books, the land that wrote itself into being. We were aware, of course, that those good-for-nothings were pressing him to sign their document, their death sentence against the written word. And we gave him a choice: sign and that great book of yours, the book about books, of which 80,000 copies were printed, bound and stacked on pallets in the printing works in Plzeň, will go the way of the other books described in it, pressed into blocks and pulped. Don't sign and you will continue to be what you are and what we all appreciate you for being, the prophet of our nation, the person who reveals the latest way of deducing, from the premise that we Czechs exist in books, the conclusion that we exist too in reality."

Macháček continued in this vein for some minutes. At one point he allowed himself to raise his voice, speaking dismissively about the "underground kafkologists" who imagine that our system of government is not just stupid—about which we can all agree—but somehow sinister in the way of those endless corridors frequented by unexplained participants in an unexplained drama.

"In Kafka," he said, with a dismissive gesture, "judgment cannot be avoided, since innocence is proof of a deeper guilt. That is just a comfortable bourgeois clerk's attempt to deal with the oppressive mental presence of his father. And the result is not truth but litera-ture. You should give us more credit than you do, Mr. Reichl. All our efforts—and they are expensive efforts as you see—are designed to spare the innocent, to warn the guilty, and if necessary to cor-rect the guilty, though only, as you must admit, with the mildest of punishments."

I record here the words of this curious character, since they struck a chord in me, just as Father Pavel's words had done in the Church of Svatá Alžběta. In pursuit of truth I had entered a labyrinth of fic-tions. Even the mysterious Other, the collective "they" of our panop-tical prison, turned out to be a fiction, playing an improvised part in a drama that none of us understood. When the car stopped in a dark wood, some twenty-five kilometers out of Prague, and the young man who had been taking notes got out to open the door for me, Mr. Macháček held out his hand. I hesitated, and then took it with a shudder of distaste. It lay for a moment in my palm, like a wet fish.

"You will find your way easily back from here," he said. "And count yourself lucky."

CHAPTER 29

I WALKED ALL night. As I entered the suburbs it began to rain, and in the early hours, wet through and with broken heels, I boarded the first Metro from Holešovice. My thoughts were of Father Pavel. I reasoned that quite possibly he had known what would happen if he took me to the Municipal House, known even that those particular men were waiting for him. But it was also inconceivable that he, who had given everything to the dissident cause, should also be a part of their network. I concluded that it was therefore not I but he whom they had been tracking, and I was merely a diversion, to be got out of the way as efficiently as possible. By keeping me close, Father Pavel had delayed his arrest, and also secured a witness to it. If I kept quiet he could be murdered in secret, as had happened to several underground priests in recent times. If I broadcast the news of his arrest he would have to be brought to trial. And his trial would be a *cause célèbre*, which would embarrass the fools who had arrested him. I therefore resolved to make contact as soon as possible with Professor Gunther, before he left for New York.

I was able to change my clothes and rest for a while before ringing Mr. Krutský from the Gottwaldova Metro station to tell him that I was ill and could not report for work. He told me that "they" had been round again, that he did not like it and that I should look for another job. I hung up without responding to the suggestion. And then I took the Metro to Vltavská, and set out for Rudolf's apartment. As I turned the corner of his street, I saw that the building had been cordoned off. Two policemen stood outside checking the identities of residents and visitors. A police car was parked opposite, and officers were carrying files, papers, and books across to it. I walked on briskly, hoping not to attract their attention.

Nowadays, and especially here in America, news does not spread slowly through a community, nor does it travel fast. It does not travel at all. The air-waves are instantly replete with every happening, the now is a universal presence, and—while this leads to an undeniable lack of understanding, since the present is meaningful only in relation to the past, which is instantly drowned by the flood of new information—the result is that there is no news. We are instantly aware of every event that affects us. Then, and especially in those countries where information was a precious commodity, to be hidden by those whom it enriched, and confiscated by those whom it threatened, news still existed, and percolated slowly through hidden channels. I bought a copy of *Rudé právo*, in the slight hope that it would contain some hints of what had happened. But it contained only the usual stuff: cheerful statistics about the wheat harvest, news of a trade delegation from Mongolia, the award of an honorary degree to a French communist, a treaty of friendship with Ethiopia.

I called on Igor, who informed me that Rudolf's seminar had been raided, and everyone—Professor Gunther included—taken into custody. Although it was possible that they would all be freed after the statutory forty-eight hours, it was being officially rumored, according to Lukáš, whom they had already released, that Gunther was a Zionist agent in the pay of imperialist powers.

I went straight to Betka's hideaway in Smíchov. I let the metal door slam shut behind me and for a moment stared at the courtyard. In the far corner two skull capped jackdaws were debating some intricate question of theology. Somehow their presence suggested that the place had been shut off from life. I bounded up the stairs, determined to speak to her, whomsoever she was with and however angry she might be at the disturbance. But the door was wide open, and inside the room was bare, like a stage at the end of a run of performances, when all the sets have gone. I stood on the threshold, practicing my gymnastics of attention on the eloquent nothingness before me. The bookcase which had held her precious collection of samizdat: empty. The desk: swept clean. The still-life painting in over-ripe colors: gone. The candlesticks and the little Russian icon: vanished. The bed: stripped bare. The case beneath it and the box marked Olga: both gone. I became aware of a presence behind me.

"You see," spoke a deep male voice, "it got cleaned after all. She was too quick for me."

I turned to discover the man with jug-handle ears, who fixed me from his deep black eyes with a round, expressionless, bird-like stare.

"You must be Vilém," I said.

He said nothing but pushed past me into the room, swearing beneath his breath. His presence in that room was a line drawn through a story that had started brilliantly, and then wandered into obscurity and doubt. His profile was handsome, despite the ears, with a fine chiseled nose and a clear intelligent brow. Only the leather jacket and trainers, signs of wealth and Western connections, belied his bookish and bohemian air. He spoke rapidly, directing his stare into the corners of the room, his top lip glossy with phlegm.

"If it had just been you I could have dealt with it. But now this American who offers her everything—*everything*. You can see it in her face when they are talking: a scholarship, a doctorate, publications, a career in some American university, and of course a certificate of marriage, which has 'exit' embossed in gold. There was a moment when I could have killed you—she so infatuated with a mere boy, who couldn't believe his luck to be taken up by a woman with looks and brains. But I knew it couldn't last. Forgive me, but you are just not one of us. There are two kinds of people in this world: those going somewhere, like me and Alžběta, and those going nowhere, like you. If I stuck to it, she was bound to come back to me. I could wait. Yes, I kept track of you. It was my right. You'd do the same if you were me. She was mine, see, mine. That was the truth, no matter what she may have said. We were going to the top, both of us, and that's where we would be together."

He continued in this vein for some time, turning every now and then to stare right through me at the wall so as to prove that I did not exist.

"Whatever was normal in her life I provided, see? I was security and culture, money and music both. I had contacts, friends, a way around the system. We could have set up house together, I was prepared to leave wife, family, everything. And then you came along. How the hell did she discover you? I mean, from what miserable corner of our world did you emerge? I don't get it."

His words were full of venom, but his tone had become hesitant and beseeching, as though surreptitiously begging my permission to abuse me and begging me too to agree with the conclusion that I didn't really exist. He described her evasiveness, her constant shifts from warm to cold and back again, her openness to the world and her flight from it, as though prompting me to discuss the point, to reassure him that perhaps it wasn't true, or that the good outweighed the bad, and we should both attempt to forgive her. I let him continue and stared at the blank room where no vestige of my Betka remained. She had become a figment, a vapor lingering above the marsh of suspicion in which Vilém's life was stuck.

A butterfly was flapping its wings against the window, where the sun slipped in at an angle. It was a *babočka*, which my dictionary translates as "painted lady." I had learned the name from Betka in those days in Krchleby, when she had given names to everything she saw. These living things fluttered about her like her own eager thoughts, each one replicating some part of her ambition, each possessing its portion of the world. I recalled her competence, her love of words, her care to call things by their names, her illuminating presence in my life. I recalled her naked body as she had first displayed it in this place, the light that shone from her face, her neck, her breasts. And there came to mind a little Czech word, one of those words in which consonants, clustered together like a posy of wildflowers, make a sound softer and sweeter than any vowel. *Srstka*—gooseberry.

I stepped past Vilém and threw open the window. The painted lady flew up above the roof across the courtyard, was caught in the steam that issued from the protruding pipe on the opposite roof, and fluttered dead to the ground.

I squeezed past the electrical charge that surrounded him, and made it to the door.

"Look," I said. "Much of what you say is relevant and true. But the battle is not wholly lost from your point of view. That American has been arrested. If he isn't jailed on charges of subversion, he will be thrown out."

He turned to me, dumbfounded.

"How do you know this?" he asked.

"Just let's say that I am giving you this information. And I would like some information in return."

"Oh?"

"Tell me where she lives."

Vilém emitted a hollow squeak which I took to be laughter.

"She lives here, in this place, which is mine."

"But when she is not here, as she plainly isn't?"

"You don't understand, comrade. She forbade enquiry. I was to know nothing about her, nothing about the other guy, if there is one, nothing about anything save what she chooses to reveal. I knew about you, because of a few mistakes she made in the first days of her infatuation. Why the hell do you think I gave her this place? At least I have an address for her."

So Vilém's case was worse than mine! I took small comfort from this knowledge, but as I turned to go, I said, "If I find out where she is, I will leave a note for you here."

He stared through me, and then cursed as I closed the door.

My first thought was that she had fled to the house in Moravia, that I should go to look for her there to tell her about the arrests. But then I reflected that, if she had fled, it was because she already knew what was going to happen. She had fled from a disaster, of which I was a part.

CHAPTER 30

I WENT STRAIGHT from her room to the children's hospital in Hradčany. My head was swimming with thoughts that I dared not confess to. I wanted the truth, whether or not I could live in it.

The nurse who admitted me to the old house in the alleyway was neatly dressed, with a blue apron rimmed in white. She had grey startled eyes above shiny cheeks, and she allowed me to pass from the threshold with a slight genuflection that suggested a person in holy orders. Behind her was a screen of frosted glass, and in the distance, the noise of children, one crying, others babbling excitedly.

When you enter such an institution in America and a person comes enquiringly forward, her first words are, "how can I help?" Helping the stranger, putting yourself from the get-go on the stranger's side, those are the two great virtues of this place to which I have come. And they were more or less unknown in my country. The nurse recoiled from me, and when I told her that I was enquiring after one of her colleagues, who was a close relative, she pointed in silence to a door marked *Ředitelka*—Director—and quietly retreated behind the screen.

The director, Mrs. Nováková, was a stern-looking matron of about fifty, sitting behind an empty desk and playing with a pencil on the pages of a newspaper. She seemed to fill in half of a crossword before reaching into a drawer of her desk and taking out a smudged old file containing the names of her employees.

"You understand that they come and go," Mrs. Nováková explained. "It's not my job to keep track of them, only to clear up the mess when they've gone."

I noticed a dingy-looking woman, perhaps a secretary, who was shuffling papers at a desk in the rear of the office, her small hands unnaturally white against the greyish paper, like hands in a painting. Across her forehead fell a fringe of mousy hair, and her grey eyes were set in a round plain face that had an institutional air to it, as though it had been once issued to her by some authority and grown inseparable through constant use. I had the immediate impression that this woman, who was certainly much older than the director, represented the true spirit of the hospital, and that the director had been appointed to crush that spirit, and to ensure that the Party's instructions were followed even in the matter of dying children.

The director told me there was no one by the name of Palková employed either in the hospital or the *internát* attached to it. As I turned to go, I saw the little secretary get up quietly and slip out of a door at the back of the office. I lingered for a moment in the hallway, trying to find peace in the broken moldings of a rococo ceiling, on which were painted here and there the images of frightened-looking saints. I heard the cries of children, infrequent now and quickly extinguished, serving to emphasize all around me the troubled stillness of disease. The little secretary stood suddenly before me. She wore a metal cross, hanging over the plain grey dress that wrapped her from head to foot. She had the manner that I had come to associate with religious devotion, of placing herself right in front of you, like your own face in a mirror.

"You are Jan Reichl," she said. Her voice was soft, accentless, with the same institutional character as her face and clothes. I stared at her in astonishment and nodded silently.

"Before she left Alžběta asked me to promise her something."

I continued to nod.

"She said that you would be certain to come looking for her, and that I must find a way to tell you about Olga. I must ask you to understand and forgive, because she had wished only to protect you."

It sounded like a prayer inserted in the liturgy—part of the office for the day. Information had been stored in this neat receptacle, like a note between the pages of a prayer book. I had a premonition that I would not like the information, and made a bid to postpone it.

"How can you live a consecrated life?" I asked. "Didn't they close the orders in 1954?"

"We Ursulines proved to be necessary—some of us at least. There is nothing in communism that can bring comfort to a dying child."

She lifted her peaceful grey eyes to mine and a spark of warm humanity showed that she was now departing from her script.

"Alžběta Palková," she told me, "was here every day. She didn't work here, except as a volunteer. I don't understand why Paní Ředitelka wanted to hide this from you."

She looked up at me with a new animation, her nose and cheeks twitching rhythmically as though sniffing the air.

"I'm telling you," she went on, "because I am so glad for what has happened. I loved Olga, we all loved her. The thought that she was going to die was hard for us to bear, and the sight of her mother, so determined to prevent it, so full of tenderness and conviction—well, it was an inspiration to us. But of course you know that intractable epilepsy has been pronounced incurable by our ministry of health. The director told us to make the child comfortable and devote our energies elsewhere. Alžběta wasn't having it, as perhaps you know, on account of the children's hospital in Boston. How I wish we could be joined to them! But then—well, you know the problem. None of our doctors would write a recommendation, and there are no better facilities in Czechoslovakia than ours. It all had to be done unofficially. I wrote letters to Boston with the details of Olga's case, while Alžběta worked on getting permission to travel."

We had emerged from the hospital and descended the alleyway towards the steps. I was studying the church of the Loreta, conjuring in my mind the Prague of Rudolf II, the place where all mysteries were exchanged and bartered, and no boundaries set limits to thinking. I imagined myself in that time, believing that all mistakes could be undone by spells, and all losses changed by magic into gains. And then my thoughts returned to the present. In my intoxication with truth, I had ignored the truth that was staring me in the face. I groaned aloud, and the little nun looked up at me in consternation.

"But you see," she cried, "Olga will be saved. They gave Alžběta permission—it was only days ago—to take her to America. Never has a little angel touched our hearts as Olga touched them."

She talked on more calmly about her plans to visit Boston, about Olga's future in America and her possible return, and about a hundred trivial details that escaped my attention until, with a choked "goodbye," I went stumbling along the street towards the city.

CHAPTER 31

AT EVERY POINT during the two weeks that followed I reminded myself that I was alone, that it was up to me to rescue what I could of the little world that had collapsed around me, and that to retreat underground was no longer an option. I left a note for Vilém, explaining what I had discovered. I went every day to work, reassuring Mr. Krutský that I would leave as soon as I had found a job more suited to my uselessness. I asked Igor to inform the official dissidents about the arrest of Father Pavel. I begged him to collect signatures for a letter to the Western press, in which I emphasized that the very public arrest of Martin Gunther while addressing a private seminar had served to distract attention from the furtive seizure of Pavel Havránek. As an unofficial priest, I wrote, Mr. Havránek risked a fate far worse and far more decisive than imprisonment. Igor told me that it would serve no purpose to sign such a letter, other than to invite a charge of subversion in collaboration with a foreign power. All that we could do was to make enquiries through official channels at the Ministry of the Interior, National Security section. I accordingly addressed a letter to the minister and, to my surprise, received a reply inviting me to the Interior Ministry on Letná, where my request, I was told, would be dealt with by the competent authorities.

The competent authorities turned out to be the two policemen who had been in charge of my previous interrogation. They were waiting for me in the foyer of that ugly tile-clad block, took me straight to the lift, marched me down corridors and through doors and partitions, and at last sat me down across from them at a large bare desk, by a window with a view of the castle and the Sparta stadium. My letter was produced, shaken in my face, and then torn in two.

"So far as we are concerned," the sharp-faced officer told me, "there is no such person as this Pavel Havránek. And if there were such a person, then the idea that he might be an unofficial priest is simply laughable."

He told me that I was lucky to be treated with such courtesy, that he would not be surprised—though as a low-ranking officer it was not his business to enquire—if I were not one of their more privileged clients, who had so far enjoyed the protection of someone up there (and he pointed to the ceiling). He made it clear that my continuing association with lawless and subversive elements was jeopardizing Mother's chances of early release, and that, if it were not for the embarrassment already caused by the stupid action of the District 7 Police Force in arresting an American as well as the hooligans who had gathered to gawp at him, they would feel far more free than they temporarily were to lock me up as well.

All these home truths I absorbed as best I could, and pondered them during sleepless nights at Gottwaldova. Meanwhile the American Embassy had made our authorities understand that, when you lock up a liberal American professor, friend of ex-Presidents and Supreme Court judges, there is a diplomatic price to pay. After two weeks, Professor Gunther was put on a plane to New York, and the few members of our seminar who were still detained—Rudolf being one of them—were released. Warnings were issued, and the solidarity of the shattered was resumed. I gathered this information in snippets, being afraid to return to Rudolf's seminar, for fear of what they might be thinking and saying about Betka.

One day I made the trip to Krchleby, walked to her house through fields now glowing with sunflowers, stood for a while beneath the image of the *heilige Jungfrau*, and then took the road to Nebíčko, Little Heaven. In the early afternoon I arrived at the Chapel of Our Lady of Sorrows, took the key from the bird box, and let myself into the sacred space of our marriage. It was a warm day, and there was no sound within the chapel save the buzzing of flies and the gentle cooing of a dove under the roof tiles. There were fresh flowers on the altar, and the floor had been recently swept. I sat in the chair where she had sat, in the nurtured tranquillity of a place where only nothing happens. In so many ways she had cared for me, and even if I would never again stand in the sun of her presence, even if everything henceforth were to be shadowy outlines, she had been mine. Of course, Vilém thought something similar. But he was wrong, and I rehearsed the proof of this from a thousand tiny premises. I remembered the kisses, the ironic smiles, the ballerina movements that she kept for me; I remembered her voice, her music, her wondrous competence at everything she attempted; I remembered her lessons, not about books only, but about life, the life that seemed so minutely forbidden but which a person like her could snatch without permission and fly away with. She had briefly appeared at the boundary of my being, like a lovely bird in a window, and she had turned towards me with the softest of kisses before her flight. I could not condemn her, but would be forever hers.

A strange transformation came over the chapel. The afternoon light, filtered through the dusty windows, outlined the pilasters with shadow so that they seemed to stand forward from the walls as though observing me. The painted saints in the barrel vault parted and reassembled. The wounds left by the wrenched-away monuments seemed to bleed afresh, like the wounds of the saints that had once stood there in effigy. The chapel slowly came alive, and moved with me to that boundary between worlds of which Father Pavel had spoken—the place where mortal things melt into their eternal counterparts, and where the supernatural reveals itself in human form. The important thing, Father Pavel had said, is not our belief, but His grace. We refuse His gifts out of meanness, for we fear the cost of them. And yes, the cost is everything.

Recalling the mysterious maxims through which Father Pavel ordered and defied the world, I wondered again on his part in our drama. Was he preparing for martyrdom, or, on the contrary, managing his escape from it? And my eyes fell on a small door that I had not noticed before, set in the wall to the side of the great stone altar. Around it had been painted a trompe-l'oeil door frame, which was barely discernible against the pale ochre plaster of the wall. The door itself was composed of clean slats of hardwood, maintained in good repair, and with a handle of brass. In the atmosphere that had filled the simple shrine like incense it seemed as though this door had been revealed especially for my benefit, that it was the door between worlds.

As I went across I had the distinct impression of being followed. Unexplained shadows swept the wall, and there was a sound of footsteps in the aisle. But turning, I saw only the empty interior of the chapel, haunted by sunlight, watching me as our Lady of Sorrows, according to Father Pavel, watches all of us always, awaiting her chance.

The door opened on to a little sacristy. A cupboard contained an old tattered surplice, and hidden beneath its folds two cups that I assumed were used in the furtive sacrament. A broom stood in one corner, beside a sink that was kept clean with a scouring brush. A small round-arched window cast its light on a bare table, with a wicker chair pushed under it, as though to make a desk. These few objects had a disposable air, ready at any moment to be disowned and discarded. Next to the cupboard was a smaller one in metal, containing oddments—some dishes, a few clothes, a tattered kneeler, some old newspapers—which had been swept there out of sight. A patch of gold leaf glistened behind the pile of junk, and after rummaging for a while I extracted a painted wooden plaque edged with rococo scrolls in gold. It carried a list of names and dates in Gothic lettering. At the top was written, *Kapelle Unserer Lieben Frau der Schmerzen*, and beneath it *Priester dieser Kirche.* The list began with Vater Peter Hindsinger, who was appointed to this Parish in 1845. And it proceeded through fifteen names until 1951, when there was a gap. The last name, written in Czech characters, was that of Father Pavel Havránek, who served the congregation between 1969 and 1971 and again between 1975 and 1979, when presumably he was arrested and the church finally closed. In 1979, Betka would have been nineteen years old. Father Pavel was her priest, her mentor, and surely her lover and the father of her child.

In that moment, Betka's life lay clearly before me. I envisaged the taut, determined girl, abandoned by her parents in a world of distrust, yet imbued with the highest spiritual ambition, wanting to know, to make music, to see God. How could such a girl not be drawn to the most powerless person in that place, the one who lived not by calculation but by sacrifice? In such a way had Betka's love been awakened. And then the disaster of Father Pavel's arrest, the birth of the sickly Olga, the need now to care for two people who were paying the price of the spiritual freedom she had so recklessly assumed. I remembered Betka tenderly wrapping Mother's food parcels, and saw her doing the same for Father Pavel. I recalled her abrupt way of moving on from every situation, of finding the hidden door through which she alone could pass into the future. I imagined the decisive steps that she had taken to move with Olga to Prague, to explore the avenues through which to rescue this child of a love that could not be openly confessed. I imagined in every detail the flirtation with Vilém, whom she used as best she could, and the contract with the StB, the only ones who could grant the infinitely precious thing that Olga needed.

And yes, I was part of that contract, someone who must be watched for the simple reason that he was a mystery—a mystery to himself and to them, but no longer a mystery to her, once she had brought him up into the daylight to see how he blinked. And then, because I was useless, because there was nothing to be gained from me, because I was a poor creature living in reckless solitude, yet with the same ambition to know that had put her on the path to her disasters, I appeared before her as an object of love—that precious love, born of the highest yearning, for which there was also the highest price to pay. She was a free being, who accepted the cost of what she most truly felt; therefore she had decided to protect me. About Olga she could not speak: to reveal that part of her life would have destroyed everything between us. The room in Smíchov was a temple removed from the world, a place from which all the calculations into which she was forced by her secret need had been excluded. We were together there in the only form of togetherness that she would allow, the togetherness that made no contact with the world of daily compromise. Right until that last moment by the Chapel of the Holy Family, when she looked into my eyes as though hoping that I could read the story there as I was reading it now in the gilded plaque of wood that I held before me in trembling hands, she had wanted to rescue both me and Olga. And when, in my anger, I had rejected her, she had sent Father Pavel to intercept me. And maybe, in some recess of her all-encompassing consciousness, she had obscurely foreseen that I would be put into the hands of Officer Macháček, and brought down by that official lever from the heights of our impossible love into the world of everyday survival.

All that passed in a moment through my mind, and I knew for the first time fully what I had lost. I walked along the road that we had taken on the day of our marriage. I lay down beside the stream where we had made love. I crossed myself at the icon of the *heilige Jungfrau* above her door, and again at the Cavalry by the nearby crossroads, where Hans Müller or Honza Molnar had been shot. And I walked on through the twilight into the forest, to lie down beneath a spreading copper beech, tired, miserable, and hungry. I awoke shivering in the early hours, my clothes saturated with dew. It was midday by the time I arrived in Prague, too late for work. I went straight to Ruzyně, since Mother had been allowed a visit for that very afternoon. And there, facing her across iron bars, I asked her forgiveness for all the ways in which I had neglected her. She smiled wanly, since direct expressions of emotion embarrassed her. She had for the last two weeks been cheered by the presence in her cell of Helena Gotthartová, Rudolf's wife, who had told her everything. The guard interrupted her at this point, but I easily guessed what "everything" included. We turned to the kinds of trivia that occupy people when they are watched and censored, and as I got up to leave, she said, "By the way, I heard from Ivana. She is marrying a policeman in Brandýs. She sends her love, and says that the wedding will be a private affair, just the two of them and a couple of witnesses. She hopes we will understand why it is best you stay away."

CHAPTER 32

A MONTH LATER Mother was home from prison. We knew now that things were changing. Gorbachev was two years into his reign as sixth Secretary of the Soviet Communist Party and the diplomatic disaster of Martin Gunther had led our police to survey us with a lighter touch. Rudolf was aspiring to emigrate, Karel to emerge from his boiler house, and Igor to be either Pope or President, I could never tell which. I found a new job in an *antikvariát*, making use of all the things that I had learned through Betka, and studying how to forget her. For a while I almost thought that it was possible. There were one or two girlfriends of a Western-leaning pop-bothered kind. One of them even suggested looking for the orgy described, or invented, by Philip Roth. I refused, of course. But only afterwards did I acknowledge to myself that it was Betka who prevented me—Betka whom I would betray with any girl I slept with. Only one person came near to replacing her in my affections, and that person, Markéta, was so embarrassed when I left a performance of Janáček's folk song arrangements in tears that she broke off the relationship.

Mother found work as a translator, and in our evenings we began to reassemble the Powerless Press. The manuscript of *Rumors* had been confiscated during the course of Mother's arrest. I wanted to start again as a writer, making use of things that had happened during my brief time living in truth. I needed those stories as proof that I was me. But the last typed copy of *Rumors* had disappeared with Betka, and I presented this fact to myself as the only good reason to regret her departure. I did not speak of Betka to Mother, and Mother did not speak of her time in prison. Instead, we set up home together in a new way, knowing that each had grown towards the other, and that whatever had happened during our eight months apart had happened for the good of both of us. When, a year later, we were arrested and charged with running an illegal business, we were able to laugh at the charges. Vilém Sládek, with whom I had become quite friendly, and whose concerts of baroque music I frequently attended, made a fuss on our behalf, contacting Bob Heilbronn's successor at the American Embassy and threatening to raise a petition which would embarrass the government not only towards the Western press but also towards our masters in the Soviet Union. The charges were dropped within a week and we were released unconditionally.

But a curious detail arose during the course of my interrogation, and I record it here since it casts a little more light on my discoveries. I had asked Igor if he knew what had happened to Father Pavel Havránek. There had been no news of a trial, Father Pavel had left his work at the garage, and the Church of Saint Elizabeth had been definitively sealed up with metal screens. Igor put on the look of distracted holiness with which he dismissed mere realities, and changed the subject. After a while I began to think that, whatever Betka had done by way of making her escape, Father Pavel had done also. It was with this thought in mind that I confronted day two of my interrogation, in the now familiar room at Bartolomějská before the now familiar policemen. I pointed out that Mother's decision to found a samizdat press was entirely her own, and that I had taken no part in the process of production. In response, they played a tape recording of a long conversation in which I described my relations with Mother, and all that her bid for freedom had meant to me. It was the conversation that I had had with Father Pavel in the Church of Svatá Alžběta. Did Father Pavel have a part in ensuring that this confession was recorded for their future use? I could not believe it; but my not believing it was more a decision than a conviction.

Some time later, when the Berlin wall had fallen, and our Communist Party had decided to negotiate a transfer of power, I happened to be passing the window that a trembling old hand had once filled with memoranda in praise of our enslavement. It had ceased to be an Agitation Center and now housed the local branch of the Civic Forum. The dusty relics in the window had been replaced by the symbols of the emerging future: posters of John Lennon and Michael Jackson, an icon of the Blessed Agnes of Bohemia, and childish smiley faces in yellow and orange saying "Ahoj," as though we were proceeding, as Karel might have said, from kitsch with teeth to kitsch of the toothless variety.

I stood for a moment in the doorway. There, behind a desk piled high with leaflets, and wearing a brown corduroy suit, sat Father Pavel, speaking to a small crowd of young people about the need for a new kind of politics, an "anti-politics," which would permit us to be no longer slaves or subjects but citizens, enjoying our freedom and our rights. The speech could have been scripted by Professor Gunther, so replete was it with clichés, and so far from the mysticism that had awoken in me the frail spirit of discipleship.

He seemed tired. His brow was furrowed and his hair receding, so that the lock that used constantly to fall from it no longer summoned the sweep of the hand. One eye had sunk lower than the other, and peered slightly sideways, as though jealous of its companion that gazed calmly from the notch at the top of his nose. The cheeks were fuller, flabbier, unstrung from those fine ligaments that had seemed to encase the corners of his mouth like the flanges of a helmet, and his lips were somehow more sensual, as though they had acquired the habit of luxuries that they could not afford, and craved always for some new sensation.

He looked in my direction, and stared beyond me to the street from which I barely intruded. I turned quickly and walked on. It was Mother's birthday and I was carrying a cake and a bottle of Becherovka with which we were intending to celebrate. In the street it occurred to me that the man I had seen was not Father Pavel, and that this last image from a vanished world was just another fiction, born of my need.

CHAPTER 33

IT MUST SURELY have delighted Officer Macháček that our new President owed his position to the books he had written—some of them while imprisoned for the other things he wrote. But now it was the turn of reality, and against reality the books were helpless. Prague awoke from its enforced slumber and became a modern city. Fast-food restaurants, porn shops, travel agents, and multi-national chain stores arose to stimulate the lust for new experience, while also ensuring that never again will experience be truly new; flocks of chirping tourists began to settle and spurt up again like migrating starlings; expensive cars came to stand bumper to bumper in the street, poisoning the narrow alleyways; the churches, once tranquil islands in a sea of fear, became busy thoroughfares where foreign voices sounded; on the dull stucco of neglected chapels and along the corniced walls—those frail membranes between the worlds where the ghosts of the old city had come to peer at us—the graffiti now were sprawling. The slaves had been liberated, and turned into morons. Pop music sounded in every bar, filling the corners where, not so long ago, we whispered of Kafka and Rilke, of Mahler and Schoenberg, of Musil and Roth and *The World of Yesterday* that Stefan Zweig so movingly lamented.

There were meetings of local committees, political parties, cultural programs, often funded by Western organizations anxious to claim credit for their part in rescuing us. Sometimes I attended, intrigued by the cheerful visitors who spoke to us in English of their harebrained schemes which would cost them nothing. The ebullient Bob Heilbronn was often there, claiming credit for a knowledge that he had never acquired, guided around the room by his handshake like a blind man by his stick. At one of the meetings, on his way towards an official dissident, he bumped into me. With a quick apology and without looking up, he took a business card from his pocket and pressed it into my hand. It said "Dr. Robert Heilbronn, President, Heilbronn and Svoboda, Public Affairs Consultants." The address was that of the carriage door in the Újezd, behind which we had built our house of dreams.

I came across Karel, too. He had been praised for his samizdat essays, now issued by a literary press, and had been appointed to a research professorship in the Academy. His office overlooked the Estates Theater in the Ovocný trh and I called on him there one morning. His *"objets d'art et de vertue"* had followed him from the boiler room beneath the hospital, and he had meticulously recreated his dissident life as an old soldier might hang his lonely room with trophies. He ushered me in with his wonted ceremoniousness, thanking me for remembering him and apologizing for the unavoidable decision he once had made to exclude me from his life. He seemed to have as few visitors in this new workplace as in the old, and I discerned a certain sadness, now that his buffoonery had lost the character of defiance. He dressed more carelessly too, without a tie or neckerchief, and with a short-cut jacket that barely touched his thighs.

Papers lay on the maplewood desk, beneath the lamp raised aloft by a pink porcelain poodle. He was still working, he said, on the abuse of language, having found so much to examine in the jargon of democracy and human rights that his work would be cut out for another decade. As he said this, however, his face took on another and more resolute aspect; his eyes fixed themselves on the theater where, 200 years before, Mozart had conducted the première of *Don Giovanni*. And I noticed that the page lying uppermost on his desk was covered with figures. He looked down at it as we passed, and after a moment of hesitation covered it with a book. A year later I heard that Karel had made a fortune on our new stock exchange, had invested it in a private academy for the arts on the outskirts of Prague, and was giving classes in theatrical performance to a select group of students. His classes, I learned, were devoted to suffering—the suffering required if a character is to emerge from a body that does not belong to it. His students had to learn voice technique, like the famous actors of old, such as Eduard Vojan and Zdeněk Štepánek; they had to practice circus acrobatics; they had to lie still in the darkness as the audience walked over them, or slide down the edge of the curtains onto the stage. They had above all to have a higher purpose than making a fortune in TV commercials, and that purpose was valid, Karel persuaded them, even if there would never again be a theater in which it could be pursued.

When at last I called on Rudolf it was with a certain hesitation, since I had not returned to the seminar since Betka's departure. It was a Wednesday in May, six months after the changes, when I rang his bell after *oběd*. He pointed me to the living room. He wore the same blue serge jacket, lustrous with use, that had covered his thin body in the days when he sat with his left hand pressed to his temples, his right hand turning the pages of a book, before the assembled room of his disciples. His eyes focused me from across the desk with the same intent gaze, relayed from the same place in the center of his skull. From his steel cheeks and unsmiling lips there issued no enquiries and no small talk. He was still locked in battle with the enemy. But the enemy was no longer outside the window. He was there in the room.

Rudolf was denouncing the foreign academies that had ignored his request for scholarships, the publishing houses that had rejected his articles, the people who had profited from his instruction and made no attempt to reward it. He was denouncing the new President, who had betrayed his calling, the new democratic process, in which only cheats and frauds had influence, the careers in dishonesty and opportunism that were opening everywhere and which he disdained to pursue. He began to question me about my future, pouncing on every lightly sketched ambition, indiscreetly tearing away its incognito, rudely calling it by name, just as it was flitting by in the course of conversation. Soon I too was denounced for wishing to be a published writer when only time-servers and popularizers had a chance of success. A vague desire to try my luck in America was castigated as an intention to discard my country in its hour of need; and my hopes to establish Mother as a professional translator were dismissed as the belated reaction to a justified guilt. I watched the dark waves of bitterness sweep one after another across his face. And I felt that I was watching a fallen angel out of Hell, ever casting himself upwards into chaos, and always scraping to rest on some black ledge lower down. How I escaped from his presence I do not know. But I recall his look as he closed the door on me: a look of metaphysical dismissal, as though I had lost the right to exist.

So it was with all the attempts that I made, during those times of transition, to revisit the world of beautiful defiance. That world was mine and it was Betka's. It was the world of all the people who had a part in our drama. And it had vanished. Prague has since become a replica—a Disneyland version, a stage-set for *Die Meistersinger*. The global market has cleared the center of its old and settled residents, and ghettoized the poor. Those who can afford it are moving to the suburbs, or retiring to sweet country cottages in the Sudetenland. The poorer people of Žižkov, where doctors and tram-drivers lived side by side, where people of every occupation came to pray in the forbidden shrine of St. Elizabeth, have been abandoned by their better-off neighbors, and look on helplessly as Ukrainian mafiosi, illegal immigrants from the Balkans, and international smuggling rings take up residence on their once silent stairwells, to settle old scores with guns. The hypermarkets and shopping malls are descending from the stratosphere into the fields around the city, while the little shops that served the shy, frugal outcasts who attended the unofficial seminars (many of whom hurried for a while like Igor from one official building to another in chauffeur-driven cars) are closing down. Those beautiful self-wrestling buildings that stood between two worlds are now dragged into the marketplace, raising their strained heads above the commotion like noble horses above a pack of wolves. That is how it seems to me, at least, when I return each summer to visit Mother in the little flat near the Metro station once named after Gottwald, and where we are sometimes joined by Ivana, separated now from her disgraced husband, and sad and childless. For I remember those alleyways and palaces, those echoing stairwells and mansard studios, when they were held in trust for that other *polis*, the twofold city of Father Pavel, hovering always between the real and the transcendental, between the transitory and the eternal, celebrating the marriage of time and eternity in a wedding cake of stucco.

But one book remained to be written. It was during that time of transition that the first major study of our unofficial culture appeared under the imprint of a New York university—the very university where Martin Gunther was Professor of Human Rights. According to the blurb, the author, Alžběta Palková, had emigrated from Czechoslovakia during the last years of communism, bringing with her much precious material, a vigorous English prose style, and a well-read and skeptical mind. Professor Palková's text was widely praised for its realistic account of the heroism, as well as the self-deception, of those who were forced by their love of books to live in the catacombs. It became a standard text for American students of international relations, and in due course I obtained a copy through the library of the American Embassy, which I had joined as a borrowing member. The book bore a dedication, "To Pavel, and in memory of our dearest Olga." A chapter on *samizdat* singled out *Rumors*, by Soudruh Androš. It was, she wrote, a leading example of "phenomenological realism." She praised the young author, whom she compared in passing to Samuel Beckett, for his way of combining stark objectivity with a suffering inwardness, and in a footnote revealed his identity as one Jan Reichl, whom she hoped soon to see publishing under his own name.

It was thanks to this reference that I received an invitation to teach in the department of international relations at Wheaton College, Washington. That was fifteen years ago, when all American colleges wanted a tame survivor from the years when they had turned their backs on us. I was assured that, with a few scholarly publications, I would soon be a full professor. After a year or two, when the excitement had died down, and the world had discovered that ex-underground intellectuals are just ordinary people with needs, jealousies, rivalries, and appetites like the rest of humankind, my future presence at Wheaton College began to look less and less relevant. The scholarly publications did not come. I retreated into solitude, not the loud solitude of Hrabal, but the kind of solitude that exists in an American city, where everyone is friendly because nobody believes very strongly in the inner life that hides behind the bright exterior. I more and more regretted the loss of the last copy of *Rumors*, and clung to the belief that it would have given me the confidence to start again, to transcribe my "phenomenological realism" into saleable English prose. Perhaps it would have found me a companion, too, as once it had.

But a few weeks ago I received a letter from my head of department, Professor Richard Lopes, and it is this letter that brought my drama to an end. His florid signature, looking like the design for a wedding cake, took up the blank quarter of the page that he always left for it. "Dear Jan," it said, "I was disappointed that you felt unable to attend the lecture of our distinguished visitor, Professor Alžběta Palková, yesterday. As you know, she is a leading expert on the Czech dissident movement, and she spoke brilliantly and critically about the influence of Western pop music on the culture of protest. It would have helped the department's standing greatly, had you been there to represent us. I have noticed for some time now that you have taken less and less interest in the subject of the Czech alternative culture, even though it is the subject that we hired you to teach. I feel therefore we must discuss our future relations, and I would be grateful if you could ring Fiona to arrange a time when you might come to my office tomorrow. Professor Palková, by the way, sends her greetings, and has left a packet for you."

Professor Lopes rose to academic eminence in the 1970s as an expert in Soviet affairs. In former days, the proud possessor of a visa that his more honest colleagues could never obtain, Lopes was much in demand. No one was in a position to deny his firsthand reports or to cast doubt on their favorable tenor. But he prudently discovered in himself a loathing of the Soviet system at the very moment when it lost its power to grant him favors. He became a champion of the dissident culture and quickly put himself in a position that made it impossible to dismiss him from teaching, even though there was nothing now that he could teach. I had been recruited as a vital adjunct to his new career.

But then, I reflected, what use could a smart American college make of a sardonic Czech intellectual, whose only published work, of which no copies now exist, had appeared in a samizdat edition, in the days when whoever wished for it could claim the title of writer, poet, artist, or composer, and pass himself off as an outcast? Betka's book had damned us with faint praise. Looking back on it now, through the microscope that she provided, it was obvious that we were cheats. We had taken advantage of our situation to escape from critical judgment, to present ourselves as geniuses at a time when nobody could publicly deny it. Few of those books that Mother painstakingly copied each evening were worth the paper they were typed on—even if the paper were socialist property and therefore all but worthless in any case. Betka's brutal realism had the ring of truth.

But what had I done for my American students, with their bright toothpaste smiles and high-five salutes, so eager to understand our country, so keen to fit this curmudgeonly newcomer into the frame of "international relations," a department which extracted $120,000 from each of them, in exchange for teaching them to read newscasts? How could I explain to these young people that there was a time when books were as important as life itself, when we touched those precious volumes, which it was often a crime to own and a still greater crime to produce, with the awe afforded to sacred things? How could I explain that a sentence, lifted from the world of mortal events and given permanent shape upon a page, can pierce the heart like an arrow, can have the meaning of a glance of love or a vow of marriage?

I look back on that solidarity of the shattered and recognize that it was, indeed, as Officer Macháček had said, a literary invention, a wondrous transformation of everyday life in the crucible of the written word. And in this crucible, rising from it like incense, was the intoxicating love that changed my life, attaching me forever to the person who loved me in the world of imagination that we shared and who was trapped, like me, in a real world of distrust. I look back on that moment, knowing that I lived in it more fully, more perfectly, and more spiritually, than I shall ever live again, and that our story was written in the purest fairy-tale Czech. And when has our language been more purely used than in fairy tales? Even the tourists who flood across our city, where the lovely twofold façades now hide their visions of the transcendental behind advertisements for cars and jeans and makeup, even those tourists know that they are in fairyland. And if one or two of them have read those books that set my story in motion—the half-forbidden books by people for whom a normality outside literature was as absurd an impossibility as an angel in the street—then it will be scholarship, not life, that leads them into this trap. We, holding in our hands the page of Kafka's on which was written, "far, far away world history takes its course, the world history of your soul," were called by those words to another life, the inner life that I searched for in those underground faces, and which led me to a farmhouse at Divoká Šárka. Did that farmhouse exist outside the world of my imagination, and was it Betka's face that led me there? How could I know? Maybe Father Pavel was right, that I had imagined that part of the story. But what, in the end, did it matter?

That's what I would say now to Betka. And I would take her back to the day of our marriage, when two souls stood bare before each other, and the light of the world shone down on them from the place in which they could not believe.

Well, I already knew, before I visited Dr. Lopes in his office, that he was right to get rid of me. The only small qualification that I wanted to add was that he would have been even more right to get rid of himself. He received me with that remarkable American affableness, which can be turned on and off at will, and which is the lubricant of business. For the Americans have a way, which we central Europeans can never simulate, of respecting people as ends, so as to reduce them to means. The society that surrounds me, and of which I can never be a part, is built upon a single premise, which is that everything happens by agreement. And of course Dr. Lopes is a liberal, because only liberals can advance to the top of the academic pyramid in America. This does not mean that he subscribes to some liberal philosophy. He subscribes to no philosophy at all. A great statue of Liberty stands above the open harbor of his mind, ushering every idea that might arrive into the riotous cavern of his body, where it disappears without trace. In all real conversation, it is Dr. Lopes's body that takes charge—a body that has floated of its own accord to the top, and which was now addressing me with smiles, handshakes, and polite, meaningless words, to tell me that it was time to move on, that with my talents and background I would be a credit to any department of Slavonic studies, but that, in the field of international relations, the witnesses to the end of communism are no longer needed.

As I left, he thrust a packet into my hand, telling me that Professor Palková had hoped to give it to me in person. I left with a curt bow and did not open the packet until I had boarded the Red Line to Friendship Heights. I like the Washington Metro. I like the smart female voice that tells you to step back, to allow customers to exit, and when boarding to move to the center of the car. I like the mixture of races, the faces with their iPods plugged to their ears, or locked to those new gadgets like mirrors, on which the tune of self can be constantly played with one finger. I like the fact that everyone seems to possess an unquestioned goal, and that no one sitting or standing in this thundering capsule could possibly imagine, in the person opposite, the secret life and the openness to love that I had imposed on my victims in those beautiful terrible days back home. I also like the fact that in so many places—Friendship Heights is one of them—the line runs deep underground, unlike the shallow metro of Prague, which mostly runs just beneath the life of the street as though to spy on it and collect its secrets.

But then, as I fumbled with the packet, I glanced up at the girl across from me, who lowered the book that she was reading and looked at me from still grey eyes. I tore away the cover addressed to Jan Reichl. Inside was another cover, which Betka had addressed in

Czech to "my mistake." I stared at it for a while, before removing it. In my hands was the only surviving copy of *Rumors* by Soudruh Androš. With the same feeling of necessity that had propelled us from the place of our marriage to our fate, my eyes were drawn to those all but invisible corrections, those little lines and marks that I had intended to guide the true, the future, publication, but which Betka had evidently failed to notice. The copy I held in my hand was the one that I had left on the bus at Divoká Šárka. Once before she had tried to give it back to me, and had I taken it, none of this story would have happened. I recalled her words as she had replaced the book in her bag. "There you are, back in my dream." And now, over twenty years later, I understood what she meant.